Also by Megan Abbott

Die a Little

The Song Is You

Megan Abbott

SIMON & SCHUSTER

New York London Toronto Sydney

SIMON AND SCHUSTER
Rockefeller Center
1230 Avenue of the Americas
New York, NY 10020

SIMON & SCHUSTER and colophon are registered trademarks of Simon & Schuster, Inc.

For information about special discounts for bulk purchases, please contact Simon & Schuster Special Sales at 1-800-456-6798 or business@simonandschuster.com

Book design by Ellen R. Sasahara

Manufactured in the United States of America

10   9   8   7   6   5   4   3   2   1

Library of Congress Cataloging-in-Publication Data
Abbott, Megan E.
The song is you / Megan Abbott
p.   cm.
1. Mystery fiction. 2. Noir fiction. I. Title
PS3601.B37S66 2007
813'.6—dc22   2006051229

ISBN-13: 978-0-7432-9171-2
ISBN-10:   0-7432-9171-9

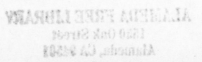

Acknowledgments

My immense and enduring gratitude to my editor, Denise Roy—without her inestimable editorial guidance, support, and talents this book would not be possible—and to my agent Paul Cirone for his ceaseless labors and ardent conviction; to my dearest friends, Christine Wilkinson, Alison Levy, and Darcy Lockman; and to the ridiculously excessive, stalwart, and deeply appreciated support of my family: Philip and Patricia Abbott, both writers who've reached heights to which I aspire; my beloved brother and sister-in-law, Joshua Abbott and Julie Nichols; my cherished grandparents Ralph and Janet Nase; and Jeff, Ruth, and Stephen Nase, whose kindnesses over the years are too numerous to name. I would also like to thank my in-laws, Dee Maloney and Bob Myler and Sam and Paula Gaylord, who continue to inspire me with their generosity of spirit. Finally, warmest thanks for their encouragement and friendship to: Karen Nichols, Mitchell Bartoy, Mary Duncan, the entire Milowitz family, Erin Barthel, the Abate-Peters family, Linda Malamy, Angie Drumm, Ken Anderson, Jaymie Kahn, Jennifer Kyle, and Lynne Connelly.

And most of all, I want to thank Joshua Gaylord, who makes everything better.

For Josh, who knows why.

*The end of a story should be
what the beginning is about.*

—IRVING THALBERG

1949

The Petty Girl

The whistle isn't jaunty, not Doris Day. It's low and slow and the actor Bob Cummings would remember its hot zing for some time.

Ah yes, that bit player of definite note.

"You sound happy," he says to her, his head half turned, leaning back in his springy dressing-room chair so he can catch a glimpse of her in the corridor.

She stops, swivels her hips, and looks back at him, black eyes crackling.

"I am," she says, almost a husky coo. She laces her long, red-tipped fingers along the door frame. "I have a new romance."

"Is it serious?" he says, flirting hard. Has he played this game with her before? He lets his arms dangle boyishly from the sides of his chair.

"Not really," she replies, tilting her head. Then, with a klieg-light leer lewd as a burlesque dancer but with infinitely greater appeal: "But I'm having the time of my life."

With that, she twists her long hips back around and, with a

kittenish wave of the hand, continues down the corridor, heels lightly clacking, matching her whistle in perfect time.

What is she humming?

He can almost name it, taste it even.

It reminds him of close quarters, mouth pressed against folded satin, sparkled fishnets, music throbbing unbearably, pressure in the chest and fast, jerky leg kicks in the air. A long-ago peccadillo with a clap-ridden chorus girl in a curtained booth at the Top Hat Café, an encounter so quick and so urgent that it felt like a sucker punch in the stomach.

Of course.

That was it.

You're so much sweeter, goodness knows . . .

Honeysuckle rose . . .

He will tell this story hundreds of times in the weeks and months to come under official and unofficial circumstances. He will tweak it occasionally, leave details out, add a shading of provocation or a whiff of heat. Or he'll tell it as if it were a cool exchange between temporary colleagues. He'll tart it up or iron it out, depending.

But this is how it really happened and it has lodged tightly, uncomfortably in his head on a continuous loop, winding itself through his thoughts, unfurling in his dreams. He may barely recall the movie they were shooting (*The Petty Girl*, right?), but he remembers everything about the costume she wore as she walked down that hall, all china silk and shocks of pleats, a curling blue flame. And the lipsticked mouth folding around the coarse and delicious whistle. His creaking, squeaking chair as he leaned back, makeup bib cocking up, he, the star, too eager, bright-eyed and chomping, aside her distinct and unfounded cool, the cool that comes from her not needing his attention at all. He could tell: she had brighter stars sniffing around her, around her creamy curves, lashes batting in chestnut hair, a turning ankle, a cloud of jasmine, a bawdy song no white girl should sing.

It was her voice that purred and snapped and stuck in his head most ferociously, making him sick with random desire, making him want to do something foul, unmentionable, unarticulated, ugly. How he'd like to fuck her into oblivion.

But someone beat him to it.

Park La Brea

"He ain't gonna pay up, doll. No matter what the judge said. Once you're out of their bed, you lose all the angles. You should've stayed hitched and played it close to the line."

These words of advice came from next-door neighbor Beryl Doolan, who delivered them as she chipped the last bit of nail polish from her curled foot, planted flat against the edge of the kitchen table.

"Are you going to listen to her?" Peggy said, drying the last dish.

They were both talking to Peggy's cousin, Jean, the tall brunette girl, the one pulling on a pair of crisp gloves and not meeting either woman's gaze. The girl, well, she was beautiful in a toothy, sharp-dimpled way. You had to look very, very close to see the thin skein of lines around her eyes. She was still a good eighteen months away from post-ingenue.

"She don't need to listen to me," Beryl said. "She knows. She can talk to the ex-hubby 'til she's blue in the face and she ain't getting more child support. She thought she married an *en-tre-pre-nure* and he was just another four-flusher."

"That's enough, Beryl," Peggy said. "Christine's in the other room."

Jean pulled a lipstick from her purse and dabbed her mouth with it.

"Christine knows all about her old man," Beryl said, watching as Jean clipped her purse shut and slung it over her shoulder. "Don't she, Jean?"

Jean finally raised a pair of finely etched eyebrows and looked in Beryl and Peggy's direction as she straightened her hat.

"Five years old," she said. "And she's already got her daddy's number. I should have been so lucky."

"Oh, Jean." Peggy shook her head, hands on her hips.

The girl smiled, all straight, shining teeth and two sets of dimples. The smile was so charming that Peggy couldn't help but smile in return. Even Beryl, nursing a hangover from a late-night party at her apartment next door, managed a grin. Everyone smiled when Jean Spangler smiled. That's why they all said she'd make it someday. And why no one had been surprised when the leading men started circling.

"Are you coming home after you meet with him?" Peggy said, walking her cousin out the front door. Behind them, Jean's daughter, Christine, came running out of the house, following her mother down the front path.

"No." Jean kneeled down and kissed her daughter hard on the cheek. "Can you watch this little darling?"

"Sure. Are you working at the studio tonight?" Peggy asked her.

Jean patted Christine's neat row of blonde bangs and then stood up. "Yeah," she said, winking at Peggy. "Wish me luck."

As Peggy watched her cousin walk away, Christine pulling at her legs and whimpering for Mommy, she felt funny. The same strange feeling she'd had all day. That morning, she and Jean were alone in the house, Mama Spangler away visiting family in Kentucky. When Peggy went to the bathroom to brush her teeth, Jean was already there, zipping up her skirt and looking at herself in the long mirror.

"I had this dream about you last night, Jean," Peggy had said, rubbing her face tiredly, her cheeks still pink and soft from her sleep.

"That so," Jean murmured, straightening a stocking.

The night before, Peggy had gone to bed with her head throbbing from the sloe gin she'd had for a nightcap—a bad habit she and Jean's brother, Rich, had picked up lately, itching to go out in the evening, like lazy-legs Jean, but with no coin to do it. Peggy was still officially in mourning for Ray, her husband, who'd died at Saipan five years back. Peggy couldn't type, sew, or run a cash register, so pocket money was hard to come by. Rich's only excuse was too many afternoons at the dog track. Too broke to go out on the town, he came by the apartment instead, often staying on the couch overnight.

Many evenings, the family listening to the radio, Peggy and Rich felt their collars scratching, the closeness of the living room, Mama Spangler's nerves on edge, and Jean's little girl, Christine, playing jacks soundlessly for hours, the most blank-faced five-year-old you ever saw. When it was late and just the two of them, they'd make a cocktail, sometimes two, with whatever Jean's boyfriends had left behind. Sometimes soft-tongued scotch, other times the tingly zing of fine stone-white gin.

Jean didn't mind and often she'd get home early enough to join them, wilted gardenia in her hair, the musk of nightclub smoke and long ocean drives radiating off of her. She had fine stories to share, of star sightings at Trader Vic's, seeing the Will Mastin Trio at Ciro's; her voice—warm and flat with strange pitches to it—seemed engineered to accompany late-night drinking in cramped spaces, the tightness of frustrated day-living giving over, lovely-like, to the breaking freedom of faint, early intoxication.

That night, however, they'd just about given up on Jean. Peggy was working up the energy to go into the kitchen and soak the gluey red bottoms of their sloe-gin fizz glasses when she finally heard a car idling in front of the apartment.

"Carriage turned back into a pumpkin," Rich murmured, reaching behind his chair to lift up a blind slat.

Peggy smiled tiredly and leaned across the end table to look through the slat, too.

"Dim that light," Rich barked suddenly, before Peggy could get a look herself.

She did as he asked.

"What is it?"

In Peggy's dream that night, Jean had touched her shoulder. When Peggy turned to smile, Jean was looking at her expression-lessly. Then, her cousin opened her mouth and black ashes issued from it in a soft gust, painting a thin layer of glistening soot on her chin, her jaw, her golden collarbone.

"Jean," she'd said in the dream. "Jean, you were on fire."

Jean nodded, saying, "From the inside out." Suddenly, long strands of inky tears dropped from her eyes.

"From the inside out," Peggy repeated, and suddenly she was crying, too.

• • •

When she woke up, she wanted to tell Jean about the dream. She might get a kick out of it. She might laugh and make some joke about having one too many cigarettes the night before.

She wanted to tell Jean so she could get the picture out of her head. That was what she wanted. The old story about the kid who dreams about a marshmallow sundae and wakes up with a big bite out of his pillow—that was how Peggy felt. When she woke up, she was afraid that if she looked at her hands, they'd be smudged with soot from reaching out to Jean's face. When she woke, she stayed in bed for twenty minutes, arms under the covers, afraid to see.

But when she tried to tell Jean, when she got out of bed and found her ironing her burnt-orange "audition dress," Jean barely looked up from what she was doing.

It wasn't until an hour later, when Peggy was putting on her hat to take Christine to play in the park, that Jean approached her.

"Tell me again about that dream." Her hands were clasped in front of her.

Peggy slid her hat off and met her cousin's gaze. She told her the dream once more. This time, she told her everything.

"What do you think about it, Jean? I tell you, it spooked me," Peggy said, laughing eagerly. "I sure was glad to see you this morning. Isn't that funny?"

"It spooked you."

"Well, sure, I mean, it was awfully strange, wasn't it? I'm not superstitious, but . . ."

"But what?"

Peggy looked Jean in the eye, those midnight-satin eyes of Jean's. She looked and looked and then saw that something had passed over from her to Jean. The picture she couldn't get out of her head had gone over to Jean's and now they both had it reeling and reeling, like a record skipping. She looked at Jean and also at Jean's hands clutched before her.

"Forget it, darling," Peggy said with a grin. And she put on her hat. "Heck, night before last it was all about Tyrone Power kidnapping me on his big old pirate ship."

The tight look in Jean's eyes loosened a little. And then a little more. She finally grinned.

"You never know, Peg. I hear Ty Power sure does get around."

"I could be next. Or you."

Glamour Girl Reported Missing

Wire Service, *October 8, 1949*

Dancer and film actress Jean Spangler was reported missing today by her cousin, Peggy Spangler. A divorcée, Spangler left her Wilshire District home at 5 p.m. Friday, kissing her five-year-old daughter, Christine, good-bye and telling her cousin that she was going to meet her ex-husband, Dexter Benner, to discuss an increase in child-support payments. Following this meeting, she was going to work on a night shoot for a new film.

This morning, after Spangler failed to come home, her cousin went down to the Wilshire Division of the LAPD and filed a missing-persons report.

Jean Spangler, a former dancer at Hollywood nightspots such as the Earl Carroll Theater and the Florentine Gardens, recently completed shooting a small part in *The Petty Girl*, with actor Robert Cummings.

Missing Actress's Purse Found in Griffith Park

Wire Service, *October 9, 1949*

During a 100-man search on Sunday, a Griffith Park groundsman found what is believed to be the purse of actress Jean Spangler, missing since Friday night. The groundsman reported finding the object near the entrance to the park. The purse's handle was broken, but it still contained a wallet and other items. Those contents include a mysterious note believed to be in Spangler's own handwriting:

> *Kirk, can't wait any longer, going to see Doctor Scott. It will work best this way while mother is away,*

The search of Griffith Park has turned up no additional clues.

Spangler's cousin, Mrs. Raymond Spangler, told police that Jean said she was meeting her ex-husband, Dexter Benner, to discuss child support and then to work. "But she winked as she said it," her cousin told reporters. Benner denied having seen Jean for weeks, a story supported by his new wife, Lynne. Police also report that a check of the studios determined that no movies had been in production the night of the seventh. Jean had last been seen at a local market where the clerk said she appeared to be "waiting for someone."

Missing Actress's Nightspot Tour with "Tall Man" Traced

Los Angeles Examiner, October 12, 1949

Through the bright lights of the Sunset Strip, police yesterday traced the dim trail of actress Jean Spangler, missing since Friday and feared the victim of a killer.

Witnesses came forward to tell of seeing her in a café and riding in a convertible with a strange man on Friday night and Saturday morning, but none could guess her fate.

The search for "Kirk" and "Dr. Scott," mentioned in a note found in her discarded purse, was fruitless.

Her friends knew of no one among her many men friends who was called Kirk or whose name might be shortened to that.

But people who knew her by sight said she was in Sunset Strip nightspots Friday with a tall, good-looking man whom none had ever seen . . .

Terry Taylor, proprietor of the Cheesebox Restaurant, 8033 Sunset Boulevard, says she sat at a front table there with a man–"clean-cut fellow, about 30 or 35, brown hair, neat, medium build, tallish." That was early Saturday morning, around 1 or 2 o'clock.

Joseph Epstein, who sells papers there, saw her between 1 and 2:30 that morning, standing outside the café. He is positive of the identification.

Al Lazaar, a radiocaster pseudonymed "the Sheik," who does table-interview broadcasts from the restaurant, approached her about 2:30 that morning, at the place. He said she appeared to be arguing with two men, and he veered away when they signaled they did not want to talk over his microphone.

Cinestar, *Gil Hopkins, Reporter*

Some days, he could scarcely believe his luck. Here he was, Gil Hopkins, just some kid from upstate New York, hopped off the Greyhound bus three years back still knocking the snow out of his shoes. Now he's strutting around the Warner Brothers lot like he owns the place. From writing crop reports for the Syracuse *Post-Standard* to interviewing Lana Turner for the reading pleasure of just under one million starstruck housewives—all in a few easy steps. God bless this crazy country.

Sure, he wasn't exactly fulfilling anyone's youthful ideal of the muckraking reporter, including his own. But he'd tried the newshound gig for the better part of a year and it never really took. Turned out he was born to *this*, not so much reporter as candyman, spinning knots of sugar into cotton candy so fine you could see through it. And yes, sometimes it was as routine as working the line at Ford Motors. Some days, he'd be counting the seconds before he could finish the frothy on-set interviews and escape to the back lot with the grips and, occasionally, some hep outcast actor like Bob Mitchum or John Ireland, to smoke reefers and shoot crap. And yes, his editor might not be pleased to know his star reporter was spending more time shaking dice out of his trouser cuffs than coaxing verbal bonbons from the mouth of yet another leading lady. But everyone at *Cinestar* liked the results, the airy cream puffs he bestowed with sticky fingers. And he wasn't one to take things for granted. He loved this god-awful burg, this frontier mirage, the kind of place where a fellow like him, saved from the salt mines of Onondaga County, could end up in a job where he's having a heart-to-heart with June Allyson about her trademark bangs one minute, and the next he's joining her husband, star Dick Powell, at an after-hours gambling den in Santa Monica. What a story. Like something he'd spun himself from so much cane sugar.

And then that day, a day that seemed like one more flossy strand of gossamer, easily flung off. A ten-minute interview with Lauren Bacall about her wardrobe choices for *Key Largo*, then Gil Hopkins—"Hop"—was back in the makeshift alley with

Moe and Leo and Stu, throwing dollars down and losing big.

Two girls were hanging around smoking and watching the dice. A colored girl, Iolene, who sang in the movie, and an extra, a sloe-eyed white girl wrapped tight in a palm-frond bra. Next to Iolene's sly grin and browned-butter looks, the white girl nearly disappeared, save the crinkling hula skirt and the brick-red pout—a little bored, a little agitated. They were complaining about being summoned for an evening shoot that ended up being called off on account of a leading lady in the hospital with a bad case of the DTs. Both girls had canceled dates for nothing.

"Take some, nice and easy, honey." Iolene passed the joint that one of the boys had offered her to her friend. "You look like you need it."

The white girl took the joint and jabbed it between her lips, but her eyes were on Hop.

"You're the pits," she said, shaking her head. "I never saw a worse crap shooter."

Hop rose from a half-squat and shrugged. "The one thing your mother never taught me."

She laughed, joint cradled daintily in her mouth. "I guess I could show you a thing or two."

"That's all you need," Iolene said, taking the joint back. At first Hop wasn't sure if she was talking to him or the girl. "You got enough trouble with fellows number one, two, and three."

"Maybe," the girl repeated, stroking her fronds with a mix of meditation and provocation.

"I don't have to be number four," Hop said, throwing down the last of his bills. "I'd settle for three and a half."

Iolene grinned. "Only a half, huh? That sure is a pity," she said with a wink.

"It's my secret shame." Hop grinned as Stu threw the dice. He came up empty again.

The girls both laughed, but he wasn't sure if it was at his joke or his loss.

"So, which one of you is buying me a drink," Hop said, eyeing them.

Stu smirked. "It ain't gonna be me," he said, picking up his money.

"Why just one of us?" the white girl said, eyes glazing over from the reefer.

"Okay, but I only cadge drinks from friends. Or at least acquaintances," Hop said, pulling on his suit jacket.

"Jean," she said, the joint dropping her voice a register, turning it throatier. "I'm Jean. And you know Iolene."

"That I do."

Two Years Later — September 1951

Cloquet

"Hop, you have no idea how rough it is," the actress said, lighting a match off the bottom of her shoe like the slickest of New York bookies.

"I know, Barbara. Believe me."

"Here I got one guy in love with me—Franchot—he reads Zig-mund Freud to me while my head's in his lap, and I got another guy, Tom, muscles like poured concrete, who'd just as soon gut Franchot as give up one night with his chin nestled in my thighs. Why make it either/or? Why not both?"

Her lips curled into a smirk and he couldn't help but laugh. She did, too, like a horse. On her it was inexplicably sexy.

"I understand, Barbara. I really do. More than you know. But you got a dozen columnists chasing this story."

She tapped her cigarette on one silky knee. "Fuck, Hop, what do I care? I'm having a ball. It's not like I compete with Loretta Young for parts. I play hookers, molls, pinup girls."

Gil Hopkins, late of *Cinestar*, had been at this new job for twenty months or more and it was getting almost too easy. From movie-mag reporter to studio publicity man in one easy step. And now his days were spent stroking actors and actresses, working the press, attending premieres, tape cuttings, and champagne-bottle breakings at every place from Grauman's to the *Queen Mary* to grocery stores in Van Nuys. He'd spent just three weeks knocking out press releases before proving to the big guys how smooth his tongue was. Now he was the one they went to. Or one of them, at least.

This case with Barbara Payton was standard issue. Her two actor-beaux—past-his-prime Franchot Tone and B-movie-nobody Tom Neal—engaged in an embarrassing dust-up on the front lawn of her apartment building. The "Love Brawl" made headlines everywhere and was only the most recent in Barbara's string of public incidents—the affairs with married actors, the romance with Howard Hughes that led Universal to cancel her contract, and the capper: her grand-jury testimony providing an alibi for a dope dealer accused of murdering an informant. Things were getting pretty complicated for Barbara. And Hop's studio had her on loan for a just-wrapped movie, *Wronged Heart*. Before the Tone-Neal fracas, they'd considered buying out her contract and had promised as much. But not now. Hop's job was to oh-so-gently push her back to Warner Brothers.

Hop hadn't bothered with Tom Neal, a side of beef in tight pants. But he'd worked Franchot Tone a bit. Over the last week, he'd carried on several soulful late-night conversations with the long-faced, highbrow actor.

"What do I care what they say?" Tone had confided. "Don't you see? I love her. Love that darling girl." And it was no surprise to Hop. Tone had long had a taste for beauties whose hems were still wet from the gutter. Even Joan Crawford, whom Tone married when she was Hollywood royalty, came with the richly thrilling backstory of a pre-fame gold-standard stag film, a seven-minute loop Hop himself had seen at more than one Hollywood party. It had been shown so many times at so many different gatherings that it had taken on the quality of a ho-hum home movie trotted out one too many Christmas mornings.

When he'd talked to Tone, the studio was still weighing their options vis-à-vis La Payton. But today they said, *Give her the air.* Hop's mission was simple: Cut ties, but do it sweet and soft enough to avoid lawsuits, and keep the door open in case the scandal dies or takes a nice turn.

"Promise nothing. Let her know her future isn't with us. But don't tip your hand," Hop's boss had told him, with a wink and a nudge.

Not one to skimp on the kiss-off, Hop escorted Miss Payton from his two-by-four office to a nearby nightspot, ushering her to one of the small, round mahogany booths in the back, the ones with the small baby spotlights that dropped onto the center of each doll-size table. The restaurant was so dark and the tables so low that you had to crouch forward from the tufted leather seats to see each other or, with its high ceilings and Nat King Cole vibrating, to hear each other. It was a place tailor-made for fugitive encounters.

Barbara's button nose, pert and bunnylike as any Midwestern cheerleader's, curved into the baby spot and above it her incomparable white-lashed black eyes batted.

"Bringing me here, Hop, what's a girl to think? Are you trying to screw me or to screw me?"

"Exactly," he said, and smiled, resisting the urge to tweak her nose as it crinkled in amusement. He was still practicing his approach in his head and she was already pushing him to the windup. What the hell, here goes:

"All I'm thinking is this, my girl, all I'm thinking is you and me: we understand things. What I've always admired about you—even back in the day, when I made you for *Cinestar* and gave you that big 'Next on the Horizon' spread and christened you 'Queen of the Nightclubs'—the one that got you that plummy part in *Trapped*—even back then I thought, 'Here's a girl who knows the score, knows it even better than the gray suits at Universal who try to stuff her into every two-bit Tex Williams oater they can find.' You and me, Barbara, we got that same grand tangle of ambition and battle smarts—like the pep squad," he said, dabbing her nose with his thumb, "for the nastiest, blackest-hearted team there is: Hollywood. We, B.P., we would and would and would, right?"

"Would, could, should, whatever you got, Hop. Life's for the living," she said, downing her gimlet and running her delicious pulpy tongue across her Minnesota-farm-girl teeth, thick and white as a bar of Ivory soap.

"Amen and all right." He signaled to the waitress for another round.

"So what's the bottom line, then, pretty boy? For the ruckus? What did my wayward boyfriends cost me?"

"You see, *that's* what I'm talking about." He jabbed his finger in her direction. "Straight to the chase."

"No finery for me. Besides, your tie looks too spanking-new. Like your shirt still remembers the rayon Woolworth tie that sat there a year ago. Right, Hop?"

"Actually, gorgeous, the shirt's spanking-new, too. But the baby-soft flesh underneath sorta recalls, wondering where the Sears Itch went."

"Sears Itch. Sounds like something you catch from a sailor on leave."

"Scout's honor, I never met the guy."

She laughed with her whole face jumping and reached out to drag her new drink across the tiny table and into her hands.

"You, Mr. Slick, may be good at the soft touch, but I still want to hear the verdict. Am I kaput, all for an honest affair of the heart?"

He flicked his finger along the sheen of sweat on her glass. "No way, sis. It's simple. You clean it up for a little while, close those lily-white gams on set and everything's apples and ice cream again."

"What does that mean exactly, Mr. Slick?"

"It means we like your face and your voice and your chops and your honey-round bottom. You'd have to fuck all of Actors' Equity to cancel that. 'Course," he said, pretending to look for the waitress as he took a silent breath, "it's really for your home team to deal with. And we don't want to interfere with Warner Brothers' business."

He forced himself to meet her eyes and gave her his jolliest smile.

She nodded her head slowly, trying to read the brush-off. "You're saying everything's fine but not so fine that I'm worth the heat. Send me back to Poppa Warner, thanks, it's been swell."

"Not at all," he said, waving his hand. "We love you, kid. We've loved having you here, loved loving you, love to have you back. It's just that your poppa's got the gate locked so tight, it's out of our hands"—he slapped one palm on her leg under the table, light and teasy, there and gone—"as eager as our hands may be."

"Gate, huh?" She grinned and placed one drink-wet finger on his wrist. "Feels more like a chastity belt. I didn't know Poppa cared so much."

"Like your old man on your prom night, B.P."

"Not my old man," she said, fingers dancing along the bottom of her empty glass. He signaled for another round. He hadn't realized he'd be going belly-to-the-bar with a longshoreman.

"Oh?" he said. This was good. Subject changed easily, no mess, no fuss, and she was already onto that old actress saw-horse—the "my father never loved me" soliloquy. If only he was as good at the kiss-off with the women in his own life. Or maybe he was, really.

By round five, the cherries-in-snow lusciousness of Miss Barbara Payton practically shimmered with I'm-easy appeal. Thankfully, with drinks, she grew not more soulful but more filthy, like a slutty baton twirler, every red-blooded American man's deepest dream.

"So I'm a little slip of a fourteen-year-old and Joyce and I are doing each other's hair, big sausage-roll curls at the hairline like Ginger frickin' Rogers in *Kitty Foyle*. And Joyce's folks are having a big party downstairs, all fast jazz and roll up the carpeting, a big bowl of Planter's Punch. Joyce falls asleep just before twelve and I'm lying there in the trundle bed, gotta pee like a racehorse. But I'm scared stiff to go down the long hall to the bathroom in my bitty white nightgown. What if the grown-ups see me? I would just die. Takes me all of a half hour to work up the nerve.

"Finally, I decide to make a mad dash. So I throw on Joyce's chenille robe and run quick like a bunny down the hall. Lickety-split.

"And wouldn't you know it? Motherfucker, the bathroom door is shut, latched, *occupado*. I thought I'd piss my pants on the spot. But the door opens and it's Joyce's dad, Mr. Magrew. All Brylcreem, Arrow shirt, and smelling like the rubbing alcohol my momma pats on my skinned knees. He's got a sliver of a mustache like Robert Taylor. He's a fine one. But he's got a big red stain on the front of his starched shirt. He laughs when he sees me, says Mrs. Corrigan pressed too close to him on the dance floor and jostled her own drink out of her glass and onto him. Awfully sticky, he says. Planter's Punch. Maybe you can help me, he says.

"I'm such a dumb cluck," Barbara said, shaking her head. "I walk in, he shuts the door behind me. The bathroom is so small that I feel half pressed against him myself. I'm handing him this wet washcloth and stamping his chest and he's pulling my night-gown up over my legs, past my little hips. Bathrobe — his daugh-ter's — falls to the floor. I start to push him away. He smiles and grabs the washcloth and tucks it in my little-girl mouth. You hear me, Hop?

"So he backs me into the tub and fucks me for five minutes, my head hitting the faucet over and over again like a freaking knockout bell. Petals whacked off the rose one by one. I was sure the whole house could hear the clanging. Then he got up, pulled the cloth out of my mouth, ran it along the inside of my legs until it was soaked-through red.

"And you know what he said, buckling his belt as I lie there, limp as my own rag doll? 'You're a delightful girl,' he said, 'and I'd like to do this again.'"

Barbara burst into a peal of hard-won laughter. Hop, one fin-ger around his tight collar, joined her, gulping his drink as she did.

"Do you believe that fucker? Like we were saying good night after the homecoming dance."

"So did he? Do it again?" Hop said, smiling a little queasily at the picture in his head of quavery pubescent and prone Barbara.

"Three times a week until Lent," Barbara said, lighting up a cigarette.

Hop nodded. Then, after a pause, he smiled widely. "You almost had me."

Barbara laughed. "Okay, okay. I graduated to captain of the varsity football team after him. He looked like he could take old Magrew. But," she said, sighing long, "you never forget your first."

He'd heard this story—really, this exact story—a hundred, a thousand times before from just about every doe-eyed, apple-breasted starlet he'd ever interviewed, drank martinis with, or taken to bed. Still, it always had its own surprising deathless power to arouse. As it was meant to, even if they didn't know it (some of them, like Barbara, did). So he'd allowed himself the churning pleasure and waited for a new twist or wrinkle in this rendition—at first waited in vain (hell, he'd even heard the best-friend's-father-at-a-party story before). Then, she introduced the bathtub. Picturing black-eyed, cotton-haired, puberty-flowering Barbara Payton with her downy legs pressed against the shower, her superb feet squeaking along the tiles as Mr. So-and-So throttled drunkenly away, well, it was . . . so sue him, accuse him of sexual deviancy, it was *awfully* nice.

"You have a phone call, Mr. Hopkins." A waiter suddenly appeared at his side, shaking him from his reverie.

Excusing himself, Hop made his way to the restaurant's secluded coven of mahogany-walled phone booths. The waiter directed him to one, where the earpiece nestled, waiting for him.

"Turns out we wanna sign her, Hopkins. Fix it." Solly, assistant head of production. So high up he rarely acknowledged Hop's existence, even when he was stepping on his feet.

"Sign her? Sign *her*? Even if, Solly, even if she wasn't tramping her way through every production she's on, she's on contract with Jack Warner."

"We're gonna buy her. The big guy wants her."

"Yessir. But you know, I can get you ten like her in your office in ten minutes."

"Listen, kid, the big guy's decided she's an ice-cream blonde like he ain't seen since Thelma Todd first gave him a hot one twenty years ago."

"What the boss man wants, the boss man gets."

"Clean up the mess, kid. Clean it all up nice and pretty. We got things waiting for her. She don't even know."

"Making a late-night date, Hop? I do all the warming up and some other girl gets the hot payoff?" Barbara grinned widely, stirring her drink with one ladylike finger.

She's not interested in me, he reminded himself. Sometimes, with these actresses, after a cavalcade of getting-to-know-you drinks, he'd forget. Barbara Payton, for example, had two tastes: dull-eyed muscle men and flush, faux-ivy debonairs. He was a long way from either. Eyes as shifty as a door-to-door and vocab straight out of the Rust Belt—all patter, but hell, his shoulders still resembled the high school running back he'd once been, didn't they? Fuck. Better switch to beer.

"Oh no, you know me, B.P. I'll be tucking in for a night of Rachmaninoff and the latest Edna Ferber," he sighed. "But, I had this thought . . . That call was from Doris Day. You know Doris? Well, back in my reporting days, I interviewed her for her part in a little picture called *Romance on the High Seas.* Knew she'd be big. She just got married a few months back to a hell of a guy. Before, she was always blue over some no-good louse. Today, she sounds like the happiest fucking clam this side of the Pacific." Easy boy, don't force it.

"Hurrah for Doris . . . ," she said, shimmying a little in her seat to the calypso tune. And far enough gone not to demand too much finesse.

"It got me thinking about you. You big beautiful doll and the damage that this hit parade of Hollywood types could do to you and that ridiculously beautiful face."

"I like damage," she cooed absentmindedly. "It tingles."

"But for how long, B.P.? You're from what, Wisconsin? Land of milk and . . . milk."

"Minnesota. Cloquet, Minnesota. Land of a thousand lakes. Didn't you write the studio bio?" she said, straightening in her seat, eyes focusing a little.

"Right, right. You're the all-American dream girl, Miss Dairy Princess and pine needles in your hair. Summer picnics and autumn hay rides and winter sleigh rides and spring bike rides and Our Girl of the Frozen Midwest."

"You want I should break into 'By the Light of the Silvery Moon'?"

"A girl like you," he began, moving right past her sarcasm, confident he was on the right track. Something in her eyes. "A girl like you, she's not meant for the bruising ride through the darker corners of the Hollywood Hills."

"What, you're saying I should go back to Cloquet? After fifteen years of clawing my way out of that town? I wasn't going to spend a lifetime of Saturday nights watching my gandy dancer husband trying to win the logrolling championship."

"Oh no, no. You can't leave. We need you, kid. You're a star in the making, if you can stomach the *What Price Hollywood?* clichés. All I'm saying is, there must be a better way for you to live here. Someone to team up with, someone who'll understand the life and also look out for you, and your interests. And you."

"I've done the sugar-daddy gig, hon. Maybe you heard."

He had, of course. Twenty-two-year-old Barbara Payton had

taken forty-six-year-old Bob Hope for a rumored thirty grand plus a fabulous, fully furnished duplex apartment on Cheremoya Avenue—all in less than six months. She was no dumb bunny.

"I don't mean a sugar daddy, sugar lips. I mean a man who will do right by you. Bells and whistles and rice and the bouquet."

"Yeah?"

He saw the look and knew he'd finally stumped her and her pushed-out siren-red lower lip.

"And I think Franchot is the fella to do it."

"Since when were you hot on him? I thought you wanted me to close my lily-white legs and all that."

"I picture something majestic, Babs. You know what I'm seeing?" He grabbed her arms with one hand and gestured widely into the imaginary horizon with the other. "I'm seeing little Barbara Payton in a white lace dress, full skirt, train, the fringe of Minnesota-white bangs peeking out from beneath your grandmother's Belgian lace veil. I see her walking down the aisle in a little country church, the finest Methodist—"

"Presbyterian."

"—Presbyterian church in all of Cloquet and the county. The townspeople are assembled, Granny in her best Sunday bonnet, the mayor, hell, the governor, and that glorious early winter light streaming through the stained glass.

"And who should be at the altar, all sophistication and double-breasted dash, and certainly the biggest star to hit Cloquet since Maude Adams did her *Peter Pan* tour in '07? Franchot Tone, of course. And who does he see, through the blinding sunlight, but his bride: this hazy vision in eggshell white, this dark-eyed, sparkling American beauty. And the moment, the locking of eyes between the dapper groom and too-lovely, petal-white bride, is so perfect, so exquisite that many of the guests—even grouchy old Mr. Carnahan, the druggist, and bossy young Miss Harley, the librarian—find tears falling from their disbelieving eyes.

"It is, Miss Barbara Payton, a moment that will be talked about for years to come, passed down at knitting parties, quilting bees, church socials, and football games until it takes on the sheen of Arthurian legend. The movie king and his rising movie queen."

Damn if he couldn't almost picture it himself. He was half ready to volunteer as best man.

"Fuck, Hop. You play rough." A hot tear sprang to Barbara's eight-ball eyes. And Hop couldn't hide his smile.

Driving home, head soft like a melon from all the drinks, he was still smiling. His first opportunity to impress the big brass and it might be a home run. Everything was falling into place.

Where the fuck did he get that bit about the Belgian lace, anyway? You're a natural, kid. A natural. The way a shot of a girl's sandalwood musk could send him into a two-hour single-minded dance of a lifetime for the chance to press his face into the center of that smell—it was the same on the job. He was always ready to take the chance, make the play, show the fellas upstairs that he could plunge his hands straight into the dross for them and still come out clean. Just like when he was a kid, always caught with his mouth on the old man's bottle of Wild Turkey, fingers in Momma's purse—she called him Little Jack Horner, forever caught with his thumb in the pie. But why pass up a hot prospect, a sweet deal, all on the chance he might get caught? After all, even then, his baby face, fast tongue—these things could be parlayed. He hadn't yet faced a punishment so bad it made even the riskiest proposition not worth his trouble.

At least that's what Hop thought about himself. His soon-to-be ex-wife, Midge, however, who'd spent close to three years on the blunt end of this worldview, saw things differently.

"All I see is a guy awfully hot to take knocks," she'd say. "You just let the punches keep on coming. Don't flatter yourself by mixing that up with ambition or smarts or charm."

His pal Jerry, with far more affection, called him "Slap Happy—or Slap Hoppy."

He was feeling so good he thought he might drive by Gloria's place, say hello. She might be out on a date, but who knows? Worth a try. He owed her a visit anyway, hadn't seen her in weeks.

Of course she might be irritated when she saw him. Last time, he'd also come late at night, high and pushy, and even though she was glad to see him, she couldn't believe it when he got out of bed afterward, buttoned his shirt and pants, and started for the door. Her face knitted together, puckered like a thread, had been pulled too tight. She threw her telephone at him and knocked over her own new chaise lounge from Madame La Foux.

So maybe not Gloria.

He could go to Villa Capri, or to Chasen's for a hobo steak, make the rounds a little. There was a waitress at Villa Capri, Bernadette something, whom he'd taken out a few times. Gorgeous Italian chick with big, black-olive eyes and tits like Yvonne De Carlo.

Yeah, that'd be okay.

Or he could try to meet up with Jerry, coming off the evening shift at the *Examiner*. At least four nights a week, he knocked back a few with Jerry Schuyler, his closest friend, with whom he worked side by side through three years of churning out copy for *Yank* and *Stars and Stripes*. Over scotch, sometimes a martini, they'd swap stories from the front, just like they'd done during the war. Jerry was the only person in his new life who knew him before he came to Los Angeles. Just possibly, Jerry was the only person who even knew where he was from, or that he was from anyplace at all.

But then Hop remembered he probably couldn't see Jerry after all. Jerry was getting pretty hard to see these days, with the new lady in his life. It would have to be Bernadette to help celebrate. He wanted to celebrate all night.

Sweet Iolene

The next morning, Hop arrived at his office with fingers crossed about the Barbara Payton deal. Today he'd have to see if what he'd set in motion had any life of its own. This girl wasn't the most reliable kid in the pen, and he wouldn't be surprised if she had ended up eloping overnight—with the bartender, Howard Hughes, the Negro parking lot attendant. That one could get into a fresh world of trouble between midnight and seven a.m.

The press-office secretary, Lil, handed him his morning trade clippings and a few pieces of late- and early-delivery mail. Nothing more about Barbara but a few small fires to put out. An item in Sheilah Graham's gossip column hinting at an on-set fling between the square-jawed adventure hero and the married actress with twins at home. More "tales of woe" in Louella about poor Gail Russell—thankfully, one troubled actress who was not with his studio. Still, there were a few unnamed "friends" cited in the column that he'd have to check on.

"Someone's waiting for you," Lil said, nodding over to the set of chairs facing her.

Hop turned. "Iolene," he said, with a start.

There she was. Just as filled with slouching, dark-eyed glamour as the last time he saw her, nearly two years before, a different decade.

"Remember me?" she said, standing.

"Always," Hop said, surprised at the itch in his voice. "Follow me."

Pressing her copper-colored skirt flat, she sat down in the chair across from him. He gave her a broad smile. Maybe she wanted to charm him into helping her get a job. He hoped that was it, and if it was, he was ready to be charmed. It wasn't until she lifted her eyes to him, the crinkly veil on her hat rising over her forehead, that he knew what this visit was really about. She didn't bother to hide the spiny fear in her face.

"Been a while. You're over at Columbia now?" He smiled, kept smiling, suddenly self-conscious of everything, from his new shirt and sterling movie-reel cuff links to the picture window behind him, the polished dark oak desk on which he rapped his fingers.

"You could say so. Not working much these days," she said, tilting her head and lowering her long lashes.

"No? You on contract? Because maybe I could call—"

"Look at the king of Hollywood. Sure look like the Jack now, don't you?" she said icily, twisting her lips into a knot.

Hop just kept on smiling.

Slanting her eyes, she shifted forward and asked in a confiding tone, "What is it exactly you do here, Mr. Hopkins?"

Hop leaned back in his chair and, out of the corner of his eye, looked out his small window at the back lot. He felt a twitch in his eye.

Putting on his game face, he looked her in the eye.

"I'm a fireman."

"Come again."

"I put out fires. I start fires," Hop said, warming up to the line. "A little of both."

Iolene gave him nothing, not even a glimmer. The shiny clicks and levers that moved so easily for him with the likes of Barbara Payton were useless here. Instead, she snapped back, "Not the same fires?"

"Not usually, no. Ideally, at least."

"Tell me, Mr. Hopkins, would you start a fire just so you could put it out?"

"Now that's an idea."

She paused a second, as if deciding whether to tussle or not. Then something unfolded in her eyes, something unpleasant.

"You're really hitting on all eight now, eh? I know all about you, Mr. Hopkins. I got you coming and going. What I could tell—it got you far with your bosses, but maybe other people would be less impressed."

"Oh." Hop set his hands on the edge of his desk to keep himself steady. Something felt funny, something he could just about taste. "That's it, huh? Looking for a touch?" he said, as tough as he could, although he couldn't seem to stop himself from swiveling back and forth in his chair.

"No touch, Mr. Shark Skin. That's not me. And you don't get off that easy."

"Who does, Iolene?" he said, treading water, unsure where she was going but wanting to play it for all scenarios.

"*You* remember what happened that night. You were there, right in the middle of it. I saw you, and you saw everything."

Of course he remembered.

"Okay," he said, nodding, businesslike. "Let's talk. Meet me at the bar around the corner, the one with the green menu board out front. Twelve o'clock."

She agreed.

• • •

For the next few hours, Hop tried to get work done, made his calls, filed some press releases. But his mind kept pitching back to Iolene.

He used to see her all the time back in his *Cinestar* days. As many times as they ran into each other at the studio or at nightclubs, she wouldn't let him make her. Iolene, lips like tight raspberries. The girl who wouldn't spread her fine legs, not ever, not for him. What could be better than that? He felt her caramel skin in his sleep nights after he saw her. She'd pretend, even, not to get his meaning (*Sure can't be your hand there on my new belt, can it?*). She liked to play it, but only so far. She wouldn't come across. Even if she was the type—and maybe she wasn't, but let's face it, in this town, they all were, himself included—she wouldn't lay for a *Cinestar* reporter, a lousy feature writer. A columnist, maybe, if he had some jingle, but not a schmuck like him. Not when she could get a three-line walk-on by laying for Otto Preminger just once.

That night back in '49, the night she was talking about, well, he'd been playing craps, minding his own business and losing his rent money, when Iolene and her friend Jean approached him. Sure, he'd offered to take Iolene and Jean out on the town. Sure, he'd talked them into swinging by his apartment first for a cocktail. They'd had whiskey sours and Hop, mostly joking, angled to try to begin and end the evening right there on his sofa. Jean had yawned and wondered aloud if he really had any idea at all where the interesting people would be. That was what she'd said, "interesting."

"What she means is famous," Iolene had said, sitting back and raising one sparkling leg over the other.

"What I mean is *important*," Jean corrected. With another yawn, she looked over at the side table and the set of framed photos on it. Nodding to one, she said, "This is your wife?"

"Can't say I know any important people," Hop said, talking over her question. "But I know they like to roll in the mud as much as the rest of us. More, really. So let's go to the mudhole, ladies."

Because he did know of a place that, thanks to a backroom betting parlor and hash den, was lately drawing some of the biz's more adventurous types.

"Make it happen for us, big boy," said Jean, smiling for the first time. And, as she did, she was suddenly jaw-achingly pretty. Well, gosh darn.

It had been late, later than late, and they'd racked up quite a tab at the Eight Ball, a sweat-on-the-walls roadhouse in a dark stretch of nowhere just east of civilization. By eleven, they'd collected a shabby but starry group. Iolene and Jean—Jean and Iolene, one of the men sang drunkenly—seemed to know everyone. But Jean never seemed satisfied, was always looking over heads, even famous heads. At one point, Sammy Davis Jr., bandleader Artie Shaw, and director Howard Hawks were all crowding into their table, pushing drinks on the girls, including a new fetch, a knockout white-blonde. Iolene, drinking only a few sips of Rose's lime juice and soda all night, mostly sat, smoking Julep cigarettes one after the other. Jean imbibed at a more social pace and played it bright-eyed, leaving the full-on sprawling party-girl routine to the blonde who, Jean confided, was a burlesque performer at the Follies Theatre, where her stage name was Miss Hotcha. "What else could it possibly be," Hop had sighed, shaking his head and smiling wistfully at her.

Jean kept flipping her matchbook over and over in her hand.

"Who you waiting for, Legs?" Hop had said to her, winking. "Clark Gable don't make it out to places like this."

She'd looked at him long and slow and it was as mean and sexy a look as they could give, these girls. It was scorching.

"She's waiting for her new fella," Iolene whispered in his ear, lower lip nearly pulsing against it in the crush of the booth. "She thinks he might come."

Before Hop could ask who the fella was, Miss Hotcha had pushed her tight little thigh against his, leaned on his shoulder, and began singing "Need a Little Sugar in My Bowl" in his ear. It was a very good night, he thought. Very good night, boy-o.

It was close to one o'clock when the biggest stars yet strode into the creaking, blaring roadhouse. Marv Sutton and Gene Merrel. Hollywood's premier song-and-dance duo. Suave Sutton with his buttery baritone and dreamy-eyed Merrel, voice like sweet ice cream, both of them acrobatic, athletic dancers with pretty faces that could be plugged into any picture formula: two Broadway hoofers and one luscious blonde, two baseball players and one sultry brunette, two cadets and one fiery redhead. It was simple, and it worked over and over again. Sutton, the charmer who got the girl, dancing in glorious tandem with the angel-faced Merrel, who watched him get her. Seven, eight years ago, they were swinging it for peanuts in East Coast nightclubs. Next thing, they're movie stars.

Drinks were now on the house, bottle on the table, thanks to Sutton and Merrel's own personal studio press agent, Bix Noonan, who kept the liquor flowing freely, kept the boys happy. Hop might well have stayed were it not for Miss Hotcha. Before he knew it, he was caroming along the Arroyo Seco with the burlesque blonde in the seat next to him. He'd always been a lucky fella.

The next day, when the brunette Jean went missing, Bix called and Hop helped him out.

End of story.

• • •

After Iolene left his office, Hop tried to conjure up every detail he could still recall about that night. But by noon, when he was supposed to meet her, he had distracted himself out of the memory. He hadn't heard a Barbara Payton update yet, but Louella Parsons had called, saying she'd heard rumblings of Barbara sending her maid to Union Station for a train ticket.

When he walked into the bar, the kind of quiet, no-questions-asked place where colored women and white men could both get service, Iolene was already there. They ordered prairie oysters and carried them to a booth in the back.

"Okay, Iolene. What's it about?" He wasn't going to bother with charm or finesse. She wasn't buying, anyway. She never had.

She leaned back in her chair and glared at him.

"What you did, Hop, it wasn't right."

Hop's eyes widened. "Hey, I think you got the wrong guy."

"You sold Jean Spangler up the river to get your lousy job."

She's so angry, he thought. Why is she so angry? What did he do that was so wrong? She was looking at him like he was something stuck to the bottom of her shoe.

"I could make trouble."

"Jesus, Iolene," Hop blurted out. "What did I ever do to you?"

She looked at him. She was thinking hard. Weighing things.

"Listen, did you want the police at your door?" Hop said. "I kept your name out of it."

"Don't pretend you did it for anybody but Gil Hopkins," she snarled.

"Listen," he said coolly, "I don't know what you think I know, but it's nada, baby. Remember, I left. You didn't. You got more to account for than me."

She didn't say anything for a minute. He could see her eyes working. The hostility began to sink visibly from her face and turned into something else. Something like resignation.

"I didn't see anything," she said, looking down at the place mat, the damp spot where her drink sat. "Not really."

"We saw nothing, you saw nothing. So what are we talking about here then, Iolene?"

"Should have guessed the way things would go," she whispered, almost as if to herself.

Something in her voice told Hop to summon the waiter and raise the stakes. "Rye," she said, not even looking up. Hop signaled for him to make it two.

When the drinks came, she tucked into the corner of the booth and laid it out for him. And it was like this:

After Hop left the club with Miss Hotcha, Iolene could see that the song-and-dance men, Sutton and Merrel, the *stars*, were working something. Were hot on Jean. Iolene slid over in the booth, wanting to take Jean aside, let her know. But Jean said, *Don't worry*, and her eyes were wide, pulsing a little from the jump she'd taken. *Jean, you have enough trouble without getting into it with them*, Iolene had said. *You got more trouble than you can handle now. Those fellows are bad business. I heard stories.*

Jean grinned broadly at her, a grin that split her face in two, eerie like a ventriloquist's dummy, dark on a stage. She grinned broadly and in that grin she told Iolene, *All the stories in the world and I wouldn't pass this up—I've seen bad things enough to shake the word "bad" loose from its roots. I can go to the far end of nothing with the best of them. I can pull the pin and roll.* At least that's what Iolene saw in the grin. She saw it and she shrugged and she figured, *Her funeral*, but she didn't mean it like that. Not like that. She just decided Jean, all colt legs and showgirl grit, could handle herself, was a big enough girl to know the danger signs and beat it, time come and things turn wicked.

So she and Jean agreed when Bix Noonan invited them to come along to a hot club down by the docks.

So they went to the Red Lily, an awful, awful place. A place women shouldn't be. And things began to happen. Gene Merrel just hung in the corner, smoking brown cigarillos and twisting his cuff links. Sometimes he'd smirk a little or take a sip from his scotch, but he wasn't the one in the center of things. That night, no crooning plantation ballads, no strumming jumpy songs on his ukulele or launching into a vaudeville softshoe. He watched as pretty-faced Marv Sutton, all pomaded pompadour and dark-eyed Jew looks that drive the girls crazy, poured champagne and, when the champagne ran out, white crème de menthe, all along Jean's now bare, golden legs. Everyone watched as Marv, who rarely shifted out of slow motion in their movies, who had nary a crease in his suit or a spot of shine on his tanned face on-screen, now walked on his knees on the sawdust floor, nudging along like a crab, sliding a dark pink tongue along every curve and shoot in Jean's endless gams. You couldn't take your eyes off the show because it gave the promise of the kind of group debauch always in the Hollywood rumor mill but rarely available right before your eyes.

Bix Noonan asked Iolene if she wanted to leave the trio alone in a private room and go play cards. She agreed. She agreed.

Hop listened. It wasn't so much new information as a new way of telling it. Should he have stayed with them? *Don't go,* he remembered Iolene saying to him, hand wrapped around his arm, first time, the only time she'd ever touched him.

But there was Miss Hotcha, silvery purple satin pressed tight against her silvery skin, a long whisper-thread of blue vein running from the beginning of her jumbled cleavage to the flutter of her neck. And there was, after all, no heat or promise in Iolene's grasp. She just didn't want to be a third wheel, a set extra in the evening. Was he really supposed to give up the cancan girl to sit out the action chastely with this cross-legged champagne pearl? How could he have known? A million nights like this in Hollywood, every night in Hollywood, and only a few turn out like this.

"Hop," Iolene was saying to him now. "Listen. Bix offered to drive me home. But I didn't want to leave her with those two. I knocked on the door to that back room to try to get Jean to leave with me. I waited and waited at that door, Hop. Then Jean said through the door, 'Go on, honey,' she said. 'Go on.' So I did."

She looked up at him, eyes glassy, spun toffee.

"So, angel face, what's the sin there?" Hop said warmly. Maybe, after all, she just wanted reassurance. He could give her that in spades. *That* he could do. That he did all day long.

"Bix said, 'You know what things people say about those two.' And Merrel—he had a habit. Bix said he'd been kicking the gong all day. Bix said he was crazy. They were going to do her up, Hop. But I left. I did." Her voice shook and she couldn't meet Hop's eyes, which was fine with him.

"And the next day you see she's missing," Hop said. "But it's not your fault. Not by a long shot."

"I've known that girl forever," she said, barely listening. "One of the most beautiful girls in the world. They should have written that for her."

Hop looked at her. "What?"

She shook her head. "Never mind. You never got it."

"We didn't do anything wrong," Hop repeated, more firmly. "You gotta put it behind you. It's over." He could see the rye was hitting her. Things could get bleak. Someone had to end this or he'd find himself at St. Catherine's, knees on the floor.

"Listen, I gotta get back to the grind, but we'll have dinner sometime," he said, setting some bills down and putting on his hat. "Catch up for real, beautiful. *You're* one of the most beautiful girls in the world." As he repeated it back, it rung in his head for a second, then shuttered into silence.

As he saw her face, struck and unmoving, watching him as he turned to walk out the door, he felt something tighten inside him and then drop away.

And her voice: "You think you can forget."

Hop pretended he didn't hear and he didn't look back as he made his way to the exit. He resisted the urge to walk quickly, like someone discreetly leaving the scene of a crime. He hadn't done anything. She couldn't make him feel guilty for something that he didn't, wouldn't do.

"You think you can forget." A second time, like the refrain in a torch song. Like a warning.

Hop walked back to work, taking the long way, picking up a sandwich at the commissary. As he moved through the lot, he thought about it all. Tried to piece it together.

What did she expect from him? He wasn't a cop, a detective. If he honestly thought those guys, or anyone else, had anything to do with the girl's disappearance . . . a girl like that, come on, was always finding herself tangled up with rough stuff. Girls with legs like that and loaded up on ambition—hell, it was surprising that more of them didn't go missing—skip town, run away with a fella, maybe a married guy, or, sometimes, sure, just know too much, simply too, too much.

Even more common than that, of course: these girls often ended up bleeding their insides out in some shady MD's run-down office on Olive Street. There was a whole stretch tucked deep in Griffith Park—not so far from where the girl's purse was found—rumored to be a doc dumping ground for such unhappy accidents. Lovers' Lane, they called it, with a nasty wink.

What did Iolene want him to do about that? If her idea was to tap him, she wasn't going to get very far. Even if he did feel cornered, he was going to be dropping whatever pocket change he had on the divorce. There'd be nothing left. And if that wasn't her idea, if she was on the up-and-up and wanted his help, why . . . why did she think he was the kind of guy who would care? Was he?

Fuck, maybe he was.

He thought for a long thirty seconds about his part in the drama. He'd kept his mouth shut. And lied to a few cops. Really, who *doesn't* lie to cops? What else are cops for? All he did was make sure a few names never found their way into the papers or to the police. And to take care of that, sure, he made the girl's name disappear from the studio logs just to be safe. And then dropped a few hints to a few cops and maybe a reporter that the girl was known to keep company with some less-than-reputable boys about town. The purse with the broken strap in Griffith Park only helped, gave more likely reasons for the girl to fade to black. The unhappy coincidence (or not) of the name Kirk in the note found in her purse and Kirk Douglas, whose movie *Young Man with a Horn* Jean Spangler had worked on, was easily taken care of. A few calls and no whiff of ugliness ever clung to Douglas's fine suit.

Even if he hadn't lied, would the outcome be any different? Sure, Sutton and Merrel, for all their on-screen geniality and grace, were maybe into some sick stuff, but nothing he hadn't seen before—at least in part. Besides, girls like that know what they're getting into. You roll the dice, you take your chances.

Still, the thought kept returning: What if he'd stayed? Would it have made a difference? Why'd he have to go off with Miss

Hotcha, trying to make her? Did he end up making her? For a second, he couldn't be sure. Then he remembered—a quick, warm flash of a creamy belly arched against his cheek. Oh, yes, right.

Remembering that, he remembered something else, too. He remembered how, after leaving Miss Hotcha that night, after driving home, he'd stood in his own doorway for a moment, reminding himself no one was waiting for him, the wife gone visiting her mother in Ohio. Iolene and Jean had been sitting there on his couch just a few hours before. He could almost see them there. Funny, even with, or maybe because of, the faint crease on the chintz cushion on which they'd sat, even with the smell of smoke and pungent honeysuckle still in the air, the apartment—his apartment, their apartment—had never felt so empty.

He was always lonely.

Girl Reporter

Leaving work that night, Hop called Jerry at the *Examiner* to see if he'd meet him for a quick nip. After some mutual job griping, Hop feigned casual:

"Hey, Jer, remember, oh, fuck, over a year ago, closer to two, that story about that missing starlet? The one whose handbag they found in Griffith Park?"

"You're kidding, right? Of course I remember. Spangler, Jean. We covered it for a week. Thought it might be Daughter of Black Dahlia. But those stories come once in a newsman's life, right? That's what the managing editor told me. We were sure they'd find her body, hopefully split in two. Or maybe split in four, raise the stakes a little," Jerry said, in full-blown burnt-out city editor mode. He curled his hand around his chin and looked wearily at his friend.

"But they never did. Find the body," Hop said.

"Nope. My guess is one of those defrocked docs downtown gutted her—probably accidentally—and buried her in one of those old caves." He lit his cigarette, then tilted his head, as if reflecting. "If we hadn't had those delectable eight-by-ten studio glossies to stretch across the front page, I don't think we'd have given it day two."

Hop almost smiled before realizing he wasn't meant to. Jerry shook his glass, as if trying to knock loose a few last drops.

"You know," Hop said. "I met her once."

"Did you now, Hoppy boy?" Jerry took a long, thoughtful drag on his cigarette. "Were you the poppa?"

"I said I met her." He grabbed one of Jerry's cigarettes. "Didn't say I *met* her."

"Knowing you, you can see where I'd get confused," Jerry said, with a flicker of a smile. "So why the sudden interest?"

"No interest. Someone came to see me. The girl who introduced me to her."

"Yeah?"

"She seemed a little scared. Even now."

"Well, I remember there were rumors that Jeannie with the Dark Brown Hair—that's what they wanted to call her if we'd gone another week with the story—was bed hopping with a couple of toughs, Mickey Cohen's boys, so I'm not surprised she's scared."

"But you never thought it was a mob deal? Her disappearance."

"Could be. Is that what this girl thought?"

"I don't know. Who . . . Do you remember the reporter who worked the story for you?"

"Jim Mackie. You know him?"

"Sure, I think I met him—"

"But didn't *meet* him, eh?"

Hop grinned. "Gentlemen never tell, Jerry. You know that."

Jerry winked at him and Hop felt, suddenly and simultaneous with the first flush of the gin, the reassuring warmth of his oldest friend, dearest pal, cracking a sad-eyed smile. He resisted the urge to shove him, press his fist encouragingly into his friend's arm.

"So how's my wife, handsome?" he said instead.

"Hell on wheels, Hop," Jerry replied, not batting an eye. "You oughta know."

Hop cocked his head and nodded.

"After all," Jerry continued, "she learned it all from you." Taking a quick belt, he added, with a glimmer in his eye, "But, when she feels like it, so nice to come home to."

"Really?" Hop said, then added, with a shrug, "I don't remember that."

After Jerry left, Hop took a seat in a phone booth. Gotta get to the bottom of this. Why speculate? Not the kind of thing to let fester. He called Central Casting. They had a number for Iolene Harper and the exchange was Lincoln Heights. He dialed.

"I'm trying to reach Iolene."

"She ain't here," a man's voice said.

"When's she due back?"

"Man, she ain't coming back."

Hop felt something unstick inside his chest.

"What do you mean? Where'd she go?"

"Where they all go," he said, and then laughed without a hint of mirth. It was either sad or cruel. Hop couldn't tell.

"What does that mean?"

The man sighed and it sounded like a far-off whistle. "Look, pal, she's gone. Long gone, know what I'm saying?"

"But I just saw her." Hop was surprised at the strange pitch in his own voice. Suddenly, things felt more urgent.

"She was here yesterday. She's gone today, greenhorn. Guess you lost your chance."

Hop felt his throat go dry. What did he mean "lost your chance"? Did this man know who he was? He hadn't said, had he?

"Who is this, anyway?" Hop asked.

The man laughed again, even more hollowly. Abruptly, Hop could half see, as if right before his eyes, the dark room, the browned bottle of Old Crow, the pulled shades and open dresser drawers. The sinking aftermath of a hasty exit. A man in a chair with a pint or two of bourbon in him. A man seeing everything shattered in a stroke.

"Buddy," he said, voice blurred. "You *had* your chance."

The click in Hop's ear felt like it came from his own gut. What had just happened? And what did it have to do with him?

Running over to a post-premiere party at the Ambassador that night, shuttling around high-strung actresses, each with the same shade of Forever Amber No. 2 rinse and the same Dior dress, and dragging the male lead from the back kitchen, where he was giving a starry ingenue her first taste of cocaine, Hop was all smiles and shiny hair and sweet nothings. But everywhere he turned, he half expected to see Iolene standing there, eyes low-lidded, sexy, filled with disgust. *It was you, Hop. Never miss a chance to climb, you knew what a little palm greasing would get you, didn't you? You showed them what you were made of, pulling curtain after curtain across that night, across Jean Spangler, until no one could see a thing. A magician without the ta-da. And magicians never reveal their secrets.*

• • •

The next morning, Hop woke up with Iolene's voice strumming through his head, accusing him, beseeching him, trying to hook him into her fear, her guilt, that weight in her eyes. If she'd left town, why? What was she so afraid of? What could the danger be now? And could it touch him somehow?

Hop called the *Examiner* office, trying to get Jim Mackie on the phone.

"He's not here. Try the courthouse or Moran's or the precinct house or . . ."

He finally found Jim Mackie at the Pantry on Figueroa and Ninth, reading the *Mirror* while shoving a plate of waffles into his mouth.

"Is this where you hide out to read the competition?"

"Fucking Hop of the World. As I live and breathe. Didn't think you'd darken the doorstep of this joint again. Don't you slum exclusively at Romanoff's these days?"

"You got some syrup on your chin, Mack. And neck."

"Fucking purple shirt you're wearing."

"Lilac, chump."

"Pardon moi, motherfucker."

"I'm not here just to flirt, Mack," Hop said, sitting down at the counter next to him. "Can you help me out? You chased the Jean Spangler story back in '49, am I right?"

"Spangler . . . Spangler . . ." He took a long gulp of coffee with cream. "Call girl? No, the actress who took a dive out a window at the Biltmore?"

"No, no. The one they never found. Just her purse strap and a note in Griffith Park."

"Fuck me, I remember. The one with the ten-foot-long gams. Ogul's girl."

"Ogul?" Hop remembered the name. Little Davy, they called him. A hood in Mickey Cohen's crew. One of his so-called Seven Dwarves.

"Yep. Right before he took a one-way ticket to oblivion. He was going up on conspiracy charges and beat town or beat the devil not long after Spangler evaporated."

"That so?" Hop rubbed his face with his hand. What was he getting himself into? Cohen may have just been sent up the river for tax evasion, but did Hop really want to go fishing in those waters?

"That be so, my friend."

"Did you follow the Kirk trail? You know, the 'Dear Kirk' note they found in her purse?"

"Yeah. Because it was a sexy angle, I spent a lot of time trying to wade through the moat around Kirk Douglas. He was in Palm Springs at the time, though, so as bad as he lied about knowing her, he couldn't lie his way into becoming a real suspect."

"You think mangled abortion?"

"It sure seemed the straightest line, Hoppy. And it's one the cops shrugged their way into."

"But you don't buy it."

"I don't have to buy it," he said, wiping a slick of syrup from his chin. "It's been bought, sold, and put into storage."

"You got pushed off the story."

"Not in so many words," he said, waving his fork. "There were just other stories with more gas."

"If you'd had two more days to run with it, where would you have gone?"

"To the Little New Yorker or Sherry's to talk to a couple of Cohen's boys. But I doubt it would have gotten me anywhere."

"Why?"

"They were all lying low because of Davy Ogul's vanishing

act. Spangler had dallied with Ogul, or so said those in the know. But they'd parted ways a while back. I couldn't find out much more, since both parties were conveniently dropped off the face of the earth."

"Some coincidence, Ogul getting invisible the same week, eh?"

"According to my PD sources, the last true-blue sighting of Spangler wasn't by her cousin when Spangler left the house. Later that night, she was eyeballed at a restaurant—I think the Cheesebox—with some goons."

"Yeah?" Hop said, trying to recall all the jazzed-up tips he'd passed to reporters and even a few cops. He was pretty sure this might be one of his own fictions being rolled back out to him. Fuck, Hop, you really make your own trouble.

"So she's no longer a possible victim of some snazzy sex criminal. Instead she becomes, well, you see it, a two-bit mob whore."

"And a much less interesting case to the press, who have plenty of richer Cohen ore to mine?"

"Something like that. And you know, this was when there was some bad blood brewing at the old LAPD. But I didn't stay for the dance. The bosses tossed me over to cover the Cohen crew shakeup. Gave Stanger—"

"Spangler."

"—Spangler to the girl."

"The girl?"

"The girl. Frannie Adair."

Twenty minutes later in the *Examiner* city room, Hop straightened his tie.

"Tell me, Miss Adair, what's it like being the only lady in the pen?"

She had been easy for Hop to spot, the sole pair of heels and the only ass worth a glance in the sweeping room full of sweat-stained, unshaven ginks. Frannie Adair, all ginger curls and round cheeks, like three months off the farm, until she spoke. Twitching her freckled nose, she shot back at him, "What's it like going over to enemy lines, turning stooge for the plastic factory?"

"It has its advantages," Hop said, rolling with it. This girl didn't look like she suffered fools.

"Likewise," she said, nodding and angling her head toward the smoky newsroom. "These boys don't tip their hats and there's the occasional pinch in the elevator, but I haven't bought my own beer yet. And you?"

"Likewise. Only they *do* tip their hats to me."

"I'll bet," she said pointedly. "I hear you've done more white-washing than Tom Sawyer."

"If I was that good, you wouldn't know about it, would you?"

"Well," she said, eyes narrowing, "it's just a rumor, but we'd all like to know how you pulled off that Simmons deal. One night, Mr. Wild West himself punches a cop in the jaw, resisting arrest—*we hear*—for getting caught with a needle full of horse in his neck, the next thing: the *Herald-Express*, our near-and-dear sister paper, runs a story about how Mr. Busted-Jaw Cop is no hero. In fact, he sent his wife to the emergency room the week before, beaten so raw they had to slide her nose back into the middle of her face."

Pausing, she poked her pen on Hop's lapel before adding, "Then, a day later, charges against Wild West Simmons go puff."

Hop tried not to smile. "I know the story you're talking about, but only thirdhand. I hear it was all an honest mix-up."

"I'm sure."

Truth was, it had been a combination of hustle and luck. He hadn't been sure the cop's wife was lying (although he was pretty sure she was). Why should that stop him from passing along the story to a salivating reporter? It wasn't his job to find out who was telling the truth. He knew what his job was.

"So it turned out the cop's wife had an ax to grind?" Hop shrugged. "That reporter should've checked his facts before condemning the guy. I'm sure you would have."

"You got that right, Mr. Hopkins," she said, capping her pen. "I don't fall so easy. Not even if you batted those long lashes at me all day long."

He took her for a bowl of chop suey at a small place around the corner. She smoked while she ate, digging for stringy pork. They sat on adjacent stools at the counter—"So I don't have to look into those big blue eyes of yours," she'd said.

"Spangler. Yeah, I had the story for about a week," she said, then lifted her eyes from her food and crooked her head toward Hop. "You must know more about it than me. She was with your studio, right?"

"I wasn't working for them then."

"That doesn't answer my question. What do you want from me? What could I tell you that you couldn't read in the papers?"

Hop pushed his food away and rested his elbows on the counter, turning his head toward her.

"Nothing. Maybe. I don't know." He was trying to be careful. To strike a balance. He wanted to find out if there were any leftover threads dangling from the case without pulling a few new ones loose in the process. He said, "A friend of mine who knew the girl came to see me. She was a little shook up."

"Why? That was almost two years ago." She was getting more interested. He could tell by the way she lowered her fork from full keel.

"I don't know. She left before I could find out."

"So go ask her. Telephone her."

"She's left. No forwarding number."

"Close friend, eh?" She wiped her lips with her napkin. "So why do you care?"

Hop tried to decide if this Adair girl was attractive or not. He thought so when he first spotted her in the newsroom, breasts like hard little peaches against her tailored suit. Big cow eyes and a firm mouth. Legs that worked coming and going.

But something in the way she spoke seemed like each word she uttered sent out a hundred-yard stretch between them. Or like she was behind a pane of glass. And not in a way that made him want to rap on it, asking for admittance.

"The point is," he said, resting his finger on the edge of her sleeve, "I can't seem to puzzle out what got her so shook up. I figure if I find that out, maybe I can help her." This wasn't all true, but it was true enough. Maybe. Hop couldn't untangle his motives. There was something about covering his own tracks— tracks he thought he'd long ago covered. And sure, there was something else. Something about Iolene's accusations. And something, too, about the coltish fear in her eyes and the idea that maybe he—the fixer—could make it disappear.

Frannie shook off his finger and speared herself a water chestnut. "Mr. Hopkins, I'd like to help—well, no, actually, I don't care. But I couldn't help even if I did. Read my stories. That's all I know."

Something in the way she returned so intently to her congealed chop suey, which was among the worst he'd ever tasted, made him more sure of her interest. She had something. He wondered what it could be and how you'd get something like that out of a girl like that.

"How would I get something out of a girl like you," he said, taking a chance on the honest approach. "And note: I'm not batting my eyelashes."

She grinned, exposing a chipped tooth. Somehow, the sight of it stirred Hop and a few dozen yards fell away.

"Let me think on some things, Mr. Hopkins." She set her fork down and grabbed for her purse, the grin slowly giving way to concentration. Slowly.

"Call me Hop."

"I can't call a grown man Hop."

"That's right."

At the end of a long afternoon at the studio spent mostly trying to coax a fresh-faced, teenage star out of marrying a Mexican mariachi musician she'd met in Tijuana, Hop drove out to Lincoln Heights to find the address Central Casting had given him for Iolene.

As he got closer, he realized he'd been in this area before, back in his short stint working for Jerry at the *Examiner* when he first came to town. He'd covered a story about a gambling shop above a Salvation Army. Bettors were strolling in, having some coffee, listening to a little of the gospel, then slipping upstairs to lay down some green on the Cardinals over the Sox in five.

He'd sized up Iolene for classier digs. In fact, he had a vague memory of her saying she shared a small apartment with a girlfriend in one of the sparkling pink and gray high-rises of Westwood. "The manager thinks I'm her maid, but I'm not particular," Iolene had said with a shrug.

This particular strip of road was a big step down. And when Hop began to get closer, he felt kind of lousy for her. Sure, a Negro girl, no matter how finely turned-out or how talented, was never going to be the next Ava Gardner, but Iolene had always worked steady in the past, small parts singing in supper clubs, dancing in large revues.

When he reached the right number, he saw it was a house, small, with a sagging overhang and split into apartments. One set of windows was covered over with sun-rippled newspapers. An overflowing, rusted metal trash can teetered on the lean strip of brown lawn.

Hop, feeling conspicuous in his pressed linen suit and his lemon-yellow pocket square, dashed up the walk as quickly as possible. A directory, just a faded index card taped beside the door, revealed no clue as to which apartment Iolene lived in, if she lived there at all. Her name didn't appear.

Hop paused a moment before trying the door, which wobbled open. There were two apartments on either side and an old pine staircase leading to the second floor.

"What the hell," Hop decided out loud before rapping on the door marked no. 1.

No answer.

He turned instead to no. 2, from which he could hear a faint thrum of bop. He'd barely completed a brisk knock when the door flew open and a petite colored woman in a red wrap stood before him.

"Honey, I, honest, don't know where he dusted. He could be clearway to Chicago with those stones for all I've been made aware," she said, shaking her head.

Hop stared at her. Had everyone in this building skipped town? "What stones?"

The woman curled her mouth in thought. "You ain't the fella from Treasury."

Hop tried a smile. "No, ma'am. Another white guy."

She laughed, tugging her wrap closer to her chest, hand still on the door. "You ain't so white."

"Well, then help a brother out," he said with a grin. "I'm looking for an old friend, Iolene. She still live here?"

"Oh, you her daddy?" She smirked, shaking her head. "No Iolene here, boy. Another colored chick."

"Are you sure? Lived with a man. I talked to him on the phone."

"So why didn't you ask him where your girl went?" Her eyes slanted, just perceptibly. "You sure you ain't law?"

"So sure it hurts," Hop said, as lightly as he could. "We worked together, sort of."

She paused a minute, locking eyes with him. Then, "A man, Barber, lives in number four upstairs. He had a woman here now and again. Name of Louise."

"Pretty, about so high, light skin?"

She nodded, tilting her head knowingly. "That the way you like 'em, Mr. High Yella?"

Hop skipped over her question. He wanted to be sure Louise and Iolene were one and the same. "With a really distinctive voice, low and soft?"

"Oh, man, what you take me for, Arthur Godfrey? Yeah, Louise sang," she sighed, as if deciding. Then, "At a joint on Adams near Jefferson Park. King Cole is the name."

Hop felt a ripple of relief. Not a complete dead end. He looked back at the woman, leaning on the door frame. "What's your name?"

She smirked. "Just call me Gorgeous," she said, beginning to shut the door.

"Thanks, Gorgeous." Hop quickly pulled out a five-spot. "You're swell . . ."

Smirk sliding away, she tucked her fingers around the bill and the door swung shut.

King Cole

It was a large place with green damask walls, long, narrow tables, and private booths with heavy curtains. On the long wall behind the bar was a smoke-patina mural of a bushy-browed king enthroned with pipe and bowl. It ran all the way behind the small stage, where it depicted three fiddlers looking more like German barmaids than musicians.

A white girl in a spangled gold dress sang Rosemary Clooney style, while a long-fingered Negro played piano. The crowd was just as mixed.

Hop slid into a seat at the bar and ordered a soda to keep things simple. The bartender didn't quite roll his eyes at the order but perked up when Hop left a two-dollar tip.

"Is Iolene singing tonight?"

The bartender lifted his eyes, pausing a second in wiping a glass.

"Not these days, pal. She doesn't come around here anymore. Not in weeks."

"That right? How come?"

"Most people here knew her as Sweet Louise. Guess you're kind of a friend."

"I am. Haven't seen her in a while, though."

"Not so much of a friend if you don't know."

"Know what?"

The bartender set down the glass and pointed, rag still in hand, to a man sitting alone at the far end of the long bar. He looked like he'd been drinking for several hours or years.

"That's the man you want to talk to. Jimmy Love. Played piano for her when she was on regular."

Hop thanked him and made his way down the bar. The man

spotted the approach and gave Hop a long, unblinking stare the whole way.

"Your name ain't Hippity Hop, is it?" he muttered. And the minute he spoke, Hop recognized him as the man he'd spoken to on the phone when he'd tried to reach Iolene.

"Uh, no, Gil Hopkins. They call me Hop, though."

"They do, do they? Who's they?"

Hop smiled. "Just about all the theys."

"Oh, then you're the one," Jimmy Love said slowly. His voice, coated with drink, still had a funny kind of dignity that made Hop sit up straighter in his seat. "I thought so when you called."

"The one what?"

"The one Iolene went to see. She said she'd done you a favor, a big one, of the 'mouth-shut' variety, and now, with all her trouble, you would step up." His eyes turned from the mirror behind the bar to Hop.

"I don't know what . . ." Hop felt three hairs above sea level, and sinking fast.

"Those boys have been closing in. Boys you don't want to make unfriendly with, Hoppity."

"Connected?"

"Hell, ain't we all?" He shrugged, taking a handkerchief out of his pocket. "You can't live in this town without it sticking to you like tar paper. But no, these fellas were up some notches."

Hop lowered his voice. "Cohen connected?"

Wiping a drop of Jack Daniel's from his upper lip, Jimmy Love shook his head. "What did I just say, greenhorn? You're much slower than she let on. She acted like you knew a damn thing."

"She was wrong," Hop said. *Boy, was she.*

"More ways than one, looks like. You didn't help her for jack, Jack," he said, shaking his head again and slipping his handkerchief back into his pocket. "Now it's later than you think."

Recognizing he'd been dismissed, Hop stepped out of Jimmy Love's way. He was starting to tire of conversations where he only followed a whisper of meaning. Each step into Iolene's world made him feel like he was pulling away filmy veil after filmy veil and never getting any closer to her honey skin. This was how he'd always felt with Iolene. With some other women, too. These days, he'd come to prefer the ones whose secrets lie only behind a thin layer of nylon, if that.

As he watched Jimmy Love drop a few bills on the bar and walk out without another word, Hop waved over to the bartender.

"Bourbon," he sighed, pushing his soda aside. "Bourbon."

"Does that mean bourbon twice or are you playing for emphasis?"

"Do you get extra tips for the Oscar Levant routine?"

"Not from your type."

Had he even made her any promises? Not that he could recall. He was very careful, his entire life, to avoid making any promises to women at all. He remembered Iolene showing up at the *Cinestar* office the day after Jean Spangler first went missing, eyes red as grenadine, hands shaking, clattering against the tortoise clasp on her purse. At the time, he was sure the girl—this Jean—would show up. That she'd just gone off on one of these joy rides that these starlets live, breathe, and tramp themselves all over town for.

"Listen, Iolene, what could you tell the cops that would help them find her, really? Stay out of it. You want to end up in cuffs on the cover of tomorrow's *Mirror*? Guilt by association, baby. Who needs it? Let me do the talking for us. Fix it real nice."

And he had. He knew what to do to make it all go away. Drop a few ideas—ideas that were code for "girl of questionable habits." "Girl running in dangerous circles." "Girl not long for this town." It wouldn't take much. He knew that, too. Girls like this turned to smoke every day.

"I guess I'm going home," Hop told the bartender at the King Cole, pushing the empty glass forward with his two index fingers. His head wobbled and he knew he'd had at least two drinks too many. *Fuck me, I'm innocent.*

"It's not even two. King Cole's booming until four o'clock closing."

"Maybe so." Hop threw some bills on the bar, his eyes moving in and out of focus. "But I got someone waiting."

"A girl?"

"Sort of. A wife."

It was only then that, in his bourbon haze, Hop remembered there was no wife. Hadn't been one for almost a month. The only place to see Midge now was tucked in Jerry's brown-walled bachelor pad on Bronson. It was the first time he'd forgotten and it made him feel lost, a ship knocking against a dock over and over that no one hears.

That's the booze talking, he assured himself.

Driving home, he missed a turnoff and ended up heading toward Bronson, anyway. Some small voice in the back of his head whispered, *But only if the lights are on.* Then he figured, hell, until a few months ago he wouldn't have thought twice about dropping in on Jerry at this hour. They'd drink brandy, reminisce about the war, talk about Jersey Joe Walcott or anything at all. That was back when Hop would do anything to avoid going home. Kind of like now.

He wasn't altogether sure what he was going to do when he got there. But that didn't stop him from leaving his car teetering on the curb and running up the drive and the four sets of stairs to Jerry's door, skidding on the last set of steps so hard he nearly tore a leg off his pants from the knee down. It was something about him wanting to see Jerry, like he always did, but now Midge was there and it wasn't fair. It wasn't fair at all.

It seemed like he'd only been knocking for a second, but when Jerry's face appeared he realized his knuckles were already sore.

"Oh boy, you're soused," was all his friend said, and before Hop could blurt out whatever it was that was ready to press through from the dark tumult of his head straight out his mouth, he heard that familiar nasal pitch. A voice from behind Jerry, scrambling to make itself heard.

"Get the hell out of here, Gil. No one wants to see you."

Midge.

"Oh yeah?" Hop found himself jamming his hand against the door hard, knocking Jerry back a few feet.

When he heard his own voice, it wasn't the cool meter he'd imagined in his head as he'd trotted up all those stairs. It didn't sound like himself at all. It sounded like the Hop only his wife could generate, spontaneously, like a disease.

"Maybe Jerry wants to see me," he said. Then, struck by his own petulance, he turned nastier. "Maybe I'm not here to take out the trash." As soon as he said it, he regretted it. This wasn't how he wanted to be, not in front of them, not now.

Still, he kept going, battering forward. He moved past Jerry, in a pair of striped pajamas that Midge must have bought—they were just the kind of smooth, shiny thing Midge was always buying.

He pushed through the familiar space, the warm brown room

with its wooden turntable and low lights and piles of books, long, tall bottle of scotch and shiny tumblers. And the new pair of acid-yellow cushions Midge must have purchased to brighten up the place, a garish splash that hurt his eyes, mustard on prime rib.

It was only then that he got a good view of his wife, her arms tugging on the door frame to the bedroom, both hands, one above the other, gripping the edge. And she in a long robe with matching nightgown, black and filmy, like a high-class hooker.

And it was also then that he saw she looked different. Her hair pinned up so tight, like a schoolmarm, a jarring disjuncture with the costume and the mascaraed eyes.

He looked closer, and something clapped loudly in him and unfurled for miles, falling and falling faster still.

"You cut off all your hair, Midge," he murmured, his voice broken, broken to bits. "What happened to all your beautiful hair," he said, fumbling across the room toward her, shin hitting the coffee table.

Then, right there, despite her shocked face, he couldn't stop his fingers from diving into the bright white-blonde curls, curls like spun satin under his nails, in the pockets of flesh between his fingers. Christ, how drunk was he?

"Stop, stop. You ruin . . . you ruin . . . ," she stammered, a hand on his chest and then a hard shove.

"All your beautiful hair," he said, repeating himself help-lessly, noticing, with a tremble, the stray platinum strand on his fingertip.

Looking back at him, she said, finally, "You ruin everything beautiful."

Hop's hands fell to his sides. "But, baby . . ."

She pulled her robe together and straightened. "You lost, don't you see?" she said, shaking her head, voice spiky. "You lost everything."

"Oh," Jerry said suddenly, and both were reminded that he was there.

Midge and Hop turned and looked at him, waiting for him to say more. But that was all he said.

When he first met Midge, he thought she was the loveliest thing in the world, her heart-shaped face, pointy chin tilted, bow lips, just like a porcelain doll. But when you touched her skin, she was neither cold nor hard but all nerve endings, hot and yielding, tensile and charged—two hands around her midriff (you felt you could wrap them around twice) and her back arched tight, and she'd shudder and ripple and undulate like some kind of wired animal. It was a kick, let me tell you. Who knew the price would be so high? Oh, Midge, I was your chump.

"Operator."

"Yeah, doll. Can you give me the number for, um, Adair, Frannie? A-D-A-I-R."

"I have Adair, F., 812 Laveta Terrace."

"Good enough."

He didn't bother to call. It would slow him down. Out of the booth on Hollywood Boulevard and back into the car. Now no longer just drunk, but drunk and cracked open by his wife's dainty high heel.

It wasn't a long drive, which, even in his condition, he could tell was unfortunate because it didn't give him enough time to think about what he was doing. He just knew that after that bang-up with Midge he couldn't stomach going home.

When he approached the bungalow, he felt the weight of his own bad behavior, but it didn't stop him.

He walked up to the door and knocked.

A moment later, a light went on and he could see Frannie's red hair peeking out the front window at him. He could almost hear her curse through the wall.

She flung the door open.

"I was expecting a satin robe. Or maybe very soft cotton," Hop said. He had been positive he'd wake her up. It was very late, he was sure. And in fact, he could tell by the long crease on the side of her face and the heavy look in her eyes that she had been sleeping. But she was wearing a wrinkled green shirtwaist dress and a pair of stockings. No shoes.

She looked down at her dress and ran one tired hand through her tangled hair. Then she looked back up at Hop.

"What the hell do I have to explain? You're the one at my door at . . ." She looked down at her bare arm. "I don't know where my wristwatch is."

"You wanna alert the neighbors or can you let a fella in?"

"You smell like my old man. How many does that make? Must be at least four hours of steady bourbon."

"Yeah? And you?"

"A girl's gotta have some social life. But I'm straight now. Can you say the same?" She opened the door wider and walked into her living room. Hop followed.

Sinking down into her sofa, he looked at her, trying to keep steady. Christ, how many had he had? What the hell was he doing here?

She brushed a hand over the wrinkles in her dress.

He was torn between his own private misery and his natural instinct to want to ask her about her night, about the kind of evening Frannie Adair had that sent her to bed before she could manage to unzip her dress.

"You got your shoes off," he noted, instinct winning out.

"I think they fell on the floor," she said, rising. "I'm getting some water. Do you want anything, bright eyes?"

"Pinch of something? Might as well keep going," he said, leaning back against the cushion for balance.

As she poured the drinks and he had a brief minute alone, he started to feel rotten again, lost his own footing, and remembered the scene at Jerry's, and the scene before that at the King Cole.

And then she was handing him a short glass of brandy and she was drinking a tall tumbler of water and something happened. Something knocked loose inside him and suddenly he could hear his own voice talking, talking nonstop, about how he'd seen Jean Spangler the night she'd disappeared, about how Marv Sutton and Gene Merrel—yes, *that* Sutton and Merrel, silver-tongued crooners, fleet-footed dancers, the whole song and dance—had joined them at a little dive called the Eight Ball. And how they'd taken her off with them and how he didn't know for sure what happened but that he knew everything had turned very bad somehow.

She listened. She listened very closely. She watched the words issue from his mouth in long, taffy strings. She let him hang himself, pull by pull. Then, finally, she said:

"What exactly are you saying? That Sutton and Merrel were involved in her disappearance?"

"Involved, involved. What does that mean? Far as I knew, they were just fixing to take turns, that's all. I don't know. I had left. I had left, Frannie Adair. I only found out the next day. And I never thought it was so bad. What I did. But now I think I may have missed something. I may not have realized what I did. Could I be the guy she said I was?"

"She? Spangler?"

"No. No."

"Who?"

"I'm not getting into all that," he said, something in him whispering, *Keep her name out. Keep names out. Iolene, whoever. You've already fucked it up enough, Hop, why can't you stop talking?* "Why am I here, anyway?" he mumbled. "I can't believe I went over there. What a jackass. I should never drink. My head feels like a sponge full of quinine. I'm a lousy bum, Frannie Adair. Why did you let me in?"

"Listen, at lunch you said someone came to see you. Was she the girl you left the Eight Ball with?"

"No, no. Not her. Let me tell you something, baby," he said, leaning forward. "Midge, she had the most beautiful hair. I wish I could explain. Like a . . . like a river of gold running down her back. Do you believe it's all gone?" He heard the words issuing from his mouth, but they kept surprising him. It was just so comfortable there—the yielding sofa, Frannie listening, hair rumpled, smelling like fresh sheets and open windows—he couldn't stop.

"Who's Midge? Is she the girl who came to see you? The one who's scared?"

"Midge's never been scared a day in her life. Midge is my wife."

"You're married," she said, leaning back in her seat. "Sounds about right."

"And the thing is, Frannie Adair, I never thought that I, Gil Hopkins, who everybody always loves, just *loves*, could make anyone—okay, a woman—so angry."

It was true. He'd always thought of himself as the kind of soft-touch, glimmer-eyed boy who begs to be smoothed over with mother love. The kind that women just wanted to curl around the feet of, like little honey kittens. Sadly, as it turned out, he was not this kind of man at all. Somehow, he was the fellow in the cartoon, the comic strip, running out the front door, pants half on, with a frying pan zooming toward his head—*zzzz*ing—thud. He guessed it wasn't Midge who had started it, but it sure felt that way. Her love like a slug in your drink.

"I wonder why Jerry let her cut her hair," Hop said abruptly.

"Who's Jerry—her hairdresser?"

"No, Jerry Schuyler."

"Our Jerry? At the *Examiner*? What's he got to do with it?"

"You know, Frannie—can I call you Frannie?—you know what Midge said to me? The last thing before she left me. She said, 'What, did you think you could keep throwing us together again and again, talking hot about me to Jerry and Jerry to me, practically shoving us both under the covers, and we wouldn't end up like this?' And yet, Frannie, here's the funny part," he said. "I *was* surprised."

She gave him a long look, reacting to something in his voice. Something funny.

Then, gently, she said, "Jerry doesn't seem the type to steal a fella's girl."

"He's a right guy," Hop said, meaning it. It felt funny to hear himself mean something so much. "A stand-up guy. He'd give me the shirt off his back."

"So you gave him the wife off yours in return?"

"My, but you're smooth." He finished his drink and raised it above his head, saying, "There goes another potato."

When he left ("I like to leave before I wear out my welcome"), he could no longer fight a sinking feeling, but he distracted himself by looking at Frannie as she walked him to the door. He stopped at the threshold and looked at her. She seemed to have the most open face he'd ever seen, at least since those Syracuse girls, snow nestling in their ringletted hair, skating around the pond behind church, making larger and larger circles, figure eights, twirling endlessly, smiling at him and waving.

"Good night, Gil Hopkins. Sleep it all away."

"You too," he said and, unable to resist the urge, reached out to touch the sheet crease still faint on her cheek.

The next morning, he couldn't remember if she'd smiled or just shut the door.

He woke up many times during the night, propelled from dreams so vivid he was sure Jean Spangler was there crouched under his tangled sheets with him. In all the dreams, she was the same blank beauty, a glamorous maw with no center. Even in his unconscious, he couldn't imagine a personality, even a sole trait for her. She was What Went Wrong. In one dream, he crawled straight inside her gorgeous violet mouth and found himself right back where he started, listening to her flat, inflectionless voice issuing word after word, none of which he could really discern—it was a low, dull stream of nothing.

The cold-hot of drunken sleep covered him head to toe, shot through periodically with the slow realization of everything he'd said and done the night before. He couldn't have possibly gone to that girl reporter's *home*, could he? He, the professional juggler of newsmen, the light-and-shadows artist forever dangling, then withdrawing, promises of sexy secrets and sexier lies, couldn't possibly have gone to a reporter's house and held forth on the carpet, no charge, no trade, tales dark enough to kill a half dozen careers, especially his own? Not him. He was the master of keeping his mouth shut, could practically count on two fingers the number of people in this town who knew his full name. Power in withholding. It's what every smart woman ever taught him, and the not-so-smart ones, too, by bad example.

You give anything away, you might as well give everything away.

Still, the more his thoughts took hold and he was able to distinguish his recollection from his frenzied dreams—the things he said from the things he merely *thought* while saying other things—the more he had to face the grim truth.

He'd told Miss Frannie Adair a lot. And he was going to have to fix it, fast.

He had no one to blame but those two girls so hard on him the last few days—Iolene and Midge weighing him down, he who so depended on being light on his feet, always moving, never sitting still.

As the sun finally crept under his blinds, Hop, half awake, forgot for a second about everything, other than a wave of brief pleasure at the flickering dream image of Iolene's coffee-with-cream thighs. But the image didn't wake up with him, just settled into his body, his bones and joints, nuzzled for a second, then passed. In its place twitched the memory of the Midge hubbub. That sure woke him. The clock read 7:30. He had to clear the murk from his head. He had to get out of bed. It was Saturday, right? Yes. Thank god.

Ten minutes later, he'd managed to make it to the bathroom, to the pulsing shower and then the medicine cabinet to scrape a night of bad living from his face. As the fog on the mirror slowly evaporated and the shaving cream slid away to reveal his bright, forever bright face, he began thinking straight for the first time in twelve hours. For a second at least. Then:

That goddamned wife, like a little girl, pulling off the legs of insects, one by one. First she steals his best friend for herself, then she gets him so worked up that he goes off and spills his guts to a professional megaphone.

And who was this Iolene, anyway? Christ, he barely knew the girl and she'd managed to throw his life into some kind of crazy funhouse mirror in a matter of days. She'd tapped into a tiny reservoir of guilt, of sympathy, of something, and now he couldn't untap it. Iolene.

Still . . .

Facts are, Hop, you fucked up. You have to admit it: you have only yourself to blame. You gotta fix it.

First, Frannie Adair. What does she know and what does she plan to do with it?

"City desk."

"Frannie Adair there?"

"Not yet, pal. Call back later."

"She comes in today?"

"She'll be in to file. She'll be at the courthouse today. Say, who is this, anyway?"

Okay. Okay.

He made some coffee and got dressed.

As he drank a cup, scalding and bracing, he thought hard.

Okay, I'm Frannie Adair, junior reporter out to prove my chops. What do I know? I know Jean Spangler met up with high-wattage stars Sutton and Merrel the night she went missing. I know they were looking to have a party with her. That's it.

What don't I know?

He thought hard about this. He never told Frannie where Jean Spangler and the others had moved on to after they left the Eight Ball. The name "Red Lily" never passed his lips, he was sure. He never said who else was there, except that there was another girl he left with. She doesn't know who that girl was (of course, neither does he). He never said anything about his story to the police, about his lies, half-lies, and whatever else he used, because, let's be honest, he'd used everything he had.

So if I'm Frannie, he thought, and I'm as smart as she maybe could be, what do I do with what I know? I don't go straight to Sutton and Merrel's people. Instead, I work the angles, the curves, the corners. I work the cops on how they missed Spangler's evening jaunt. I work the Eight Ball. I work me. Hop, that is. Good luck there, Frannie Adair. Last night, you got the biggest piece of me you'll ever get.

He decided to call Sutton and Merrel's manager, Tony Lamont. Hop had met him a half dozen times, had drinks on occasion. Nice guy. Low-key. Not the fly-off-the-handle type.

"Listen, Tony, there's a reporter sniffing around an old missing-persons case. A, uh, Jean Spangler. Trying to pull out a story."

"What's it got to do with me?"

"Nothing, and let's keep it that way."

"You wanna clue me in?"

"You know, Tony. Jean Spangler." He knew Tony remembered. They'd made a lot of calls that week following the disappearance.

Tony paused a second. Then, "You being overly cautious or is there a reason I should batten down some hatches?"

"Nah, nah. Well, somehow this reporter found out Spangler was at the Eight Ball that night. If she talks to employees there, your boys could come up. You know."

"She hasn't talked to anyone there yet?"

Hop could hear wheels turning, knocking around, charging faster in Lamont's head.

"I don't think so."

There was a click on the other end.

Three minutes later, the phone rang again:

"Hop?"

"Yeah."

"Problem solved. I renegotiated some arrangements, if you will. Our boys were never at the Eight Ball that night. Or any other night. No one can remember ever seeing them there. Or seeing anybody else, ever."

"It's amazing the place stays open for business."

"Ain't it? Who else we got to remind that there's nothing to be reminded of?"

"I'll do some work on that."

"Hell, yeah. I can't keep doing your job for you, Houdini. Ain't that what our fat studio contract is for?" He was laughing now.

"Just in case, where were Marv and Gene that night?"

"They were with their wives at a show, then a late dinner at Chasen's, and then a nightcap at my house with my wife and her sister. You can ask Freddie Condon, the maître d', Tino, the headwaiter who served them, Loretta, the hatcheck girl they tipped twenty-five bucks, George Thomas, their driver, who deposited them at home at two thirty a.m., at which time Jessie and Iris, their respective servants, greeted them and tucked them into their cozy little beds just about three."

Hop smiled. "Nice. Could you run my life, baby?"

"Some challenges are too great, my friend."

After hanging up, Hop paused. How fast Tony was able to make the story. For a night almost two years ago. And how urgent he must have seen the need. Was this an alibi they had prepared, knowing they might one day have to account for that night? Or was this just a ready-made excuse because occasions like this were so profuse, like lipstick on their pillows? How many lost nights in beery roadhouses with prone or pliant or made-pliant B girls? Possibly hundreds.

He shrugged. This is my bread and butter, after all. Dropping sheets over the Talent's monkeyshines. If they didn't have lost nights in beery roadhouses with girls like that, I'd be out of a job. Or still writing about Susan Hayward's tips for new brides.

But the thought kept returning: Lamont didn't even seem that surprised.

There were only a few possibilities. Either these guys do stuff like this all the time, or they know a little something or a lot about what happened to Jean Spangler. Or they don't know anything but just don't want their bedroom high jinks in the public record. That's really it, of course. Stop thinking so sinister, Hop. Christ.

So if Frannie Adair is going to hit a rock-hard dead end with Sutton and Merrel, where might she have better luck? He poured himself one last cup of coffee and stared at the cornflowers on the pot. In a flash, he remembered three dozen times Midge spun around the kitchen in some fuchsia chiffon nightgown, some silky robe, that chartreuse dressing gown, twirling and tipping the pot, maybe rapping her talons on the ceramic, trying to get his attention, maybe, more than once, it was true, slamming it down in front of him while whispering, snakelike (or whimpering, soft-soft—that, too), "Son of a bitch." Or "lousy bastard." Always about the women, the girls, the Girl, that Woman.

But, Christ, how was he supposed to help himself when there they'd be, all jasmine and sparkling skin, like a sheen of soft dew hanging over them, dappling their faces, hands, wrists, the glint of supple pink behind pearly ears. Good God, come on. Who could really blame him, the way they leaned over him, radiating such welcoming warmth, a coal oven in winter, and their tender, milky breath on his face as they pressed in to show him where to put his hat, his coat, his whatever while he waited?

Really, if they're going to wear those darted sweaters tucked tight in those long fitted skirts cradling heart-shaped asses, skirts so tight they swiveled when they walked in them, clack-clack-clacking away down the hall, full aware—*with full intention*—that he was watching, even as his face betrayed nothing, not a rough twitch or a faint hint of saliva on his decidedly not-trembling lip. It wasn't he who was *unusual*, so lust-filled or insatiable. It was they who packaged themselves up so pertly for utmost oomph, for him alone, really, even if they hadn't met him yet when they slid on their treacherous gossamer stockings that morning, even if they hadn't known why they had straightened the seams on their blouses so they'd hang in perfectly sharp arrows down their waiting, waiting breasts.

Christ. Christ, was he really such a cliché? Truthfully, sometimes he bored himself.

And, if he thought about it, even trying not to, lots of things—not just Midge—could be blamed on his own thrumming head, always lurching forward, looking for the angle. What's the angle? What's the angle? How do I get the story, the lay-low, the closed mouth, the Girl?

And then there's Iolene and the mystery of her angle and angles. The one who got away, so much air between his fingertips. And if he hadn't been drooling over her like some horny kid, he never would have gone off with her and Jean Spangler that night.

But then he would never have gotten any of the rest, either . . . the shiny job, with all its rewards, with its rich promise. One day, one day, if he waited and toiled and hustled and flashed his grin and talked his talk, the keys to the kingdom would be offered and he'd be primed to take them.

So somehow his own pitching desire both imprisons and liberates—don't it, though?

"City desk."

"Frannie Adair in?"

"Adair!"

A pause, then:

"Adair here," her voice chirped.

"Color me red-faced, Miss Adair."

"Oh, it's my midnight Romeo."

"You recognize my voice already?"

"You leave quite an impression."

"I promise I won't make a habit out of last night's backstage confessional." That's it. Keep it light, easy.

"You'd be hard-pressed to top that one. Unless you'd like to share your scoop about who killed William Desmond Taylor. You can't have been around for that one, too. You would've still been in short pants."

Hop laughed, trying to read her, his heart banging so loud he was sure she could hear it. "I shot my wad, I promise. I have a few drinks and suddenly I'm imagining myself Mr. Hollywood."

"Right," she said, and he could tell she was trying to read him, too. "So have you heard from your scared friend? What's her name again?"

"Mae West," he said, not falling for the ruse.

"C'mon, give a girl a place to hang her hat."

"You always have that from me, Frannie," he said. "Okay. Listen up, Scoop. Here's the lowdown: doomed comedienne Mabel Normand really did put that slug in William Desmond Taylor. The rumors were all true."

"Spoilsport."

"Oh, Frannie-my-Frannie, I'm close sesame now. That moment is past but good. Unless I trip into a bottle of bourbon and feel impossibly sentimental again. But I'm not a sentimental guy by nature."

"I bet you say that to all the girls whose doors you show up at in the middle of the night."

"Maybe, but usually I get sleepover privileges for it." Why was he expending so much energy with this back-and-forth? Get it together, Hop. Fight your own disposition for a second. "Anyway, it was all a mix of rumor, speculation, and misplaced guilt. Sorry to have bothered you with it."

"Anytime. Anytime at all."

Sitting there, Hop tried to think what to do next. One night and now he had to hang for it? He could still hear Bix Noonan, that hapless publicity agent in charge of Sutton and Merrel, on the phone, his voice tight as piano wire.

"If Marv and Gene get called on this, Hop, I'm deader than Pomona on a Saturday night."

"I'm not telling. You're not. They're not."

"How about the colored girl?"

"I can talk to her."

"How about the girl you left with?"

"Ah, she didn't see anything," Hop said. "She was too drunk to notice, anyway."

"Hop, we gotta do something. The cops—"

"How would they put it together?"

"Who knows? They're cops."

"Exactly."

"Hop, we don't know what they did with her. I left an hour after we got to the Lily. She was still in there with them."

"I have some friends in the PD. If it ends up playing out, I'll see what their take is."

And he did just that. His angle came to him but quick. When the cops found Jean Spangler's purse in Griffith Park, the note in it sure sounded like a girl on her way to an abortion: *Kirk, can't wait any longer, going to see Doctor Scott. It will work best this way while mother is away.* Hop couldn't have written a better one himself. Hell, he half believed it was true. So why not tip the hand all the way? And remove her as far as possible from the studio, the Eight Ball, and, most of all, Sutton and Merrel? He went to the studio and he and Bix took her name off the studio records for the night in question. No night shoots at all. Sorry, she was lying to her sister-in-law. Must have not wanted her family to know. He and Bix closed all the doors, spread some money around.

And Hop called the LAPD himself.

"I saw the story in the paper about Jean Spangler. I have some information. I'm not sure how helpful it is."

"What you got?"

"I saw her Friday night."

"Is that so? Okay, pal. No one left but my dead aunt Gertie who didn't."

"Lotta cranks and crackpots calling, eh?"

"You don't know the half of it. Let me guess. The men's room at Union Station, third stall down from the left, waiting just for you."

"I should be so lucky. Listen, I know you've had an earful, Sarge, but I'm legit. I know the girl. I'm a reporter for *Cinestar* magazine. I've met Jean at the studio before. And Friday night, I ran into her at the Cheesebox."

So Hop told him he'd recognized Jean by her killer legs and green eyes. Waiting by a phone booth, she seemed to remember him. They chatted a few minutes while she waited for a call. She seemed a little distracted. Then the phone rang. She excused herself to answer it. Being polite, he said his good-byes. By the time he'd gotten in his car down the street and driven past her, she was exiting the booth. She waved over to him, as if to beckon him. He pulled his car up to the curb and she approached. She seemed relieved. *Sorry about that,* she said. *Everything's fine now.* He guessed she thought she'd been stood up and that her date finally called. *Can I give you a lift?* he'd asked. *No, I have someone taking me. He'll be here any minute,* she'd replied, and smiled—beautifully.

"Taking me?" the sergeant prodded. "She said 'taking me'?"

"That's what she said. I remember because I thought it was a funny way to put it. But, you know actresses."

"Oh, tons of 'em."

"So I said, 'Where's he taking a pretty girl like you? Someplace nice, I hope. And she stopped smiling. 'Not so nice, but it'll be over before I know it,' she said. I told her she sounded like my wife."

"Why do you think she told you this, buddy? You Father Confessor or something?"

"It was like she couldn't help herself. She was nervous and had to tell somebody."

"So she tells a reporter?"

"I'm not that kind of reporter. I tell housewives what kind of cold cream Linda Darnell uses."

"What kind does she use?"

"Oh, wise guy, eh?"

"Hey, my wife's birthday is tomorrow."

Remembering all this now, remembering all his handiwork, Hop thought the one to talk to was Bix Noonan. Bix could help him untangle some things. Confirm his memory, help reconcile it with Iolene's ragged tale.

He called Bix and asked if he could meet him for coffee. After Hop was hired by the studio, Bix had been bumped down and ended up moving on to another studio, cranking out press releases. Hop felt bad about it, but any guy who needed that much help doing his own job didn't have the stomach for this business.

As he was driving, Hop suffered mightily with the kind of self-reflection he'd only heard about. Here was the thing. Sure, he'd helped cover tracks. Because yes, helping Bix would help him into so much more. And within two weeks, he'd gotten the call from the chief of publicity. "We've heard a lot about you. We like your style. We'd like you to join our little stable. Would you like that, Mr. Hopkins?" Yessir, he would. He'd been grateful to *Cinestar*, liked his job, but was he supposed to go on for another three, five, ten years trotting along after the actors as they tried to hunt geese on their five-hundred-acre ranches in stupor-inducing Chatsworth? They were all the same, one after the other, insecure girls and blowhard guys, plastic-faced boys and full-flight bitches—all hiding the private sagas of abject misery in cold-water flats or abject boredom in small towns and cities across the country. None had ever read a book or thought a thought. Left to their own devices, they'd drink too much and tell Hop tales of swimming coaches fondling them, gang bangs by the football team, botched acid-bath abortions, mothers burning them with curling irons, fathers whipping them with brass-buckled belts . . .

Most of the time, however, they weren't left to their own devices. Instead, the press agent—sometimes two—sat right next to the actor or actress, shading the answers, making corrections, laughing loudly to mask bad language or bad form. These guys fascinated Hop. What kind of men got that job? Protecting the fortress, guarding the gates. And so bad at it all. So transparent. And so unsubtle that even a *Cinestar* reporter could only roll his eyes and take the press release instead. Why write the interview, why coax interesting answers out of this thick-tongued, hayseed actor or gum-snapping, garter-flashing actress when he could just take their press-office copy and go on a bender?

But then there were the big guys, especially the best ones, the ones like Howard Strickling or Eddie Mannix at MGM or Harry Brand at Fox—the guys so good at what they did that they no longer arranged publicity stunts or chased gossip columnists or dirtied their hands with press releases. Their job was no longer about getting publicity. It lay instead in collecting secrets and erecting steel-cast fortresses around them. He knew guys like this in Syracuse, where his pop was a plumber for the city. A hardcore union man, Pop was always on the front line, fighting the city, the mayor's men, the shiny-toothed fixers. The fixers who fixed everything. They made his father sick every day of his forty-two years, before a ceiling collapsed on him on the job while Hop was overseas.

He met Bix at a nondescript coffee shop on La Cienega.

"Any reason you picked a dump like this? Just 'cause I'm working over on Poverty Row now doesn't mean I can't afford a corned-beef sandwich at the Derby."

Hop couldn't tell if Bix was kidding or not and decided not to guess.

"It's all square, baby, it's just I can't have anyone overhearing us, you know?"

"I don't go for boys, if that's where you're heading. Even ones as pretty as you."

"Well, there goes my first idea." Hop smiled, streaming cream into his coffee. "Okay, plan B. Listen, remember that night . . . ?"

Bix looked at him. "You mean the night that set you up at my studio like an A number one whore and left me begging for press coverage of glorious stars like Regis Toomey?"

"That's the one," Hop shot back, guessing sympathy was not a wise tack with a boy this bitter.

"What about it?" Bix said, shoulders straight, hands cupped around the sugar dish.

"They never found that girl, you know."

"I know it. You did good work, my friend."

"What do you mean?" Hop said, face tingling. "It's not my fault they didn't find her. All I did was keep them from finding our boys."

"However you frame it, Hopkins," Bix said, relaxing his shoulders even as his hands still cradled the sugar dish. "What about it?"

"I've been thinking about it lately. I ran into that colored girl we were with that night, Iolene. She got me thinking about it."

"What's it got to do with me, Hopkins? C'mon."

"When you left, what was going on, anyway?"

Bix leaned back against the booth, grinning. "Developed a conscience now, have we?"

"Well, let's not get hysterical."

"Why should I rack my brain for you? So you can feel better?"

Hop shrugged. "How about I put a word in? You know. With the big guys."

Bix stared at him hard, disgust mingling with a kind of hunger Hop knew well.

After a minute, he leaned forward and shrugged. "I got no pride or I wouldn't be in this town, right?"

"Hey, likewise, I'm sure," Hop said, trying for camaraderie.

"Okay, okay. But you gotta make the call now. I don't yap until I see it."

"It's Saturday."

"Since when did that matter? Especially for a big shot like you."

Hop lifted his hands up as if in surrender. As Bix watched, stone-faced, he slid out of the booth and walked over to the pay phone in the corner.

He dialed the home phone of the head publicity secretary, Lil. As he waited for her to answer, he shook his head to himself. How far out of the big leagues was Bix to think Hop could get his bosses on the phone on a Saturday to ask for a favor?

"Hello?"

"Hi, it's me."

"Oh boy, Hoppy, I got a date in an hour and I can't—"

"It's nothing. Just let me talk to you for a minute. Get it?"

"No, but since when did that stop you?"

"I want to put in a word for a great guy." Hop raised his voice very loud. Bix looked up from the booth, squinty-eyed.

"Whoever he is, I get my own dates," Lil said. "And I don't do favors for publicity men. I learned how that works my first week on the job. They ask you to go to this actor's apartment and the next day, when they decide not to sign the guy, you don't even get the bonus."

"Yessir, he used to work for us and he's doing great stuff over at Monogram and we gotta get him back," Hop said.

"Oh, I get it," Lil finally said. "Couldn't you just talk into a dead phone for this? Why you gotta take up my Saturday? First, Mr. Solomon calls me trying to find you."

"He did?" Hop blurted out, then, lowering his voice, asked, "What did he want?"

"You gotta call him."

"Great. So we'll talk more when you get back in town. I see big things for this fellow, sir. Big things."

"I'm hanging up now."

"You have a swell weekend, too." Hop hung up and strode back to the table jauntily.

"They're really excited, Bix," he said, grin foisted. "Always looking for chances to bring back the fabled fish that got away."

"When you gonna know for sure?" Bix said, still squinting.

"Well, a week or two at most. They're doing a hiring cycle at the end of the month. They're going to get rid of some dead wood, some fellas in the department that I've been carrying on my back."

"Mmm."

"Before you know it, you'll be out of the graveyard and back in the palace, baby."

Bix's eyes brightened a little. Hop couldn't believe it. This guy was the easiest sell this side of Kansas City.

"Now you do me, buddy."

Bix finally loosened his pose and even took a smacking gulp of coffee.

"Those guys were ticking time bombs. I had to clean up their messes before."

Hop pretended to be surprised.

"That was the reason I was there that night," Bix said, meeting Hop's eyes. "I was supposed to be keeping them out of trouble. I guess you knew that."

"What kind of trouble?"

"That kind."

"What kind?"

Bix looked around anxiously. "I gotta say it, huh? Weird stuff, Hopkins. And not just the needle and hose."

"No?"

"No." He lowered his voice even further. "Merrel rented this house out in Seal Beach. One day, the brass calls, tells me to go out there and pick up some boxes that were shipped there by mistake from his house back East."

"And?"

"I couldn't find the boxes at first. I even went into the wine cellar."

"So?"

"No wine down there. But I did find a girl tied to a chair." He waited for Hop's reaction. Hop was too busy thinking, frantically, to do a jaw-drop for him.

"Was she alive?" Hop asked distractedly.

"Yes . . ." Bix looked at him a little funnily. "But a mess. I untied her, carried her upstairs. And when she came to, she said Merrel had left her like that for almost two days."

"Fuck me. You think that's what happened to Jean Spangler?"

Bix rode his shoulders up and turned away. "I'm not a total SOB. I put in an anonymous call to the cops about the house. I don't know if they went there or not."

Rookie, Hop thought. What good is an anonymous call? Who couldn't figure out it was you? You either cover your tracks or don't play the hero, schmuck.

"You're a right guy, Bix."

"Sure. Sure, why not?"

"So, when you stayed after I left—try to get a piece of Iolene?" Hop didn't know why he asked it. It just came out.

Bix raised his eyebrows. "If I thought I had a chance. Not the type to come across for day players."

"So why'd you stay? For kicks?"

"Sure. You know, and . . ." He took a small bite of his sandwich and stared out the window. "And, you know, I didn't want to leave her alone with them. I mean, the Spangler girl seemed up for it, not the other one. And, well"—he looked back at Hop—"those guys seemed the type to . . . No rules at all with spook chicks. Get it?"

Hop looked at him. "Right." He felt something twitch under the skin of his brow. It didn't strike him until now that one of the reasons Iolene might have wanted Hop there had to do with being a colored girl alone with these men. If they'd do these things to a white girl, then . . . Momentarily, Hop felt something slip away from him, something he thought he knew about himself. Bix Noonan, fuck you for being such a schmuck and still a better guy than me.

Bix took another sip, also lost in thought. "Gee, what do you think they did to that Spangler girl?"

"I don't know, baby. I really don't."

Ten minutes later, Hop was ducking into Schraft's to use the pay phone.

"There's my bright boy. I've been trying to reach you all morning."

It was the old man, Solly. The one who'd given him the order to woo Barbara Payton back to the studio. Hop felt his blood pound, press against his skin.

"I'm sorry, Mr. Solomon. Personal commitment."

"Ah, the ball breaker."

"You're in the ballpark." Hop was surprised Solly would know about Midge. Things like that spread like—well, like things like that.

"You count yourself lucky she's gone, bright boy," he said with his patented imitation of paternalism, all jobbed off watching Andy Hardy movies. "Besides, since she took a powder, look at the gems you've polished for us."

"I do my best."

"When I asked you to work that little round-heels—that Payton girl—the other day, I, truth be told, my boy, didn't think you stood much of a chance. Girls like that don't settle down easy."

"Well, she can't help herself any more than anyone else. But I'm not sure I sold her. Only time will—"

"Time told, bright boy! I thought you knew. What rotten flack like you doesn't start the day with Louella, even on a Saturday?"

Hop stretched his arm as far as he could from the phone booth to the store counter, swiped a copy of the paper, and turned the page to Louella Parsons's column.

"Well what do you know," he said, playing it cool but dancing a jig inside.

The headline read, "Barbara Payton Over the Moon: New Bride Seals Deal with Tone in Midwest." It seemed Barbara Payton had hopped the Super Chief to Minnesota with Franchot Tone, just minutes behind Hop's hopeful (that is, premature), sunny press release hinting as much. Just minutes ahead of every soft-hearted columnist—both of them—whom Hop had, on a wing and a prayer, tipped off. And all the rest, too, including the studio-unit reporter Hop had sent on his own to cover it in fawning detail.

Truth was, as much as he liked Barbara, he'd been growing weary of the type. The itchy colts, always fixing to run into a fence, a tree, anything. Barbara Payton, hell, she was all tits and mouth, and he'd been around her kind just long enough to know that no amount of "potential" in the world could save her from her deathless desire to ruin herself. In five years, maybe less, he knew there'd be crimson spider veins on that milk face, either two handfuls too much or too little on those ivory-for-now, soon-to-be ashen-gray hips. These types always went to seed, you could hear it rattling around under their shiny hair every time they shook their heads.

Was Jean Spangler one of those girls? Or would she have been had she had a little more success, a little more stardust thrown in those fulsome eyes? He wasn't sure. He just was glad for some good news to ward off the dank cynicism he could feel sinking into him, heavy as his hangover.

Riding high, he got change for a ten and worked the phones for an hour, calling the columnists, ordering a room full of flowers at the honeymoon suite of Cloquet Carriage House Inn in Minnesota, arranging for wedding photos to be wired to the studio, writing up tender quotes from the presiding minister ("Never have I seen a couple more in love") and Barbara's parents, Mr. and Mrs. Erwin Redfield ("We couldn't be happier for our baby—this one was written in the stars, in more ways than one"), to feed to the papers. It was a hell of an hour, during which he didn't have to think for a second about missing starlets or bad dreams.

Stardust Eyes

For a short time, Hop had been able to forget about Frannie Adair. But the trepidation about what she might be digging her pretty unpolished nails into soon returned. He called the newspaper again, but whoever answered said she was on the phone. Unwilling to wait, he made the twenty-five-minute drive to the *Examiner* office, determined to work all his charm and see where it'd get him.

He parked in front of the building. Then, recalling that when he'd gone to lunch with Frannie, they'd exited by a back stairwell, he double-parked the car around the corner until a spot opened up. As he sat, he ran through what he'd said to her the night before. He thought he could remember everything, just not the order in which he'd said things or the precise shading he'd given them.

And every once in a while, he flashed to the memory of looking across at her, at the delicate line running down her face where her cheek must have pressed drunkenly into a crush of sheets, this memory mingled uncomfortably with the memory of the line of his own finger on Midge's face an hour earlier, touching skin where her bright locks should've been.

Fuck it, Hop. Get it together.

Against all reason, his mind ping-ponged instead to the things Midge had said at Jerry's place. How was it that she could hate him so much?

"You have no one to blame but yourself." That's what she told him before she left him. It galled her that after two or more years of Hop pressing her and Jerry in corners together, inviting him over for her pot roast, then leaving them alone together before coffee—while he went off on some job scooping up a starlet from an opium den in Chinatown—having Jerry pick her up at nightclubs when she was too smashed to drive home, making her take his old pal shopping for new suits at Bullock's, asking him to take his place on her birthday, buy her a steak Diane at Perino's so he could drive to Caliente and bail a director out of jail. Could he really be surprised? Or, now that he thought about it, was he only surprised at the twinge of anger, frustration, the thin strand of regret (no, not that) he felt now that the transaction was complete?

"Life's touched him," Midge had said to him at the very end. "It just rolls off you." Like everything Midge said, there was some truth in it, and some plain malice. Jerry, he had this readiness for Midge that Hop had never had. A readiness that came from year after year of spending days covering stories of husbands strangling their wives with phone cords, of young girls leaping in front of streetcars or swallowing mercury bichloride, of little boys strangled under Santa Monica Pier, of another Miss Lonely-hearts burned to ashes from falling asleep, cigarette in hand . . . In the end, it turned out Jerry didn't want any of those cool, long-necked beauties he always had on his arm, their faces as blank as their histories, who asked nothing of him but a box of fine chocolates and a civilized evening of drinks, dinner, dancing, silk sheets. Turns out, the more time Jerry spent in Hop's house, with Hop's wife (no blank face there, a face all too alive with anger, despair, desperation), the more he realized he wanted a house, kids tugging at his pant legs, a dog running down the driveway, a lawn to mow, and, most of all, a lovely, loving wife — a wife with so many sad stories of her own that she'd be waiting eagerly, gratefully on the front porch when he came home from the gloom of the city beat. A wife so glad to see him that he might cry. A wife like Midge.

Hop knew when it all finally began with Jerry and Midge, when there was nothing left to happen but that.

It had been a halfhearted attempt at best. Razor scratches on her wrist and a handful of pills. Neither would have done the job alone, and together they canceled each other out, the pills slow-ing her blood flow to heavy molasses. It was Midge's friend Vicki who found her (Hop was throwing money down at Hollywood Park with another reporter, two studio flacks, and a couple of blondes from Pomona on their first tear). The emergency-room doctors made her stay in the psych ward for three days before releasing her. The doctor who signed the final papers gave Hop one long look before he left, and Hop found himself saying, too loudly, "You don't know anything, pal. Not a goddamned thing."

The truth was, Hop shouldn't have been too surprised. After all, when he'd left for the track that day, the last thing Midge had said was, waving his razor, "You'll be sorry, little man." He hadn't guessed she'd actually go through with it, though, and when she did, he did feel sorry—and guilt-ridden enough to go on a twelve-hour bender. But he couldn't match Jerry, who spent every second of visiting hours all three days glued to her bedside, invoking alternately soft and firm warnings to Midge, insisting she promise that she'd never, ever do anything like that again. Hop watched from the doorway as Midge focused on Jerry's dark hooded eyes, listening to every word, nodding and nodding, and slowly, slowly losing all interest in Hop—even in making him sorry, which had been her most favorite thing, the only thing she enjoyed, for so long.

Later, Hop would be sorry without her even trying—sorry for Jerry when, ten months later, she moved out of their house and into his bachelor pad, consummating what was, when he thought about it, an eventuality long in the cards, a romance begun even before they'd met.

He was suddenly jarred out of his thoughts by a loud thump on his driver's-side window. With a jolt, he turned his head to see Jerry himself, tidiest reporter on either coast, in a finely cut blue suit—a vision of order disrupted only by three red marks on his face, three dainty curves, the unmistakable mark of Midge's tiny, witchy little nails. He'd worn those marks many times himself.

He rolled his window down all the way and gave Jerry a knowing smile.

"What did the other alley cat look like?"

"You're too embarrassed to show your face so you stake me out like a cheating wife?"

"Bad example," Hop noted, grinning up at his friend, playing it jokey, wishing it were. After humiliating himself last night, he couldn't quite look him in the eye. But the claw marks helped.

"These, my boy, were meant for you," Jerry said.

"Yeah, but somehow I think they're all yours now. It's the price you pay for those spectacular breasts."

Jerry looked down at his own chest. "They're okay, I guess." Then, leaning closer to the car, he said, "You know I won't ask why—"

"I know," Hop said quickly, his voice creaking strangely.

"A drink?"

"Ah, I can't. Work." He wanted to tell Jerry about the fix he was in. That was what he did with Jerry. But telling him anything meant telling him everything. He wasn't ready for that.

"Maybe later?"

"Sure. Definitely."

"Musso's at seven?"

"That'll work."

"Okay." Jerry kept eyeing him, trying to get a read. It made Hop nervous and ashamed. "You're just going to sit out here?"

Hop shrugged, smiling. "Taking a minute for myself, big guy."

"You're a lousy liar, Gil."

"I think you know that's not true," Hop said, looking straight ahead. "Fuck me, Jerry. Okay, I'm waiting for Frannie Adair."

Jerry's eyebrows lifted. "Oh . . . is that how it is?"

"We'll see. I think she likes me, baby."

"Maybe so, heartbreaker, but she just left . . ."

Hop felt his chest leap. "You don't say," he said, looking over at the rear glass doors he'd been watching for more than an hour. "Thought she was a backdoor girl."

"Driving over to your studio, in fact. Maybe to see you?"

"Maybe, maybe." Hop turned his key. "I'll find out."

"See you at seven." Jerry stepped away from the car just as Hop punched the gas.

"Yeah, yeah, sweetheart."

• • •

From across the soundstage, Hop could see Frannie talking to Alan Winsted, a sight that made him cringe. Alan, twenty-two years old, gawky, long-necked, and dateless — wouldn't he love the opportunity to help Frannie Adair and her fire-engine-red hair?

He moved as close as he could, creeping over the cables and behind large sets of lights, cranes, whatever those things — arc lights? — were called. Hop knew very little about actual movie-making ("only starmaking," he'd told many a young ingenue, with a confident wink).

He could just make out Frannie's sincere tone: ". . . trying to find out what movies were shooting on a particular night two years back. Could you help me with that?"

And Alan, sounding official: ". . . through the press office? They deal with reporters. I just . . ."

Good boy, Hop thought. You tell her, Al. All reporters — even the ones with curves — gotta go through *us*. Me, to be precise.

". . . appreciate that, but I'm on a tight deadline and thought you might help a gal out . . . very exciting story about Mickey Cohen. You'd be playing a part in a big exposé . . ."

She's taking a gamble with this tack, Hop thought. How can she know this particular lie won't scare him off, not tantalize?

". . . gee, that sounds really important . . . I do know a lot of guys who know guys like that . . . can't really get as far as I have in this biz and not see things . . ."

Motherfuck, thought Hop. She knows her mark.

". . . I bet. You'd probably be of real help to me in the long haul . . . someone like you who's so keyed in . . ."

He could see her lean in toward the puny runt, probably letting him smell her Girl Reporter perfume, all printer's ink, starch, and chutzpah.

". . . anyway, Mr. Winsted, the date in question is October seventh, 1949 . . . an associate of Mr. Cohen's may have been at the studio that night, but we need to know if any productions were shooting that night . . ."

". . . I get it, I get it. A Cohen boy right on the lot, eh?"

"Something like that . . ."

". . . have to go to the log . . . come with me to the office . . ."

Hop watched them walk away together, Winsted placing his pimply hand on Adair's back like some exec, or an overly friendly maître d'.

Knowing where they were headed, Hop took an alternate route into the adjacent building so he could approach the production office from the other direction.

He thought back to his handiwork with Bix. Hop had rewritten the entire day's production schedule log and thrown the original away.

As he came closer, he saw the door to the office was slightly ajar, most likely because it was a Saturday near dusk and the place was close to empty.

Hop couldn't hear their initial interaction, but as they started to move toward the door, Winsted's voice became audible.

"That's why you can't just check the day logs, Miss Adair, or even just the week or month logs. If there's a mistake, it's often not corrected until the movie finishes shooting and the final budget is submitted. Looks like they forgot to record the October seventh shoot at the time. From the budget notes here, it looks like they postponed a big scene after setting it up, but I assure you, Miss Adair, they did plan to shoot that night. Cast called in, the whole bit."

"Well, color me surprised, Mr. Winsted. This explains a lot."

Hop felt pinpricks dance over his chest. But what good, really, could this do her? A lot. She speaks to other actors on the shoot, someone mentions that Jean Spangler was pals with Iolene . . .

"Would it be possible, Mr. Winsted, to see that list of every-one who was on the set?"

"Well, sure, don't see why not. We have no secrets here, after all."

"Do you mind if I take some notes?"

Hop knew he was standing too close to the door, but what did he have left to lose by now?

"And the extras?"

"On this page."

"Spangler, Jean. Interesting."

"Yeah? Know her?"

"Well, isn't she that girl who went missing a few years back?"

"The one who got cut in half?"

"No, the one they never found."

"Don't remember that. Let me look up her file."

"Why not? Just for curiosity's sake."

A few minutes of riffling, with Hop standing not two feet out-side the door, whispering Hail Marys to himself for the first time since catechism school.

"Yeah, I guess that's so. This was her last job for us, that's for sure. Creepy, huh?"

"Creepy, huh. Guess you don't remember her."

"I was still in Tustin in '49, taking tickets at my dad's movie theater."

As he listened, Hop thought about bursting forward, muzzling this lousy Winsted character. Stopping Frannie Adair in her pert little tracks. But he took a chance: better not to tip his hand. The more she senses fear, the more she'll think she's onto something. Gotta act like there's nothing to find.

Before he left, he went over to the casting office. He had an idea he might need something. A "just in case" scenario. There was one clerk in that office on Saturdays and she knew Hop well. It was part of his everyday job to get photos and bios to oil the publicity machine, so she didn't even blink when Hop asked her for a few glossies. He hoped Jean's was still on file.

Ardmore, Jan
Clifton, Rod
Spangler, Jean
Bliss, Ann

"Here you go, Mr. Hopkins."
"Thanks, doll."
Back in his car, he pulled out Jean's photo and set it on the bench seat. Jean, a stunner as ever. Dark hair, widow's peak, dimples, eyes sparkling out at you, asking you to come on in. A real knockout. Better than in person, Hop suddenly thought. That night, he'd found her bored air kind of sexy, but nothing to get excited about. He wondered if this picture was several years old, before some hard living and desperation, before some of the glitter got knocked out of her eyes, making her a little tired and a lot wary.

He slid the photo back in its folder and turned on the ignition. As he drove, he began thinking: if he could find his pickup from that night, if he could find Miss Hotcha, maybe he could be sure all the holes were plugged up but good. There'd been no one left with a story they'd care to tell. No one with the real nitty-gritty for Frannie to find, unless she was lucky enough to stumble on Iolene.

Miss Hotcha. He could remember a few details about her apartment—at least he thought he could, unless he was confusing her with some other girl, some other apartment. It was on the ground floor, right? There'd been two beds and he'd asked where her roommate was. They were twin beds, and as soon as he saw them he'd said to himself an hour, no more. Vague memory of her platinum hair, a soft cloud in his face. The side of his head crashing into a frilly lampshade on the bedside table. A long blue vein on her thigh, visible from the light of the streetlamp outside.

Not much to go on, Hop.

He could recite the names and numbers of every gossip columnist and movie-magazine writer and Hollywood-beat reporter in town and across the coast, but this . . .

Love Is a Memory

As he drove to Musso's, Hop tried to think of a way to get Jerry's counsel without telling him everything, without having to tell his friend the whole sordid story and his own role in it. With Jerry, there was nothing behind what you saw, nothing waiting to reveal itself. This was something Hop could count on. Maybe the only thing. Hop wondered how it happened. He wondered if that was a quality he'd ever had and, if so, when he'd lost it.

Pulling into the back lot, he could hear Jerry's old refrain from back in his *Cinestar* days buzzing in his head: *Why don't you leave that tinhorn newsletter and get back to the what's what.* He was always trying to talk Hop into returning to the *Examiner*, where Hop had worked for his first months in New York, the pay so bad he couldn't get off Jerry's couch and into his own place.

"You moved out here for what," Jerry would always ask. "Not for this."

"What else I got up my sleeve?" Hop would say, shrugging. He wouldn't say as much to Jerry, but he could admit it to himself: he liked shiny shirts, good gin, and the occasional entrée to Ciro's. Was that so wrong? The only price he'd paid so far was picking up some bad habits. "Jerry, I run with the tide. Can't fight gravity. Can't—"

"Say no?" Jerry would say, smiling almost wistfully. "Just keep moving, Hop. The minute you let your feet hit the ground, you're doomed."

"I know it," he'd respond quickly—so quickly he'd surprise himself.

Just after seven o'clock, Hop and Jerry were leaning against the mahogany bar at Musso's.

"Remember that girl I told you about?" Hop said, sliding Jerry's drink toward him on the bar. "The one who came to see me about the Spangler thing?"

"Yeah."

"I've been thinking about it a little. Funny, huh?"

Jerry lit a cigarette and looked at Hop in the mirror behind the bar.

"Not so funny. Happens a lot to me. You run down those stories and a lot of 'em stick in your head, knock around there a little, sneak up and say boo when you least expect it. Happens even more with cops, but with cops it's about saving them. I think it's different with reporters, but I'm not sure how. Wanting to know, needing to know everything."

Hop nodded vaguely.

"Five years ago," Jerry said, "I chased a story—just a one-day ditty—an actress, hair like buttercream, found facedown on the kitchen floor. I heard the call and was at the scene with the PD.

"There was something sad about the way her face was, her body, her waist turned and her legs bent almost like she was running. She was wearing this dress with a red check, like some farm girl. When they flipped her over, her eyes were wide open, big green beauties staring up at me, like they could still ask me something. Kind of like they were asking me something."

"So what gives?" Hop asked. "How'd she go?"

"Accidental overdose of diet pills—trying to win a spot as one of the Babylovelies in Ken Murray's *Blackouts*." Jerry shrugged, rubbing his stubble. "Funny, now that I tell it . . . if it happened today, doubt I'd blink twice."

"Eh, you're not so hard," Hop said.

"So this Spangler girl. How do you think she bought it?"

"She had the longest legs you ever saw," Hop said out of nowhere, the fizzy haze of the gimlet now descending. "And that sharp, dark-eyed face they look for, or used to. She'd been through some things. Maybe been knocked around a little by life. You could see something in her face. A look." Hop's eyes unfocused.

"I know that look," Jerry said.

Hop turned and looked at him. "Right. That's right."

As he drove down Hollywood Boulevard with Jean Spangler's face looming in his head, Hop thought again about Jean Spangler herself. Jerry always clarified things like that, blew off the dust. Hop had been so absorbed in everything else, but now there she was. Maybe, he thought, she could tell him things. And she was beginning to take on a quality he must have missed when he actually met her. She'd seemed flimsy then, a paper doll. Now there was something behind her, something roiling away.

How does a girl like that, a girl who'd been around the business, hoofer, showgirl, extra, bit player for a few years or more, get into a room with two fellas like that, fellas with such awful, awful looks in their eyes, like he'd seen many times in men at the top, high on their own glamour and glory and with an open door into every dark urge they'd ever had? They were bad guys and you could see it. He saw it, Iolene could see it, Miss Hotcha—why not Jean Spangler, or didn't she care? Could she just not care?

He remembered her at the Eight Ball. Sutton or Merrel—he couldn't remember which one—patted his lap, gestured for her to sit on it, and when she did, the other lifted her legs off the floor until they were stretched out across his lap, those legs encased in red stockings with red lace high heels. Her head struck back, laughing. Didn't she have dimples as deep and tempting as he'd ever seen? Why hadn't he paid her more attention that night? He could have pulled her aside, tilted his head and let it fall on top of her dark hair, and whispered to her, "Stick with me, sweetheart. Those guys are bad news, anyway."

Instead, he goes for the two-bit burlesque dancer, and one apparently not lucky enough to have her own place, or even her own bedroom.

Hop, you hit it. Where *did* she work . . . ?

That was the idea.

Hop pulled up at the new Tiny Naylor's on Sunset, got change for his dollar, and ducked into a phone booth, nearly jerking the directory from its chain.

He called the Follies Theatre, where he was sure she'd said she performed, the Burbank Burlesque Theater, the Cha-Cha Parlor, the Curly-Q on Sunset, the Girly-Q in the Valley, and a half dozen other places.

"Does Miss Hotcha still perform there? Did she ever?"

Finally, "Have you ever heard of a performer called Miss Hotcha?"

No dice.

Was he remembering wrong?

He drove home, not sure what to do next. He had some idea of dropping it all, cuddling up to a nice warm bottle and taking his chances.

The elevator doors opened to his floor.

He saw the shock of bright hair first and the long silver raincoat. In a heartbeat, something surged hot and prickly in his gut. But he recovered.

"You threw away your key?"

Midge turned and looked at him, one hand clutching her coat collar, the other pressed on the apartment door.

"I don't live here anymore. I don't let myself in places I'm not invited."

"You and Count Dracula. Well, you always were a talented little bloodsucker." He pushed past her and unlocked the door.

"You've got a lot of nerve after what you've just put me through," she said, her voice low and stretched out. About three vodka sours, Hop guessed.

"So I came by last night for a friendly visit," he said, walking in ahead of her, leaving her to dart in behind him before the door swung shut.

"That was rotten enough, but par for the course with you," she murmured.

And he flipped on a light and finally turned, looking at her full on, finally hitched up his shoulders and looked at her face-to-face, looked at her tiny little face. As ever, god-awful pretty and full of contempt.

"After all," she continued, untying the sash on her coat, "you can't surprise me on those counts anymore."

With slightly shaking hands, she patted the soft edges of that short haircut, that violation, Hop thought to himself, of all that is lovely in this world.

"So how could I surprise you?" Hop asked. "With flowers and bon-bons? Vows of fidelity?"

"That would surprise me only if I believed you."

"You believing me—*that* would surprise *me*."

She ignored him and looked around the apartment, at the not-so-fine layer of dust coating her meticulously planned decor.

"Couldn't spring for a cleaning lady?"

Before he could snap back an insult, he felt himself struck by the sight of her standing in their home. Standing there, touching the edge of a Wedgwood ashtray brimming over with stubs. It had been barely a month but truthfully it was much, much longer. Had they ever really lived here together, like a married couple, reading the newspaper and eating toast and jelly, doing what married couples do, like . . . What do married couples do?

She kept hovering on the other side of the sofa, running her fingertips along the edge of the narrow table behind it.

Hop, for his part, stood in front of the sofa, hat still in hand. Watching her, he'd forgotten how small she was. She never seemed that way when she was coming at him, fists balled.

She blew dust from her fingers and met his gaze. "So what kind of mess are you trying to drag me into now?"

"What do you mean, Midge?" He dropped his hat on the coffee table and folded his arms. "Why don't you just spit it out?"

"I mean this reporter calling me."

There it was. The punch in the stomach. And he had no one to blame but himself for this one.

"Reporter?" He tucked a finger under his collar, which felt close against his neck.

"A Miss Dare," she said, watching him closely. Must be sensing fresh blood, he thought.

"Only you," she added, "would have a *girl* reporter on your tail."

"What did she want? Other than my tail."

"She was asking me about this night way back two years ago. I told her I'd blacked out everything from my wedding day until last week."

"What happened last week?" he said, straining for a joke.

"I threw my wedding ring off the Santa Monica Pier," she shot back stingingly.

"You're a cold little piece of work, aren't you?"

"You drained all the warmth from me the last time I found you rolling around with the elevator girl at the Roosevelt Hotel."

"That was the one that did it, huh?" he said, the sound of his own cool voice making him sick.

Midge walked around the sofa and took a tentative seat on the wing chair.

"I couldn't begin to pinpoint which one did it," she said, crossing her legs tightly.

"You're not so innocent," he started, then stopped. He shifted uncomfortably. Were they really going to go through all this again? There was nothing more unpleasant to him than seeing the version of himself she brought out in him.

Needing to do something with his hands, he began emptying his pockets and tossing the change, matchbooks, paper, and keys onto the coffee table.

"So what did she say when you pleaded marital amnesia?" He sat down on the coffee table, facing her.

"She asked if I remembered about a girl who disappeared that fall—fall of '49."

"What a funny kind of question."

She leaned forward, eyeing the matchbooks. "Same old

haunts," she said, fingering the one from Villa Capri. "Guess you're on a real spree now." Before he could respond, she continued, "So I told her I didn't remember anything like that and what did it have to do with me. Or you."

"And?"

"She said you told her you were with the girl the night she went missing." Her eyes looked up to meet his. "And I said oh, so did he murder her, too? Because I'm damn sure he took her to bed."

"Thanks, dear. Thanks a lot."

"My pleasure."

"And I didn't. Either one. I'd just met her. It was right before I met the fellas at the studio who helped me get my job. Which is why I remember it so well."

She sighed deeply, wringing her coat sash in her hand. "I don't care. I don't care. Just spill it, for God's sake. Why's this number calling me?"

"Just chasing an old story. She called me. I told her all I knew. I don't know why she's bothering with you." He thought quickly, maybe too quickly. "She works with your boyfriend, Jerry. Maybe she thinks you'll be more agreeable, shacking up with a fellow scribe and all."

She looked at him with that prison-yard stare of hers.

"You're a lousy bastard," she said, shaking her golden, shining head.

Looking at her, feeling very much the lousy bastard, Hop surprised himself with the urge to reach out and cup that hateful, heartbreaking face in his hands.

But he didn't do anything. Really, how could he?

"Gil, I don't know what kind of game you were playing to get the girl, this Miss Dare, in bed. Seems kind of sick to me. I asked her if, when you told her this tall tale, you'd been drinking. She said yes. So I asked her if, when you told her this tall tale, you were at her place, and she said yes. And I asked her if it was the wee small hours of the morning. And she said yes. So I told her that, under those circumstances, she shouldn't believe a goddamned word you said."

Hop smiled to himself. For once, Midge's bottomless disgust for him paid off. Even if Adair didn't buy it wholesale, she'd have to think twice about it, or at least about the part he'd played. Sweet mother, he only wished he *had* made a play for the girl reporter that night to complete Midge's portrait of a lying lout.

"I'm sure she won't bother you again, Midge."

"We'll see. You've got an awful lot of tricks up your sleeve." She rose, refastening her coat and running a set of silver-edged fingertips through her hair.

"Going home already?" He stood, too, looking her in the eye, trying to read something in her. She came here in person for this? She couldn't want a toss for old time's sake, could she?

"Of course I'm going home." She began walking toward the door. He followed her.

"So things are pretty cozy with you and Jerry."

"Funny how it can be with a real man."

"I can't imagine."

"Gil." She looked at him as they stood at the door. "Don't get yourself in any messes, okay?" she said, almost softly, an old voice he knew from long ago—maybe a thousand years ago.

Then, recoiling, she blurted, "And leave me out of it," slamming the door behind her.

He opened it again and stood in the doorway, watching her walk down the long corridor, silver coat swaying, one cool bird, that one. Wow. If only she'd been so interesting when they were married.

• • •

When he met her, Midge seemed a beautiful 180 degrees from his old Syracuse fiancée, Bernice, with her long, plaintive letters asking when Hop was going to send her the money to come West and join him so they could get hitched. Bernie and her upturned eyes, freckles like pale confetti over her nose, across the slightly chunky spread of her girlish back. And Midge, well . . . she may have come from a small Ohio town, but there was nary one hint of Main Street, county fairs, pearls-to-church-on-Sunday about her. By the time he met her, she was a premium, hard-cut Hollywood diamond, gleaming and icy with a hundred sharp edges and a hundred mirrored faces.

You must really hate me. That's what Midge always said, lips twisted like a candy wrapper. *Why did you marry me if you hate me this much?* And what he wouldn't tell her, what he didn't know the way or have the heart to tell her was that *that* was precisely why he had married her. He couldn't, never could, still couldn't separate out the heady brew of desire and contempt she elicited in him. The pouty face he couldn't resist was the same one he often wanted to smash in with the hard heel of his hand. When he felt this way, he disgusted himself. How could a woman be so stupid as to marry him? And how could he be weak enough to marry her?

Men he knew, they'd always say, Oh, I understand. They really trick you, don't they? You marry the fleshy beauty popping out of the strapless dress, the one who's dolled up and ready to play, knocking back cocktails and dancing with her heaving chest pressed so close against you that you think you've died and gone to tit heaven. Then, three days after the honeymoon you think, Where'd that girl go and what is my mother doing here ironing clothes in the living room and yelling at me for not buying milk as her waistline grows an inch a day?

But Hop couldn't really play along with the boys'-club patter.

Truth was, Midge hadn't changed one bit. The same WASP waist and black underwear and chilly distaste for anything unattractive or cheap. Never was a girl to cradle your head in her lap and coo words of comfort and never would be. She still drank martinis and slid her pointy feet into spiky satin shoes, and she still had the flat white belly he'd once licked a pint of Early Times off of in a Palm Springs hotel room. She hadn't changed at all. It was a crying shame.

Twenty minutes later, Hop had showered, shaved again, and put on a new suit. All the while thinking about Frannie Adair's ambush. Calling his wife. Pretty low. It didn't make him mad, exactly. He knew things would be all right. They always were. Still, something softer than the girl-reporter routine or Midge's pointed nails would be nice.

He resisted the urge to pour some bourbon, sit down on the couch, and begin working the phone, trying to get a girl to swing by or invite him to do the same. Tonight, he'd want something sweet and wide-eyed. A Midwest girl or a ponytailer from deep in the Valley or Glendale.

Maureen. Maureen, the dark-haired file clerk in the shorts department with twitchy nose and sprightly thighs. She was always willing to send her roommate to Schwab's for a butterscotch sundae so she could give Hop a quick tumble and an earful of studio gossip. Breasts springy as her bouncing head and the inside dope on the latest star dipping his wick at queer joints over in Silver Lake—wouldn't that be wonderful? Hell, the hour or two it'd take, what could Frannie Adair find out?

Before he could look up Maureen's number, the phone rang.

"Is that Hop?" It was a juicy female voice that made Hop sit up straight in his chair.

"Sure is."

"This is Barbara."

Beautiful Barbara Payton, there to remind him of all the good things coming his way if he could only . . . "Congratulations are in order, Mrs. Tone," he said.

"Thanks, kid. And thanks for the flowers. Our room smells like a French whorehouse," she said, and he could hear the smile in her voice.

"Must be the middle of the night there, B.P. Shouldn't you be consummating or something? Got the honeymoon jitters? I promise, it's not so bad."

She laughed. "I kicked that butterfly out. He was drunk as a skunk and crying like a girl. I miss Tom," she sighed.

"Gee, I'm sorry, kid." He wondered if she would blame him. Who else could she blame?

"Hell, it ain't so bad. There's a lot of lumberjack types out here."

"And your family's good?"

"I guess so. They're in Texas."

"Texas?"

"They moved us all to Odessa years ago, when I was eleven. They didn't want to come back to snowy old Cloquet for a lousy wedding. They drink like it's 1933, you know."

Shaking his head, Hop thought of all the stories sent out over the wire about the heartwarming family wedding. "Well, we'll keep all that between us, gorgeous. Mum's the word."

"That's what I got you for, Mr. Blue Sky."

"That you do."

She sighed again. "Well, good night, Hop." She sounded far away.

Hop felt funny. She was lonely and he was willing to spare a minute. "Barbara?"

"Yeah?"

"Let me ask you: you've been around this dirty town a few years. You've never been afraid to dig your heels in."

"Hell no."

"You ever run into Marv Sutton and Gene Merrel out on the town?"

"Yeah." She paused, which she'd never done once since Hop met her.

"What's their story?"

"Fuck if I know, Hop."

"C'mon, Barbara. Between you and me. You don't need to pussyfoot with me."

There was another pause. Then, "Look, I don't like repeating what I ain't seen firsthand."

"I'm a clam, Barbara. It's my one and only virtue."

"Well, that Marv's cuddled up to me a few times, but there was something about both of them that rubbed me the wrong way. A girl gets a kind of radar."

"Yeah?"

"And I heard things."

"What things?"

"Okay, here goes," she said. "A girlfriend of mine once stripped for them at a private party at Gene's place out in the desert," she said carefully. "After she came back, she locked herself up in her apartment for a week, drinking and crying so loud the neighbors called the cops. She wouldn't talk about it. Not ever. And she was the kind of girl who loved to trade fuck stories." Barbara breathed in deeply. Hop could almost see the cigarette burned down to the nub. A shaking head worn down by everything.

"She left the biz soon after. She said, 'You can't unsee things you've seen. Can't undo things you've done.'"

"Fuck me, Barbara."

"I never minded a little bad fun, Hop. And live and let live and all that. But that ain't all. There's things out there darker than all this."

"Wish I didn't know that, B.P."

The wind knocked out of him, he took a short drink and stared at the wall. Little Maureen from the shorts department just didn't seem like a possibility anymore. Did girls like that even exist in this town? Had he made her up in his head?

Why couldn't Sutton and Merrel just have pulled your average droit du seigneur? Why'd Iolene have to drag him back into this? Why couldn't he have kept his big mouth shut? He knew where he had to go. The Red Lily, the last place he knew Jean Spangler was. Tracing her steps from me to oblivion, he thought.

In all Hop's experience, which involved accompanying stars and execs to Chinatown whorehouses, to dark parking lots, alleys, and motels off Central Avenue, to one Mexican hothouse that trotted out prime San Quentin tail, he'd never been to the Red Lily, never even heard it mentioned more than a handful of times and always in choked whispers late into lost nights, nights when the warm glow of eleven p.m. had turned into something quaking and nasty by two.

He'd been half sure the place was mere rumor, black fantasy, a vision that came in the night with the sandman. The few who'd mentioned it to him had never actually been there, had only known someone who had been. Or knew someone who knew someone.

There were tales of rough orgies, of Hollywood royalty throbbing violently against world-class dock trash, floaters from faraway ports with rough faces and pliant bodies or pliant faces and rough bodies, bodies coursing with diseases from centuries past.

Dark and ancient folk who'd moved from port to port for centuries, or so it seemed, carrying a taste for sexual devolution. Their eyes held secrets back to Babylon.

Oh, it was too much for Hop.

"Hell, who needs all that brimstone poetry," he always said. "Give me a good Tijuana whorehouse—or hell, a makeup girl from Van Nuys, any day."

He'd discovered long ago that asking women nicely was all he'd ever needed to get whatever he wanted.

Getting into his car, he wasn't sure he was going to be able to find the place. He had a vague sense of the area, down in a waterlogged strip of warehouses and bars on the harbor, and an impression of it being like a 1920s speakeasy with a sliding peephole and a secret password. Then he remembered, that night at the Eight Ball, the manager had given Bix directions of some kind. Had even told them to slip the folks at the Red Lily his name.

Two birds with one stone, Hop thought, as he veered north toward the Eight Ball. He could make sure everything was locked as tight as Tony Lamont made it seem and then also get directions to the fabled Lily. It's not even ten o'clock, Hop thought. By morning everything will be sealed up for good.

Thudding along the parkway, he kept his eye on the rearview mirror the whole way to make sure Frannie Adair wasn't on his heels. Every time he assured himself he didn't see her, however, he wondered instead who she might be talking to, getting information from.

For chrissake, she's probably sound asleep. It's just a whisper of a story for her, that's all.

He played the radio loud and tried not to think too hard, and finally the ugly old belly-burner, the Eight Ball, sprang from the horizon in all its ramshackle glory.

Stuck out in some unincorporated plot of land, the Eight Ball was one of the few places in town that had seen more than thirty years of life. Rumor had it as an old gold miners' saloon back in the day, and it sure had the booze-swollen, dust-caked mien of the Old West.

Saturday night and the whole greasy-walled place was a crush of gamblers, drinkers, and rounders. Hop tried to keep the lowest of profiles, even ducking into the men's room to avoid running into Van Heflin and Gloria DeHaven. You could always count on finding slumming stars at this place. And yet he'd never known a single story to slip out its front door and make its way to a solitary reporter. Or at least to a reporter who would run it. It was a bona fide tight ship, if there was such a thing.

He made a quick tour through the back poker room but didn't recognize anyone, not even the croupiers, who may have been there in 1949. Finally, he asked the bartender if he could speak to the manager.

"It's still Freddy Townsend, right?"

"Yeah," the bartender said, barely listening. "Freddy's upstairs."

"Can I talk to him?"

"Free country for your kind," he said, pouring a drink.

"So I hear," Hop said, dropping a bill on the bar before making his way to the back. Stepping into a long, narrow corridor, he spotted a wrought-iron spiral staircase with a piece of twine suspended across the entry point. A handmade sign read PRIVATE.

Hop ducked under it and went up the stairs, winding around and around until he reached a small upper hallway and a door marked MGT.

He knocked.

"Better be good," a gruff voice sounded.

Hop tried the knob and it opened. A sour-faced man in shirt-sleeves sat behind a desk. He had an account book open and wore an empty shoulder holster. Hop guessed the gun was in his hand or resting on his leg behind the desk. The Eight Ball was robbed regularly, even though the word was it was protected.

"Sorry to bother you, Mr. Townsend," Hop said, playing his cards with care. "I'm with a motion-picture studio. I bring a lot of our actors and actresses here and I—"

"I think I seen you here. I'm good with faces," Townsend said, chewing on a splintery-looking toothpick. His tone was just agreeable enough to assure Hop that the man liked the Holly-wood trade he got, liked the money they dropped, and wanted to keep it coming.

Hop took a seat in a metal chair facing Townsend. Setting his hands on the desk between them, he played it like an honest broker. Which, in a way, he was.

"I'm really just here to check on something. Something that happened here—or began here—one night back in '49."

"You positive you ain't ad vice?" He squinted.

"I may be a lot of things, but I'm not vice," Hop said, smiling. "I'm just a studio flunkie doing my job."

"You feed stuff to vice, though, don't you?" Townsend looked like he was never more than 10 percent convinced of anything.

"That would be the quickest way to lose my job."

"That don't stop everybody."

"My only interest in vice is in keeping them from arresting half our talent department."

He eyed Hop for a second, then said, "So what night?"

"It was in October '49 and a big group was here spending on all fours. At the center was Marv Sutton and Gene Merrel."

"They've been here more than once, my friend. Sutton prac-tically gets his mail here."

"I believe it. But they were causing quite a stir that night. They were with a colored girl and two other Hollywood numbers."

"Keep it coming."

"And one of the girls, you might have seen in the papers, she ended up, well, disappearing."

"Bingo," Townsend nodded, leaning forward. "Sure I remember it. I wouldn't, but people keep reminding me."

"People?"

"Tony Lamont just called me today," he said. "And it ain't the first time. But hey, I'll tell you what I told him: I did my job, friend. You never saw the name of this joint in a single newspaper story, did you? And the cops never knew, either. I know how it works."

Hop nodded. "Yeah, yeah. You were shut tight as a drum. So what do you remember about that night?"

"Nothing other than your little gee from the studio—"

"Bix?"

"Okay. He tells me the boys want a real good time and can I help them to find someplace hot and closemouthed. And I mentioned a few places and he says we know all those places and they're dead. What's a place, he says, you know the kind of place I mean. And I didn't, but whenever anybody says something like that to me I send them to the Red Lily. Because they got a corner on the stuff-you-can't-say-out-loud market. So I told him, the Red Lily. The Red Lily can't be beat. I even said they could drop my name, for what good it did them. Probably cost them."

"And that's all you know?"

"And I ain't saying a word about it to anyone, don't worry. I read about the girl, sure. But I was taken care of right after it happened—"

"Bix."

"That Bix guy, yeah," he said. Then, just realizing, his eyes went wide. "I get it now. That night—that's one of the times I seen you here. With some blonde hanging on you. And you," he said, sitting up straight and waving one finger at Hop. The other hand remained behind the desk. "It was you who called me, right? And the other fella brought out the care package."

"Right." Hop remembered the call. It had lasted under ten seconds. This boy knew how to play.

Townsend leaned back again, drumming his free hand on the desk. "I learned a long time ago there was more soup in keeping quiet than in yammering," he sighed, lifting his other arm from behind the desk and depositing the gun that was in fact in his hand back into his holster. "Besides, I say let dead dogs lie."

"Dead?"

"Look, I don't know nothing on that count. But you gotta be guessing that's the end of that story, too, or you wouldn't be here. Otherwise, what's the problem?"

Hop tugged at his shirt cuffs and thought for a minute. Was there any other possible end? "So," he said. "Tell me, how do I get to the Red Lily?"

"What do you want to go there for, kid? You don't want to get into that. Honest." He looked at Hop and his lids went heavy. His whole body seemed to sink deeper into itself. "It's not a place you wanna be unless you can't help it."

"I just need to make sure—"

"Kid, they sure as hell ain't talking there. You don't have to worry about that." He shook his head.

"All the same," Hop said, waiting.

Townsend sighed, turned his head, and seemed to be staring at the picture on his wall calendar, the topless girl with high black boots straddling the top of a fireman's truck, the hose wrapped around her, releasing a few stray drops.

Without turning back to Hop, he flicked a small card from a container on the top of his desk and tossed it at him.

"All the same," he said. Then, looking back at Hop, he added, "Watch what you wish for, kid."

Hop walked back down the spiral staircase and down the hall-way until he was back in the main room, which was even more jumbled with people. A small jazz band had taken the stage and was playing a raucous version of "That Old Master Painter."

"Oh, if it isn't Hop . . . ," he heard some girl chirp, reaching out to him, fingertips just barely on his arm, but before he could turn, the crowd had pushed him on. The brief smell of her perfume passed through him and he almost stopped, but the scramble to get around the dance floor shoved him further along and suddenly he was back near the far wall and the crammed tables filled with the serious drinkers.

As he moved past, intending to make it to the front door, he saw a flicker of auburn hair out of the corner of his eye.

Frannie Adair, alone, wearing a deep green dress with amber buttons that glittered, sending flocks of light across the wall to her side.

She gave him a small wave.

He walked to her table. "I don't see how . . . ," he started, but couldn't finish. Trying again, he said, "And dressed for the part," trying to match her nonchalance.

"It's my job," she said with just a trace of self-consciousness as she straightened her satin-edged collar. "I'm good at it. Like you."

"But you didn't follow me."

"No. This is just your bad luck. I followed him."

She pointed across the room to a small corner table clotted with random girls. Hop peered closer.

And there he was: Marv Sutton. Alone and holding court, tie loose around his neck and a cigar in his hand.

"So where's Hardy?"

"Looks like Laurel's flying solo tonight. Maybe he'll only get in half the trouble."

"You're going over to get a quote," Hop said, suddenly realizing. He tried to hide a distant panic. "Maybe I can handle it for you. I'm imagining something along the lines of, 'I'm a happily married man with three beautiful children. I love my wife dearly. I never even met the girl.'"

"A little too late for that."

"How about, 'Sure, I took her for a ride. A hell of a broad. I'd do her again . . . if only I could find her.'"

She looked at him.

"Over the line? Sorry. I'm all classed out." He slumped down in the seat next to her, the weight of everything beginning to settle in his shoulders. "You trying to lose me my job? Or worse?"

"Hey," she said. "If you're clean—or as clean as you types get—I'll leave you well out of it. I'm not out to break a story about some studio flack with loose lips. Where's the headline in that?"

"So," he said, pulling his chair closer to her. "What'd you find out today?"

"Oh, all kinds of things. But no, I'm not getting a quote from Sutton. Not yet. I don't want to tip my hand. I'm just watching."

"Sounds more like a private eye than a reporter."

"What does that make you?"

"The bastard child of both, baby."

"I thought you were the palace guard."

"So you've been bracing the staff? The waiters, the busboys, the bartenders? Did they give you the lowdown?"

She shook her head. "Actually, it's amazing, Mr. Hopkins: they were all hired in the last six months." She gave him a stare, then added, "I didn't know you had such pull."

Hop tried not to smile. "Let's have a drink."

"I never have drinks with men who are prettier than me."

"Neither do I," Hop said. "You never know what might happen."

"Ah, but I do," she said, grinning.

"So sure, huh?" Hop waved the bartender over. "You give me too much credit. C'mon. Help a lonely fellow out. What's your tonic?"

She sighed, hands curling around her russet handbag.

"Whiskey highball."

"Make that two."

She turned back to him. "But only one round. I'm on the job, sailor."

"Me too, baby. Me too. So before I came over last night to pour my bitty heart out, what were you doing?"

"Sleeping, remember?"

"Before that." He leaned toward her ever so slightly, as if in confidence.

She looked at him. "Why does that matter?"

"It doesn't," Hop said, easy. The way she was tensing next to him was interesting. He was just grazing something, almost by accident. And whatever it was, it was turning her into something else. Something he knew.

"I was on a date. Sort of. A fellow who could maybe help me with other stories. Down the line." She looked at Hop only out of the corner of her eye, seemingly focused on trying to see through the crowd to Marv Sutton. "The way to get it, the things you need, with these guys—well, you have to give them a long line. You have to dance on the hook a little."

Hop thought for a second. "You can't be both the fisherman and the fish," he said.

"What?"

"Your comparison. The *metaphor*," he said, drawing out his five-dollar word. "The line and the hook—which end are you on?"

"Don't you know?" she said. "Just like in your biz, I'm always on both ends at once."

"And the job is telling them apart."

She looked at him. Then, slowly, she seemed to be trying to regain her balance. "So why did you want to know what I was doing last night?"

Eyes on her, Hop folded his arms across his chest and reclined a little in his chair. He was playing it soft—this thing he was playing. He almost always played it soft. Those guys who couldn't do it, who were always rushing the gate, he found pathetic.

"I don't know, Frannie," he said evenly. "There was something about it. About the moment I rang your bell. The idea of you on your bed. One shoe off. Your breath on your pillow. I have a picture of you in my head. And you're such a smart, strong girl, it feels like I'm the little boy caught at the peephole." He paused for effect, then repeated, "I keep thinking of you on your bed, one shoe off."

She listened intently and he could feel her taking the words and weighing them, weighing him, caught between puzzled irritation and something else.

And he knew she was seeing the image he'd just described. Of herself. And she was wondering, was that an alluring image? Wasn't it just forlorn? Was it something, really, that would run hot through a man's veins? Is that what he is saying?

"Funny the way you put it. Almost like it was me exposing

myself last night," she said, voice thick. Then turning smooth fast. "Instead of you."

Either he'd really misread her, Hop thought, or this was her last defense.

"Hey," he said, flashing her a smile, fingers spread on his chest. "I got nothing to hide. And I'm easy."

She couldn't hide her own grin. "You're half right."

"And you'll notice," he added, "I haven't taken back a single drunken confession."

"Wouldn't matter if you did." She finished off her drink. "In vino veritas. Or so the Fathers used to tell me."

"Let me get you one more, then."

"No thanks," she said, reaching for her handbag. "I don't want to tilt the mitt too far with Mr. Sutton. And besides, in this case"—she waved her finger between the two of them—"I know just which side of the metaphor I'm on."

She stood, and as she did she laid her palm, for one split second, on the lapel of his suit. It was warm and he felt it there.

"It's okay." He rose, pushing the table out of the tight corner so she could leave. "I've got a long line."

She half turned in response, but before he could see her face, the crush of clubgoers swallowed her up.

He sat for a while, catching glimpses of Sutton. He knew the ones like this. He knew them even back in Syracuse. Even there, there were ones like this. Something in the way they carried themselves, the way they walked through a room, parked their cars, lit their cigarettes, groomed their hair. It wasn't something you could put your finger on. A kind of unruffled self-satisfied contentment wrapped just barely around a seething center. Something was in there, wedged deep, dating back to the time they saw their pet dog run over, lost their sister to polio, felt Mother's overly tender hands on their bodies, got teased at school for the club foot, caught Daddy shtupping the nanny, or watched as the neighbors fished a dead body out of the river. Who the fuck knew? And who knew why the thing nestled tight in them made them like *this*, when plenty of other fellas had bad memories and never wanted to hog-tie a girl or lynch anybody?

He'd leave that to the head doctors.

All he knew was Marv Sutton had that look, even if you didn't see it on the silver screen but only in places like the Eight Ball or the Red Lily.

He thought about going over and talking to him. But what would he say? And why would he say it? What good could it do? He ordered a second bourbon. As he sat there, he felt a wave of uncomfortable recollections stream in and begin to settle in his head. Of looks that had passed between Sutton and Merrel that night, of the aggressive Marv and the strangely cold Gene, famous baby face set in stone, sitting with Jean Spangler between them and one of them flipping the string of beads that hung down the front of her dress. Flipping them like she was a doll or a department-store mannequin. Of Iolene looking at him, looking at him again and again, leaning backward to catch his eye as he pretended to listen to the fluttery nothings issuing from Miss Hotcha's candied mouth.

And later Iolene's hand on his arm.

"You'll come, right? To the Red Lily?"

"Sure, kid, I'll meet you there," he'd said. "Right after I do my gentlemanly duty and escort this charming young lady home." He'd been glib and winking about it and she was straightfaced and yes, he saw it, anxious. Maybe frightened.

As he watched Sutton now, he began to think: Was this a

coincidence, Sutton showing up tonight? Or willful? Tony Lamont warns him to stay away and the guy can't stop himself from showing up, thumbing his nose at fate?

Before he knew it, Hop was walking over to Sutton, drink in hand.

The long ruffle of girls that had been curled around his table had narrowed down to two redheads in the Rita Hayworth vein, one in bright yellow and one in midnight blue. A grinning fellow in hound's-tooth rounded out the group. What am I doing, he half thought. I should be steering as clear as I can from this guy. I don't want any connection at all between me and the lead Frannie Adair's got. Why am I doing this . . .

"Marv Sutton as I live and breathe," Hop said as he reached the table—with as much loud bravado as he could muster.

Sutton looked up with his famous dancing eyes, just as they appeared in *The Crazy Caravan*. A face that looked so bright and jubilant on-screen hung snide in real life.

"This is, honest, déjà vu," Hop added, swinging the glass in his hand so it came just short of splashing bourbon on the table.

Sutton didn't say anything. The man in the hound's-tooth straightened up in his seat and scowled a little. By the Dan Duryea imitation, Hop guessed this fellow for a studio employee. "Care to introduce yourself, buddy-o," the man said.

"Easy, Bob," Sutton said, smooth as an oil slick. "You do look familiar, pal."

"Gil Hopkins—in the press office." Hop shoved his hand out.

Sutton pretended not to see it and let loose an easy smile. "Sure, kid, sure. Pull up a chair."

Hound's-Tooth Bob seemed to relax and took Hop's outstretched hand instead, yanking him down into a chair.

"So what's doing tonight?" Hop ventured, settling in the seat, half pressed against the face of the redhead beside him. It was a face so empty Hop felt he was looking straight through it, so light he thought it might blow away. Was she a paper doll?

Hound's-Tooth Bob was trying to get his attention, tapping his shoulder to get him to turn toward him.

"You're the one who banged my secretary," he said, wagging his finger.

Hop thought for a second. "Me?" he finally said.

"My secretary, Ruthie." The grin was wide. "I do Marv's books. And I only know about you and Ruthie because Tony Lamont wanted me to give her the sack. He said she was laying a publicity man in the file room every day at three instead of taking expense receipts to accounting. Tsk, tsk."

Hop suddenly remembered the girl with the short bangs and cat's-eye glasses and the baby fat around her middle. It was only for a week or so during the first month he was at the studio. A way to congratulate himself on the new job.

"I'm not the only fella in publicity," Hop said. "You sure it was me?"

As he said it, he noticed Sutton's growing interest. He seemed to find Hop a hairsbreadth more interesting.

"I think it was you," Sutton said, looking Hop in the eye but not moving, sitting as still as a king or a statue.

"Yeah?" Hop said, finishing his drink and setting it down with a smile. He could see something in both men's eyes. Something he could work. "Okay. Guilty as charged. But let me tell you, fellas, it only lasted a week. On Monday she was a virgin, covered her face with her hands for the entire lock-kneed deflowering. But"—Hop let loose as nasty a smirk as he could fashion—"by Friday she was ready to take on the entire USC Thundering Herd, front to back, top to bottom. I never saw one turn so fast. She had tricks for *me* by week's end and she even let me do her sister after work."

"Is that what killed it?" Bob grinned.

"Nah." Hop waved his hand. "She found out I was married, called my old lady, and threatened to twist a broken bottle in her face if she didn't divorce me."

"Bitch," Sutton said, shaking his head, the first real animation Hop had seen in him. "Listen, pal, they ever give you a hard time like that, two quick ones to the face. Open hand. Like this." He took the face of the redhead next to him in his left hand and feigned a hard cut to her jaw with his right. Even though Sutton didn't connect, he still managed to jerk the girl's face hard enough to crack her head against the wall. Not the stuff of *Crazy Caravan*, that was for damn sure. "Ow," the girl murmured, rubbing the back of her neck.

"So you're the one who gave that lesson to my wife," Hop said. "Well, you forgot to tell her about the open-hand part."

"Get a load of this one," Hound's-Tooth Bob harrumphed, looking over at Sutton, who almost joined him. "A bona fide court jester."

"I remember you now," Sutton said, lifting one manicured finger a sliver of an inch. "One night we rendezvoused with some ladies you brought, right?" He shot a wink at Bob before adding, "You're good at bringing girls. That's why you're a comer."

"Is that why?" Hop smiled, as he always did with these types. "I wasn't sure you remembered that night. But I think I left before the party really took off." Hop couldn't imagine why he was bringing this up to Sutton. How could this help? But he couldn't stop himself.

"Is that so?" Sutton said blankly.

"Yeah, you went off to the Red Lily, if I remember correctly." Hop watched for any flicker of meaning from either man.

Bob rolled his eyes. "That old rat trap."

"You been there lately?"

Sutton's jaw twitched ever so slightly, but it was hard to tell if it carried any significance other than bored dismissal of the question. He seemed like a man always on the verge of boredom. Tapping out a cigarette, he groaned, "I thought you publicity guys were supposed to be in the know. That place has been dead for months."

"I guess it depends what you're looking for."

"It does," Sutton said, looking off onto the dance floor as if thinking, gropingly, about something he couldn't quite reach.

"It's purely for the hulking masses now," Bob sighed. "It's lost all its native delicacy."

"These places have a shelf life," said Hop, trying to get a bead on Sutton. Was he just a lout or was that thing Hop thought he'd seen in him from across the room as deep and malignant as it appeared? He watched him and thought he saw something twisting around behind his hollow gaze.

"But Gene still drops in?" Hop ventured, using every angle of his springy, anything-goes tone.

"Maybe," Sutton said. "We don't socialize much anymore. Can't keep that one out of the harbor and skid row. He got a whiff of the docks and he can't get enough of it."

"It's epic. The stuff of high melodrama," Bob said. "Gene Merrel, that shanty-Irish baby face, that ululating voice. Dancing his way from the slickest of soundstages straight into the gutter and back again. His feet never touching the ground. Mr. Muckety-Muck can't get enough of the muck."

"Yeah, well, he better make sure he keeps those wings on his feet," Sutton said. "I don't want to see my gold piece sinking in that muck."

"Marv here prefers to be the muckiest part of any scene," Bob added, evidently a little high and feeling bold. "He was upstaged."

Sutton shrugged and lit a cigarette, open cuffs dangling. Hop looked over at him, working at an idea. Maybe the high-life degeneracy that used to intrigue him lost its gleamy allure. Maybe there was some real thinking going on behind the movie-star mug with its long jaw and massaged and scented fleshiness.

Sutton, one eye still grazing the room, began talking to Bob about racehorses. The redheads were starting to look bored.

"Let's dance, Marvy," one said, hooking her shimmery hand around Sutton's lapel. Sutton looked over at Bob, who took his cue.

"He only dances for a fat bill," Bob said, shaking his head. "Won't sing a note, either. That's the sound of money, honey. Opens his mouth and you can see the pretty dollar signs flutter-ing out into the air." Bob held his hand out to her. "But I'll twirl with you, sugar. And we'll get someone for your girlfriend, too."

The three rose and made their way to a spot on the shivering dance floor.

Hop ordered a double scotch and tried to remember what he was doing there. Making sure everything was nailed down or try-ing to peek under the floorboards? The job, kid, he told himself. It's all you got.

With that, Hop took a swig of his drink and tried to imagine a way to exit . . .

"Hey, pal, bring me a pocketful of that," Sutton said abruptly, without breaking his mile-long stare. He was pointing to a young, damp-foreheaded waitress carrying a heavy tray of glasses, her uniform pulled too tight across farm-girl hips. She was a real San Gabriel Valley hick, a teenage face lit with shooting nerves.

"That one?"

"I'd like to fuck her blind," Sutton said, turning to Hop. And in his voice stirrings of something that edged into the grotesque. Hop somehow knew Sutton meant it. An ugly thing, thought

Hop, even to him, who had brought a hundred girls to a hundred movie stars in the last twenty-odd months. It had never been like this. Had it?

The thing he was seeing in Sutton now—had he seen it that night with Jean Spangler? Fuck, sure, he saw it, but what did he care? How was it his business what these fellows needed to get them hot?

Hop looked again at the girl and took a long drink, thinking and then deciding not to think. The job, kid. The job.

Hell, he'd done this a million times before—made an introduction like this. Greased the gears for these boys. It was just an intro. Why the fuck not.

Catching her as she leaned over a tub of dirty glasses by the bar. Placing one hand gently on her arm and talking as softly as he could amid the din. The girl's eyes as wide as a hoot owl's, mouth falling open. A babe.

"But you don't have to be interested." For the second time, Hop interrupted his own spiel. His own velvety patter. He couldn't keep it up. Looking at her downy cheeks, her raw, pliant face, her guileless, insipid eyes, he couldn't. "You really don't."

"Why not?" she said again, with a dreamy smile.

"Because he may not be a nice guy, Ann," he said. "People talk. Say he's rough with the ladies." He wanted to close her gaping mouth with his fingertips and send her home to Paw.

"People say things," she said, shrugging. Then, "I saw him in a picture just last week."

"Ann, how 'bout I just tell him you're taken? I say you got a strapping ranch-hand boyfriend on his way here to pick you up and take you home?"

But Ann didn't hear a word. She pulled a small lipstick—a child's play toy—from her apron pocket and applied a waxy coat of what Hop guessed might be called Apricot June.

"Can you take me to him now?"

Fifteen minutes later, having put off wet-eared, thick-ankled Ann as long as he could, Hop found Sutton coming out of the back room after a few quick hands of blackjack.

"Three hundred just nestled into my lap. I'm primed for that Cinderella."

"You don't want her, Marv."

"What do you know about what I want?" Sutton asked, more surprised than angry.

"I talked to a few people about her. One of the bartenders and one of those"—Hop pointed to the five-piece jazz band—"and I heard the same thing."

"What? Virgin tail?" Sutton said.

Hound's-Tooth Bob, who had sidled up beside them, the red-head in midnight blue on his arm, grinned. "Doesn't matter to him. A few hours and we can have her dumped back here on the doorstep with some beautiful memories."

"Believe me, Marv, you'll carry the memories a lot longer than she will." Hop cocked his head in the waitress's direction. The girl, twenty yards away, waved eagerly. "Got a dose worse than a two-dollar whore."

"Well I'll be . . . ," Sutton said, eyes wider than a half-squint for the first time that night. "The question is, am I sober enough to let that stop me?" He rolled a toothpick along his tongue.

"Look at the dewy-lipped beauty painting her pan at your own table," Hop said, gesturing toward the redhead in yellow, pressing powder into her face with the concentration of a master builder at work. "She's ready and waiting. I'd give my eyes and my kneecaps for a taste of that."

"She's all yours," Marv said, tapping his toothpick on Hop's lapel. "I'm going to take a chance that the cunt's fresher meat than the word on the street."

He headed toward the girl, Bob scurrying behind him with both their raincoats. Sutton looked over his shoulder at Hop and added, "I been lucky all my life."

Hop watched as the waitress's face turned red and she threw off her apron. She barely had time to grab her own coat from behind the bar before Bob had her in his maw, hound's-tooth arm nearly covering her body and Sutton not so much as bothering to look her in the face. Even from the other end of the bar, Hop was sure he could hear her panting, squealing, squirming — and the sounds were playful and fearsome at once. It was impossible to tell the difference.

And then they were gone.

As he walked back to the table with the idea of finishing every drink the group had left there, he wanted to laugh. He nearly laughed. Rarely in life do you get a second chance and look what happens. He wanted to laugh, but the sound wouldn't come up his throat.

As he downed the rimy bottom of a gin and tonic, the redhead in yellow made her way back from the ladies' room to find only Hop left.

"Did Vera skip too?" she said wearily, leaning her impeccable curls against the wall beside Hop.

"The other girl? Yeah."

"Since you finished my drink, how about ordering me another?"

They drank a round.

When they finished, she sighed, "I'm going to call a friend to pick me up."

"I can take you home," Hop said, playing the gentleman.

"No, we're going to Café Zombie. But you can have a smoke with me out back until he comes."

Hop waited while she made the call. Then they stood in the loading area by the back exit. Hop felt glad for the air and for the chance to distract himself from thinking about Sutton and the waitress.

As they breathed in the dusty wind, the redhead abruptly turned to him. "You never even bothered to get my name, did you." As she said it, she lifted her leg slightly from behind the crinkly yellow pleats of her dress.

The leg was nice.

"Name, huh? Let me guess," Hop said, going with it. "You look like a . . . Ethel? Mavis? Clara Mae?"

The leg nudged out farther. To Hop, it looked like it was dusted with gold.

"Hazel? Millicent-Ann? Lazy-Eye?"

"I may have lost the big gun, but hell if I'm writing off the night," she said, giving Hop ten yards of leg now. "At least a publicity man has a shot at getting me in Winchell."

"Is that what the other publicity men have told you?" Hop said, shaking his head.

Looking around, she pushed open the door of the storage room she was propped against. Her hair was so red it was almost blue in the dim hallway light.

"I *have* been having a really bad day," Hop said, a tad wistfully.

She backed into the small room and he followed. He reached his hand out, meaning to slide it around the back of her neck.

But instead he saw his hand cover her face, the heel of his hand on her bright red mouth. He half wondered why he was doing it but then forgot to care. As her head knocked hard against the wall she made a sharp, excited little noise.

When they walked out of the room, the girl tugging her bodice higher over her flushed chest, two of the jazz musicians looked up from packing their instruments. Hop recognized them from a bigger gig they'd had the week before at Moulin Rouge. One grinned at him as he snapped his trumpet case shut. "There's our boy," he said.

He could barely get to his car fast enough, his head foggy from the smoke, noise, drinks, and especially from the close, overripe smells in the storeroom and the girl's loamy perfume, which seemed to have tunneled down into his throat. At last in the safety of his sedan, he rolled down the windows and took a deep breath. He considered smoking a cigarette, but just the thought of the smell clogged his head all over again. He stared ahead, out into the black desert, letting a gritty breeze coat him. Then, shaking himself out of his trance, he tried to flatten the wrinkles on his suit. Twisting the rearview mirror closer to him, he saw a map of the redhead tracing down his face and neck. A skein of mascara on his jaw, a bloom of lipstick on his neck, a shimmer of pancake down one side of his face.

I'm meeting with Carl Heinrich at Casting on Tuesday. He'll get a call from you, right? she'd said as she rolled her skirt back down.

Sure, baby, sure.

The Red Lily

It was a long drive from the Eight Ball to the harbor and Hop's mind jammed itself with doubts and self-recriminations. Especially about what he thought he was accomplishing by nudging his way back into these places, these lives. A movie-star tour of one very bad night.

He looked again and again at the card Freddy Townsend had given him, its cryptic notations guiding him to a sludge-brimmed corner of the San Pedro docks.

As he drove, he remembered writing pieces about Sutton and Merrel back at *Cinestar*, fizzy bits of dross about their "peculiar duo magic." They were coming off their famous string of wartime musicals—*Merry Marines* (1943), *Air Force Follies* (1944), *Sailors' Serenade* (1944), *Army Antics* (1945)—all box-office bonanzas, as they say. As Hop wrote. Endlessly.

Merry Marines was the one that started it all, sealed their fame. Seventy minutes of splashy patriotic-themed numbers choreographed to regimental perfection by drillmaster extraordinaire Busby Berkeley. And then that famous last number. Gene Merrel's final solo, shot in glorious close-up, with his curlicue forelock dangling and Irish blues shining, face lit soft and luminous as Lillian Gish. It was "God Bless America," with Merrel, using every bit of his God-given, milk-and-honeyed tenor and wet-eyed boyish looks, famously looking straight into the camera and, in so doing, transforming himself into every audience member's son, brother, fiancé. As he hit the second verse, Marv Sutton, every inch the dream American man, entered the frame, pointed his finger directly into the camera, and, with that gesture, took hold of the heart of every warm-blooded moviegoer in the land as he beseeched the audience, "Sing along, America. Sing along for our boys."

The timing couldn't have been better, the whole country at its war-craziest, Stars and Stripes bursting out of every mouth. In theater after theater, audiences sang along, full-voiced and buoyant. And then, one afternoon, three days into the picture's release, a returning soldier, one arm lost from the elbow down in the Coral Sea, stood as he sang, stood up right in the movie theater, and others followed suit, setting off a wave of similar phenomena. Finally, to seal it, the celebrated *Life* magazine photograph of the cavernous Electric Theatre in Kansas City, filled to capacity with twenty-two hundred audience members on their feet, hands over hearts, illuminated only by the projector's smoky ray and the screen itself, where Gene Merrel's face loomed, beatific.

Fuck, if that don't make them stars . . . America's goddamned sweethearts both.

Now, as Hop arrived at the docks, the flickering movie image in his mind darkened, blurred. Merrel's on-screen face shed its balmy innocence, its patriotic glimmer. In its place was something else. Something he didn't want to think about. America's sweethearts, sure—who in their offscreen time liked to pick up eager starlets and bang them into no-man's-land. For kicks.

Townsend's card in hand, Hop got out of his car and wound around the docks in search of the storied Red Lily. At first, he felt pretty ready to admit to himself that he was a sap. Letting that skinny-legged colored-girl extra pull him by the nose into a third-rate fleshpot scavenger hunt—how'd she pull it off? But the more he wandered, the sound of water agitating beneath him, almost bubbling, the more the whole thing had a bad feeling—the smells, the creaking boards, ropes pulling on wood, the echoing sounds of someone calling out somewhere, calling someone's name—it felt all wrong.

Finally, he found the narrow passageway marked with the crimson X on one side of a glowing streetlamp. He knocked intermittently on the sea-warped door for close to five minutes before it opened. He didn't know what he was expecting, but it wasn't this: a girl no taller than five feet, one skinny arm beckoning him, her eyes as heavy, as world-wise as a veteran seaman, her body elfin and forlorn as Margaret O'Brien's.

Dressed in an oversize, billowing pinafore of some kind, she walked in front of him without saying a word. They moved down a long, low-ceilinged hall to a parlor filled with slack velvet sofas and a large Victrola. Whorehouses are whorehouses wherever you go, Hop thought to himself, a little disappointed with the Red Lily. Another Hollywood legend up in smoke.

"Have a seat, mister. Someone will be with you right away," she said, turning to go.

"Wait," Hop said. "That's not why I'm here. Let me explain something."

"You don't have to explain anything here, honey bear," she said, her voice taking on a practiced lilt.

Under the henna glow of the standing lamps, he got a better look at her. She was of indeterminate race with a kind of muddy skin and a spray of freckles across her nose and chest. She looked about thirteen with a thirteen-year-old's body—a downy curl under her chin, spindly legs longer than fit the compact body.

"Come here a second," he said, bending over slightly to speak, feeling like Lionel Barrymore to her Shirley Temple. "So what's your name, anyway?"

With a keen look of suspicion as old as the profession itself, she ambled back in the room. "Lemon Drop," she said, tongue flashing for an instant behind her teeth. So much for Shirley Temple.

"So how'd you end up in a place like this?"

"Gee, you're the first person to ever ask me that," she said, hip popping out as she adopted a seen-it-all slouch.

"Tough guy, eh? Listen, I really want to know," Hop lied. The whole place was making him uncomfortable, disgusted, and vaguely aroused at the same time—a combination he'd become very familiar with.

"Listen, if you're here to ask questions, you're in the wrong place. This here is just the wrong place. The Wrongest Place there is," she said, clicking her teeth with her rosy tongue.

"You see a lot here, eh?"

"It's all here." She pulled at the faded blue ribbon on her pinafore. "It's all I've ever seen." Lifting one thin arm, she gestured around the room. "I've never been anyplace else."

"You get some famous faces."

"No faces," she said, with just a ghost of a grin. "No one has a face. Not even you."

The way she said it inexplicably unnerved Hop. Something in her gold-fleck eyes.

"Listen, Lemon Drop," Hop said, then shook his head. "What's your real name, anyway?"

"You think a girl born in a place like this has any other kind of name?"

"Okay. Okay. But listen, listen." He wondered why he was saying everything twice. "I need your help. I really do. I'm no cop and no private eye. I'm just a fellow looking for a lady."

"This is the place, sailor."

"One lady in particular."

The girl eyed him. "She work here?"

"No, no. But she came here one night about two years ago. And she hasn't been seen since."

Her tiny jaw tightened. "Happens all the time, mister. It just does. It's a place people come to vanish. Or the vanish meets them here."

"Maybe you remember," Hop said, taking the curled publicity photo of Jean Spangler from his raincoat pocket and holding it in front of her eyes, which were, he saw now, green and gold both and as tired as his great-grandmother's.

Expecting nothing.

He expected nothing.

But it was there. A flicker of recognition.

Ah, Lemon Drop . . .

"Somebody might help you. If you got the green."

"And who might that somebody be?"

"Somebody might be Lemon Drop if you got twenty dollars."

"What's a little girl going to do with twenty dollars?"

"Get me a new hat and a pair of gloves for church," she said serenely.

"Smart acre, eh." Hop pulled two tens from his wallet and waved them.

"I'll give you one now and one after I hear what you got."

"Come here," she said, taking one bill from his hand and summoning him through a rickety door to their left.

He expected to end up in a red-lit bedroom, but instead they came out into a dank back alley filled with the thick smell of urine, vomit, seawater, and something perfumey like gasoline. He looked up and saw a dozen windows with scarlet blinds drawn shut. Through one, he could hear a woman cooing, as if to a baby, but it sounded broken and it quickly crumbled into a long, low moan of "No, no, no . . . no-no."

"Okay, listen up," Lemon Drop said, her voice taking on a new urgency. "Stay out of that place with questions about your girl."

"She's not my . . ." Hop tried to keep focused, but the smells and the woman's persistent voice were mingling uneasily in his head. Now he could hear a man's low voice talking constantly, nonstop, as if reciting a worn prayer.

"She was here. I saw her. There was five. The girl and another girl—a high yellow—and three men. The two from the pictures and another fella who kept hanging around the door wanting to leave before things got even worse . . ."

"What things?"

"I just know they took a room and the girl went in with the two fellas. They bought some crazy, doped-up ole mule—"

"Mule?"

"Moonshine. Corn. They bought it and a few bindles of junk and took it in with them. The yellow girl and the other fella stayed in the parlor with me and tried to play cards. But they were both scared. They asked me if I would go stand outside the door and see if I could hear anything."

"And did you?"

"I heard crying. I heard her crying real soft. I could hear the little one—you know, the one who sings into the camera like he's going to cry in their pictures—talking to her, muffled and saying crazy things. Saying what he was going to do to her. Things he was doing to her."

"What did he say he was doing to her?" Hop asked. He heard the woman's voice again, breaking slightly, "No-no . . . no . . ." Then, "Oh no, oh no. Not that. Not that."

"You know," she said, ignoring his question. "That one, he comes all the time. He was here just last Tuesday. We all say his mind is gone and the girls better not go with him. One night he came running down the hall and I saw him and he had an old bottle of grenadine in his hand, held it close like a baby. He was out of his mind on the pipe and walking from one wall to the other. I'll never forget: he looked at me, leaned down with the devil in his eyes, and said, 'I could use this,' and he pulled out the stopper—it was the color of a harvest moon. And he said, 'I could use this to take out your eyes. I could put this right in your eye.'"

"Is that what he was doing to her?" Hop waved the picture, his voice hoarse and funny. "To Jean?"

"The other one, the handsome one, he just liked to knock them around or shove things in them. The usual."

"What did they do? *To her?*" He shook the photo at her. His hand kept thrusting forward with it.

"All I know is they sent one of the houseboys down to the docks to pick up a couple drunk merchant marines. I don't know if he found any. And the noises, the screams were loud. I went back later and I could hear a flash. A camera flash going. Over and over."

"What next?"

"I told you: that's all I know," she said.

"Do you think . . ." Hop ran the back of his hand across his forehead. "Do you think they killed her?"

"Listen, mister, word in here was it took Frenchie and Big Arthur two hours to clean up the room. The bucket kept brimming over red."

Hop handed her the other ten dollars and leaned against the wall, which felt swampy against the backs of his hands. He didn't say anything. Couldn't imagine what he would say.

He listened again for the woman's voice but could no longer hear words. Only what could have been the whimper of a lost dog or the plaintive mewl of a cat. And then not that.

The girl looked at him. And her eyes were still working.

"Maybe you know a little more," he guessed, looking at her, at the way she was lingering, one leg bent behind her, slippered foot grazing the brick.

"You wanna come down there with me for a second?" she said, pointing to a set of splintered cellar doors at the far end of the alley.

Hop stood straight. "Not for playtime?"

She smiled—a little sadly, Hop thought. "No, mister. Not me. Not like that. Not yet."

He followed her as she walked toward the entrance, trying not to dwell on the thought of what might be down there.

She opened the doors and a buried smell blasted in their faces, ocean sewage and rot.

"Out of the frying pan into the fire," he tried to joke as he followed her down a short set of steps.

The crabbed cellar was pitch-black and wheezed with every throb of the nearby surf. From the faint glow of the alley, Hop could see the girl pull a pack of matches from her pinafore and light a hanging lamp that swung above them as if in the hull of a pirate ship.

Under the lamp, he could make out a cellar wall lined with pony kegs and another stacked with overflowing laundry bags. In a flash, the girl had slid into a crawl space between the tightly wedged kegs. Like the heroine from some old children's book he'd once paged through in the children's room at the Syracuse Public Library, some gilt-edged, dusty-smelling book with line drawings of ringletted adventuresses finding treasures in old attics—like this, Lemon Drop knocked a plank of wood loose, revealing a narrow crevice into which she slipped an umber arm.

Hop watched, rapt, as she began tugging at something, all the while watching him intently. Watching him like a striptease artist might. *Look at what I may or may not give you, show you,* she seemed to be saying, her eyes narrow and cunning.

Good God, how old is she, anyway, Hop thought, trying to blot out an uneasy feeling that—

"You ready, my man?" she whispered through her doll mouth.

"I am," his voice managed, throatily, even as he found himself backing into an empty pony keg, which rolled noisily from side to side.

From inside the hole, she pulled out her arm, first elbow, then wrist, then her hand clutching something. Hop peered under the dim, strobing light of the lamp, which seemed to teeter with every step made on the floor above it.

Bit by bit, it came out of the hole.

A pale pink sheet or blanket of some kind, festooned with dark flowers, or wreaths, some dark red flowers blooming in crazy patterns.

Hop stepped closer. She had finally fished the entire thing from the pinched hole, her eyes gleaming.

She rose to her feet, unfurling it as she did.

It was a blanket, yes.

But the pattern on it was no pattern. For a moment, he thought it was a drop cloth for painting. How else to explain the red—no, that was the streaming light from the alley; it was more of a ruddy brown—splotches all over, wild rings of various sizes and one deep blot about the size of a dinner plate?

"What is that? What are you showing me?" he demanded, voice strangely constricted.

"Come get a look," she said, although Hop couldn't have been more than five feet from her.

He stepped toward her, conscious, with the swollen ceiling, of his height, of the way he towered over her, his shadow swallowing her like a monster in some old movie.

But she wasn't frightened at all. He could even see the shine of her teeth. She was smiling.

It was when he stood within a foot of it that he had to admit it. Admit what it was.

"They wrapped her in it," she whispered, tongue clicking along her teeth as she spoke.

"How do you know that?" Hop extended an arm to his side, intending to lean his hand against the wall beside him. Trying to look casual. His hand on the wood, a piney knot, a plush tread of moss or sea slime. Standing there. Looking at this little devil.

"They left it in the room," she said, nodding slyly. "I snuck in and got it before Frenchie and Big Arthur could get there."

Hop looked more closely at it. At the striations and stippling. He could picture it once red and moving, wrapped around itself, now gone to rust. Jean Spangler, all tight-bodied, sure-faced, ready for anything, but, as the broadsheets would say, not this.

"Why don't you give me that?" he blurted, without even thinking. What was his idea? Something in the back of his head—something about getting it from her and tossing it into the water. The last bloody strand of the story slipping into the dark murk of the harbor.

"Mister, what do I look like?" She dropped her arms. The blanket swam around her reedy legs.

"What good's it going to do you? It could be anything." He tried to keep his face cool and logical. Like it was all a put-on in which he was barely interested.

"It's my lucky charm. Can put it to use when I need it."

"What? To put the squeeze on? It doesn't prove anything."

"Then what you want it for, big man?"

"I'll give you ten dollars for it. And that's more than it's worth," Hop said, finding it hard to look at the thing. Its encrusted folds calling to mind past rivulets. Like some horrible shroud. All this and he was bargaining with her, trying to make a deal. He fought a raw taste in his mouth.

She looked at him. "What are you going to do with it?"

"That's my business, honey," he said, voice turning, losing its precision. He only called girls "honey" when something was slipping away from him fast. Mostly, they called him honey.

"Sorry," she said, shaking her head. "Sorry. I just don't trust you."

Hop raised his eyebrows in genuine surprise. "Really?" He wasn't used to this.

"You look like more trouble than I got luck for."

"Maybe I'll just take it," Hop said, voice harder than he meant. Something was clanging in his head. Why didn't she trust him?

"Then I call Big Arthur."

Hop surprised himself by saying, "Would he hear you down here?"

There was a glint of recognition in her eyes that made Hop's face burn. She nodded, then, chin out, said, "He'd hear me, mister. He's closer than you think. He'd be here in a minute."

Hop tried to look away from the blanket, forced his eyes away. Tried to regain focus, and a sense of himself, of who he was, and wasn't.

"Hey, I don't want it. I don't need it," he said, talking mostly to himself. He took a breath, rubbed his forehead. What did she think he was going to do? Did she really think he was someone who would steal her imagined ticket out of whore town? Who would rough her up? Who would—

"I'm not that guy," he said, backing away, backing up the cellar stairs. "I'm not that guy."

"Whatever you say, mister." The oldest eyes in the world.

Go home, he kept telling himself. But he couldn't. Not after that.

It was clearer now than ever. There's things for Frannie Adair to find, if she's good enough at looking.

No matter how far ahead of her you are, if you stop, she could still catch up.

But he wasn't sure where to go. And so he decided to go to the only place left.

The snaky devil at the center of this sordid tale: Gene Merrel. That fast-footed, puckish American boy on-screen was a bouncing shadow concealing a lathering brute.

He couldn't very well call Tony Lamont and ask for Merrel's address. So how?

Dot.

Of course. Dot Hendry.

A good-time girl who never missed a rising star. And with a black book to make Winchell himself jealous.

"Dot? It's Gil Hopkins." From a night-chilled phone booth on Western Avenue.

"Hop, even you should be in bed by now." All Tennessee drawl.

"Without you to warm my toes?" he asked, trying for endearing, inviting her to recall the last time they saw each other, Dot unrolling her stockings behind a set at the studio Christmas party.

"Aw, I had too much Tom 'n' Jerry that night, Hop. You know I don't go for publicity men. Only talent."

"Ouch." Hop laughed. "Listen, doll . . ."

The house was in posh Holmby Hills. Merrel wasn't the type to bring girls like Dot to the family homestead, but she was a resourceful girl and had collected the address from a receipt tucked in a corner of the box holding the fur-lined gloves Merrel had given her as a come-on.

"But that was a few years ago," she'd told Hop. "I hear he's hitting the pipe too much. The girls I know won't go near him."

• • •

He pulled up in front of the creamy-walled Moorish house.

Now what, jackass, Hop thought to himself.

Every time he shut his eyes he saw the stained blanket.

He could be home asleep.

He could be anywhere.

What do I think I'm going to see, Hop wondered. What could I possibly see?

And then he was trudging up the sprinkler-beaded lawn.

And then he was chest-high in shrubs, searching for a window without the blinds pulled shut.

Fuck.

It was close to three a.m. and Hop could see very little of the house's interior other than the shine of marble floors, the hushed glow from a single light throwing a dusty glitter through a set of curtains in the upstairs windows.

Hop smoked a cigarette while contemplating the odds he could survive an effort to scale the gutters, gripping turret edges to make his way to a second-floor balcony.

Slim, boy. Real slim.

He wasn't sure how long he'd been standing there when he heard the sound of rustling mock-orange shrubs. He turned slowly, too dumbstruck by the night's endless surprises to be startled.

There stood a sharp-jawed man with a dark felt cap and all the loose-backed calm of a veteran groundskeeper.

"Hunting rabbits?" the man said, hands in pockets.

Hop managed a wan grin and not much else.

"Ah, don't bother. Listen, if you're with one of those Hollywood rags—'cause I'm guessing by the suit, even if it is pretty wrinkled, that you're no cop—you're out of luck."

"Yeah?" Hop said.

"The king of the castle, he ain't here." The man looked at the ground, his cap momentarily shielding his face. He sure as hell wants to say something, Hop thought. Stroke him a little.

"That's okay. I'm patient. And open to suggestions," Hop said, wondering if the man was looking for some bucks, or just a comrade.

"That I don't have," the man said. "Suggestions, that is. Patience I got in spades."

"So where'd milord go?" Hop said, working the comrade angle.

The man gave a cold smirk. "He's gone to . . . let me get this right: *Palacio Sano.*"

A bell rang in Hop's head. "Ah," he said. "The Lourdes of the smart set."

"You been there yourself, my man?"

"Thankfully, no. But I've been in this town enough years to know what going to Palacio Sano means." On Hop's second week at the studio, rumor was a star's wife had been paid off to keep her from going to the press about her husband's trip to Palacio Sano. It didn't stop the star from drinking a fifth of Mexican tequila and smashing his car into the side of his house rather than think about it any longer.

"If only Merrel had seen all those movies they showed us in the army. The ones with the sexy French actresses all the way from Dubuque," Hop said. He wondered if Merrel had been infected before or after the night with Jean Spangler. "Too far along for the penicillin?"

"Hell, I'm no MD, blue eyes, but he sure thinks he's on his last dance card."

Hop wondered how the studio would garnish this heartwarming tale. "Beloved Musical Hero Struck Down by Aneurysm"?

"Lost to Heart Condition—His Family's Curse"? Would he himself write the press release?

"The duo will do no more," the man sighed liltingly. "No more fighter pilots prancing through aircraft hangars, singing about love in the clouds. No more pirates dueting on top of skull-and-crossbone masts for the pleasure of fair lasses. All that crap those fellas been hustling for ten years."

"Sutton'll grab a new pair of pipes to frolic with in no time," Hop said.

"You bet your life."

Hop looked across the dark expanse of the lawn. What more did he need to do, anyway? As much as he knew, there didn't seem to be any danger of anything coming to light. The groundskeeper, he didn't seem the type to pull out the megaphone—he hadn't yet—and even if he did, a movie star spreading a social disease, even a bad one, was hardly proof that he'd killed someone. And Lemon Drop—she'd likely bide her time with that blanket, and by the time she found a use for it, no one would even remember why they cared. All that was left unstitched was the tiny hole he'd opened for Frannie Adair. And how many days could she really spend on this, an unassigned story based on the ramblings of a drunken press agent probably talking big talk just to get under her garter?

"So, does everyone in the house know? About the big S?" Hop's mind clicked back on track. On some kind of track. He offered the man a cigarette, which he took.

"No. Just me. Ask me how."

"How, my man?" Hop held out his match to him. As the man's crisp-eyed face moved closer to light his cigarette, Hop could see something twisting in his eyes.

"Ask my girl."

"Why don't you tell me instead."

"I am telling you," the man said, scowling up at the house. "I brought her here one day to try to get her a job. A kind of secretary for the old lady. Before I knew it, he'd cornered her into the laundry room."

"Did he—did he hurt her?" Hop asked, even as he knew.

The man didn't answer. Then he shrugged and said, "I guess she had stardust in her eyes." He stroked tobacco off his tongue, his face a cold grimace. "But he was done with her an hour after meeting her. Only he stuck, boy. On her, he stuck."

Hop remembered Sutton's carefree attitude when Hop had lied about the waitress with the clap. He bet Sutton didn't know about Merrel. That would be some career-staggering surprise.

And then the groundskeeper, like so many others, endless others, told Hop everything. Hop had always had that gift, that look of open-faced guilessness. A supreme gift and one Hop blamed for giving him his guile to begin with.

The man told Hop that, after it was over, Merrel confessed. Told her all about his condition, even said he was sorry, in a way. But in another way, he wasn't. And then he cried like a baby and told her she was polluted now, too. He said he'd had it long enough that he was sure he'd lost his mind. And she would now go like he did, go to places inside his head, and find that all rules, all laws, all reason would slip off her, too, like a coat falling to the carpet. Nothing seemed real anymore, he said, and there was no longer any difference between his waking life and his dream life. It was all the same and you had to realize it as the true state of grace, because that's what it was. And he wondered if she would feel as free as he did to taste everything, run his polluted tongue over the blackest ridges and furrows in the worst places. He saw pictures in his head, of dark, rutted lesions, of cancers, ringed holes that were just under his skin—and he had to make the pictures real. He drew pictures of these things—

rows of red circles—on cocktail napkins, newspapers, menus. The laundry girls would find them in his pockets. The maids would pick them up off the desks and bureaus. He told her he couldn't stop thinking of them, of red-ringed sockets and red-ringed necks and cervices, and then everything started to look like how the disease looked in his head. And if it didn't, he'd make it so. The darkness he felt all around, he said he'd had to decide a long time ago to swallow it whole.

Hop felt his mouth go dry. He felt his cigarette slip from his fingers. The green dark of the lawn, it seemed suddenly filled with the red circles, the circles from the blanket the girl had shown him not an hour before.

"The funny thing is she passed the Wasserman. Her doc said he'd probably had it for years and was no longer infectious. But he never seemed sick to me."

"Why don't you go to the police? The papers?"

He looked at Hop, an ember of his cigarette crackling. "She wouldn't like it."

"Oh," Hop said.

"He told her that he got it from some mongrel cunt on a trip to Panama," the man said. "That's what he said. To my girl."

Hop nodded.

"I met her at the church picnic in Lomita. She was about to take a job as a carhop at the Hot 'n' Tot when I talked her into coming here."

Hop nodded again. He didn't know what else to do.

As he drove, he tried not to think of the look on the man's face. Tried not to think of the waitress at the Eight Ball. Tried, most of all, not to think about the red-ringed blanket that had hung before his eyes. (Was it his imagination or had it smelled so strongly of blood that he might have been in a butcher's back room? It couldn't still smell, could it?)

He'd seen his fair share of lunatics in his years in Hollywood: hysterical actresses who liked to smash windows with their bare hands, gloomy-faced actors who played with loaded pistols at parties and then retired to darkened rooms for days or weeks at a time. Glamour girls who pulled their dresses over their heads in public. The elegant leading man who stole teacups from restaurants, and another, same sort, who asked his lovers to throw tennis balls between his legs from across the room. Hop was rarely surprised these days. But this . . . this disordered man. And everything so close, right before his eyes. That night . . . that night in 1949 when he'd bid good evening to those two long-limbed girls—girls from other places, one a mother no less, and both someone's honey-kissed daughter—and they had walked out the door of the Eight Ball straight into this man's fevered head. A head filled with horrors.

Why had he come here? Why did he have to keep asking questions? You can't unsee what you've seen, unknow what you know. Sweet Jesus, Hop, you'll dig your own grave yet, just for the endless feel of dirt between your fingers, the promise of something underneath to redeem . . . everything.

Gotcha

At around four thirty in the morning, Hop found himself in front of Frannie Adair's house again. The thought of going home to his empty apartment was unbearable, especially remembering that Midge had been there hours before. Everything would smell like her. So he kept driving until he was at Frannie's, like he was stuck in a loop and ready for more drunken confessions at the feet of the russet-haired maiden. Only he wasn't drunk and was determined to keep his mouth shut. He leaned back in his seat to think about what he might say, and before he knew it, he was asleep.

He awoke, crick-necked and cotton-mouthed, to the sound of Frannie's front door slamming. There she was, in a sober navy dress, flitting down the steps and over to the car parked in her driveway.

Hop slid down and waited until her car was halfway down the block before turning his ignition.

He followed her along Alvarado to Beverly. Traffic picked up and he nearly lost her a few times. He squinted at his watch and saw that it was nine o'clock, awfully early on a Sunday. And she wasn't headed toward the *Examiner*.

As he drove, he began to remember a dream he'd had, was still having when Frannie's front door jarred him awake.

He was at Earl Carroll's, back when Midge still worked there, taking photographs of patrons and bringing in as much as a hundred dollars in tips on a given Saturday evening. In the dream, he was walking toward the hatcheck room with its ornate cutout window. The hatcheck girl was turned with her back to him, adjusting a coat on a hanger. As he came closer, he began to feel funny, like he wished the girl wouldn't turn around—and what might happen if she did? He fixed his eyes firmly on the half dozen rows of neat, dark curls coiled around the nape of her neck and tried to will her to remain still.

He knew who it was.

He thought, I'll just leave my hat on the counter and walk right past. I'll just walk right past and not even look.

But as he reached up to take off his hat, he realized he wasn't wearing one. He looked down, as if to find it on the floor.

When he looked up again, the girl had turned around and

the amber spot above the window hit her face and there she was. Jean Spangler, pearly, iridescent skin skimming out of a green dress edged with sable. Dimples to cut glass. And she was leaning forward, her breasts nearly curling out of the bodice. And she was waving a hatcheck ticket in one long-fingered hand.

"Hey there," she sang, and her voice was low and thick, almost vibrating. "Lose something?"

Just as he was about to speak, he was blinded by the flash of a camera clattering to life.

He squinted, trying to regain his vision, and when he did, he saw Midge standing before him. She was wearing her old photog outfit, the one with the bare midriff and short sequined skirt.

"Gotcha," she said, turning her silvery head to Jean and laughing. They both laughed, and the sounds of their laughter gathered together and then—

Frannie's door squeaked open and shuddered shut, swallowing the laughter and bringing a feeling of relief so intense that Hop almost crossed himself, which he hadn't done since catechism school when he was eight.

He kept pace as Frannie streamed along the near empty lanes of Third Street, through Hancock Park, and for a minute, he wondered if they were going to Beverly Hills. But as they approached the enormous new apartment complexes of Park La Brea, she made a sharp turn. He could see her looking for a number on the string of town houses that had been growing like crabgrass since the end of the war. It was at this point that Hop began to get a strange feeling.

He watched as Frannie parked the car on Colgate Avenue in front of one of the complex's many buildings. She got out of her car and began to walk toward one of the garden apartments.

It was like something charged and electric vibrating in him, sending sparks up his spine, along his temples.

He'd been here before. Not just nearby, but here. In one of these buildings. He'd definitely been here before. The feeling— it was like dreaming he was having sex with a script girl and waking up in the middle of sex with his wife.

Before he knew what he was doing, he opened his car door, slid out, and bounded across the street and up the slope of the lawn, nearly colliding with a sparse new peppermint tree as he did so.

Hearing his approach, Frannie Adair turned, startled, her mouth a small o.

"Thought I'd join you," he said breathlessly.

"You really know how to give a girl the rush," Frannie said, touching her hand to her hair, unconsciously slipping a strand back in place under her small blue hat. "How did you . . ."

"Listen, where are we?" Hop said, his voice breaking a little. Was he still dreaming?

It was at that moment that the door opened.

"Peggy Spangler?" Frannie was saying. "I'm Miss Adair. We spoke on the phone."

Hop wasn't sure which happened first. He noticed the small geranium pot on the porch and suddenly flashed to nearly tipping it over with his foot in the dark and trying to upright it, dirt coating his hands. In the same moment, he caught sight of the woman standing in the open door, white-blonde hair, flushed cheeks, round shoulders, even—he guessed it was there and then confirmed it—a small beauty mark popping out from the top of her fawn-colored housedress.

Miss Hotcha.

"I hope I'm not too early."

"No," Miss Hotcha was saying. "I was expecting you." Those flat Midwestern tones.

". . . and I appreciate your willingness to talk about your cousin."

"Please come in."

At that moment, Miss Hotcha looked over at Hop. Her eyes fixed on him. And there was some kind of crackling mix of recognition, resentment, and panic. It was a look Hop knew well. Women had been giving it to him half his life.

Hop smiled. "Good morning. I'm a colleague of Miss Adair's."

Frannie shot him a look, which Hop ignored. He was wondering what Miss Hotcha—Peggy Spangler—fuck, Jean Spangler's kissing cousin—would do.

She looked him up and down, trying to regain something. Then, "What, like a photographer with no camera."

Aha. Smart girl. Or at least smart enough.

Hop laughed. "Something like that. May we come in?"

She avoided Hop's eyes as she let them pass in front of her. They walked into the small living room, stuffed with a large radio cabinet, hardy sofa set, and heavy fringed curtains.

Frannie sat down and Peggy Spangler took a seat in a chair across from her, folding her hands on her knees. Hop began walking around the room, trying to see if he recalled anything. But all he remembered was the bedroom and not much of that beyond twin beds and the doily-edged lamp he'd knocked down. His mind raced: What had Peggy Spangler been up to that night? And what was her idea now?

"I want to thank you for all the time you gave me on the phone yesterday."

"I'm just glad someone's still out there trying. Sometimes Mama Spangler and I feel like we're the only ones left who care, Miss Adair."

"Call me Frannie."

"Frannie. As I told you, it's been almost a year since I've seen Jean's little girl—that's Christine . . ." She picked a large, gilt-edged photograph from the side table. Angel-faced four- or five-year-old in starched organdy. "Mama and Jean's ex-husband are in a custody dispute. Christine was Jean's darling but mine, too. I took care of her every day."

Hop watched her as she spoke. He was not particularly impressed by the performance. Low-rent Olivia de Havilland. Peggy Spangler was practically wringing her hands. He wasn't sure if he would have bought it even if he hadn't recognized her.

"Jean's mother thought a boyfriend was involved in her disappearance," Frannie said, looking at her notes.

"Yeah—yes. She thought it was the movie actor Kirk Douglas, on account of the letter. Jean went on a few dates with him. But she dated a lot of showbiz types."

"You didn't buy the theory, then?"

"No." She shook her head, glancing fleetingly at Hop as she did so. "Those fellows didn't scare her. She had them sized up."

"You told the papers you didn't believe her when she said she was going to work that night."

Peggy smiled. "It's not that she was lying. It's just Christine was there when she said good-bye."

"So she didn't want her daughter to know where she was going. Where was she going?"

Hop watched her wrap her ankles around each other, adjusting her dress and stalling for time. What was her game?

Then, Peggy looked up suddenly with big blank blue eyes. "She was with child, Miss Adair."

"She told you that?"

Something roused in Peggy's face and her voice sped up, lost its maidenly poise. "She went to take care of it and some sweaty-palmed SOB cut her the wrong way and killed her. I think her boyfriend—that sharpie Davy Ogul, probably, like I told you yesterday—hooked her to a bad doc, maybe knowing she wouldn't come out alive."

"And the note?" Frannie asked.

"My guess? She tells another fellow that she's knocked up, thinking he might make it right. When he drops the ball, she decides to go ahead with the operation and starts to write a note to him. Something interrupts her or she changes her mind about telling him. Maybe she figures she can get more jack from him if he doesn't know another fellow already anted up."

Hop wanted to laugh. In this brief analysis the thin veneer of respectability and refinement Peggy Spangler had put on fell away. Closer to Miss Hotcha after all, he thought. Leave her to her own devices and she reveals herself. He tried to catch Frannie's eye to see if she saw it, too.

"Quite a picture you paint of your cousin," he found himself saying. Then he stopped himself. For fuck's sake, Hop, who do you think you're working for, anyway?

Peggy looked at him, eyebrows tangling, her face stuck in arrested motion. Wouldn't she love to squawk at him now? But she won't. Hop wasn't sure why, but he knew she wouldn't fess up to a thing.

The Q&A went around for a good half hour. Peggy detailing Jean's wild ways, her constant stream of dates with unreliable and questionable men. Boy, does she hate her missing, probably-dead cousin, Hop thought. He looked at Peggy's tired face, the dyed and curled hair and the pressed dress, the full makeup and the round legs growing thick. A girl who was running out of time. In a few years, that kind of country-turned-city mouse beauty can turn frowsy and sad. She was watching her chances fall away each day.

"Thank you for your time," Frannie said, rising.

"Hope to see you again, Mrs. Spangler," Hop added, tipping his hat toward her.

She said, with a nervous wave of the hand, "I don't know what more I can tell you."

He said, "Maybe we'll have some things to tell you," and smiled hard at her.

Frannie and Hop walked to her car. Then, at a safe distance, Frannie turned to him.

"Listen, are you just going to follow me around from place to place? Is that the plan?"

"Hey, last night at the Eight Ball was a happy coincidence, remember?"

"And this morning?"

"Thought maybe I could help."

She gave him a look. "Well, whatever you're doing, it's working. No one's talking about Sutton and Merrel above a wink. Not even their driver, the busboys at the Eight Ball. Locked shut. Like clams, I tell you. I can't get a soul to place them at the Eight Ball except you. And even my broadsheet won't let me roll with that—'cause I'm guessing you won't go on the record."

Hop just smiled lightly. His head hurt. His mouth felt like a dried-out sump. He tried to ignore the uncomfortable feeling of sweat cleaving to his shirt. The prickle on the back of his neck assured him Miss Hotcha was looking at him from her apartment window.

"And Peggy Spangler," Frannie chattered on, "she knows zip. She's either dumb as a short plank or she knows when to keep her mouth shut."

"She seems like just a simple kid. Who can say, though?"

"Still, I don't give up so easy. The way you're on my tail, I guess I'm beginning to think I'm onto something." She moved closer toward him and pointed her finger at his head. "I can almost see the tiniest little bead of sweat on your left temple."

"Rough night." Hop smiled. "You should have taken me home with you to keep me out of trouble." He leaned toward her. They were close enough now that he became conscious of the fact that he'd slept in his car. And that he'd never showered after his storage-room rendezvous with what's-her-name. "Listen, Frannie. Sure, I want to keep my nose clean. But I also want to try to help or else why would I have laid it on the line for you to begin with?"

"A fifth of bourbon laid it on the line for me."

"The bourbon was the courage, sure. But I was still trying to make things right the best way I could without losing my shirt. That's all you can do."

"You even talk like a press release."

"Well, here's one in all caps: Jean Spangler is probably dead. Slipshod abortion. The cousin told you as much."

"And Sutton and Merrel?"

"One last sad fling for a party girl who'd had one too many."

"That doesn't end the story. If it was a butcher job, I'm going to find out who the butcher was. I'm talking to some girls who work the clubs on the Strip," she said. "But here's where we part ways, cowboy."

Hop opened her door for her. Then, as she slipped by him, grazing his arm, he said, "You're not going to phone my wife again, are you?"

Frannie stopped halfway into her car and turned. "So she told you."

"In four-letter words—all caps."

She looked a half shade redder. She sat down in the front seat and, focusing on fitting her keys in the ignition, said, "I'm just doing my job."

"That's what I always told her," Hop said. "And now I know how lousy it sounds."

Hop got in his car and drove around the complex a few times. Then he parked on Fairfax and walked back to the Spangler apartment. Peggy was sitting on the front steps, a hand over her mouth.

"You were a lot nicer the night we met," she said as he walked across the lawn toward her.

"I've lost a lot of niceness in the last few days," he said as she rose and opened the front door. They walked inside. Hop turned to her, her powdery face, the white-blonde eyebrows raised high in expectation. The mouth. He felt something rotten charge forth from his belly and end up in his wrists, temples. Had she laid for him that night to keep him away from the real story?

"Listen, what's your angle?" he said, walking so quickly toward her that she backed up, nearly stumbling on the carpet edge.

She straightened her shoulders and took a breath. With an attempt at a smile, she said, "You want something to drink?"

He folded his arms and took a breath, too. Stay calm, kid. Nothing's ever gained from getting hot. "How about ten gallons of black coffee?"

He followed her into the kitchen. As she worked the percolator, he peered across the hallway into the bedroom. Doily lamp. Twin pictures of ballerinas.

"Scene of the crime," Peggy said, almost smiling, then cringing at the bad joke.

"What's your angle?" he repeated.

The percolator began to bubble.

"*My* angle?" she almost barked. "I'm a war widow from the Midwest. I admit it: I got tangled up in this because of my own vanity. I wanted to have a little fun."

"Fun, huh? Fun for your beloved cousin to take a flying leap into nowhere?"

This time, she did flinch. "How did I know? And how is it my fault? I went along that night to enjoy myself for once. I figured, why should Jean get all the good times? My figure's just as fine." She ran a hand along the tops of her breasts. "I can laugh and dance and, well, other things, too. You know." She nodded her head toward the bedroom.

Hop didn't smile. For the first time he could recall, he passed on a cue.

Abashed, she dropped her arms to her sides. "I wanted to join her on one of her nights. Is that so awful?"

"So you were playacting?" Hop felt worn through with patience. "The country-cousin routine, huh? Okay, got it. Now, Mrs. Spangler, what I need to know is what the hell your game is."

She visibly bristled, even backing up a little.

"I've got no game, Mr. Hopkins," she said. "Oh, yes, I remembered *your* name."

"Because I actually gave you mine, Miss Hotcha."

Peggy touched her cheek, slightly red, with the back of her hand. "That was Jean's idea of a joke. In her own way, she was full of jokes."

"What about Iolene?"

"Who?" She looked at him.

"Iolene. The colored girl. Jean's friend."

"Oh, her. I don't know. Never saw her before that night. Or after. Jean didn't mix us, her family, in any of that."

"Any of what?"

"Showbiz. Whatever biz."

"It's funny because I really don't believe you."

"That's not my problem," she said briskly. Then she began looking at him closely, setting out two cups and saucers. This one's raw and ready, Hop thought. She's running out of chances to play this card and she knows it.

"So I know her," she blurted out. "Iolene. She called a few times after Jean disappeared. Wanted some long green."

"For what?"

"How should I know? I told her she was barking up the wrong war widow."

"When was the last time you heard from her?"

"I don't know. A while ago."

Hop squirmed in his chair with irritation. "Listen, I'm losing my patience. I never lose my patience. Do you want to join me in seeing what it looks like?"

"She was mixed up in some schemes with Jean, okay? She was getting Jean involved in some things Jean had no business in."

"Like what?"

"What else? Parties. Good times." Peggy paused, then added, "Photographs."

"Photographs?"

"Yeah, photos."

"Blackmail."

"Yeah, yeah. Can this be new to you, Mr. Hopkins? You seemed to know Iolene."

"Not really."

"Well, she's bad news. You should just count your lucky stars it looks like she's beat town."

"How do you know she's beat town?"

"I'm guessing that's why I stopped hearing from her," Peggy said waveringly.

"You might think about this, Miss Hotcha. Iolene was awfully scared last time I saw her. Scared enough to run. Hope whoever she's scared of isn't thinking of you next."

She crumpled into a chair. Looking up at him, eyes turning pink, she poured Hop a cup of coffee and one for herself. He could see it all in her face. He could see it happening to her as she told it to him. The whole sad affair. She told him everything. All those evenings stuck in that apartment, watching her twenties pass by. So when Jean called home to check on Christine, Peggy tricked Jean into giving her the number of where she was, in case of emergency. Since Jean's mom was in Kentucky visiting family, Peggy got the next-door neighbor, Beryl, to look after Christine. She put on one of Jean's dresses, a pair of her stockings, even her perfume. She took a bus as far as she could and then hitched a ride to the Eight Ball, her heart pounding the whole way.

"And you," Peggy told Hop, not quite looking him in the eye. "You with your shiny hair and the way you talked to me close. As soon as I got there, Jean whispered to me, 'He's all yours, sweetie. Eat him up.' I thought you were an actor."

"You must have been disappointed."

She shrugged, still not looking him in the eye.

"So you don't know anything about what happened to them after we left?"

"Sure I do. Iolene told me. She said Sutton and Merrel put Jean in a room and things got wild. Iolene snapped photos of them. The two men, they took turns on her. I think there are even pictures of both of 'em taking her at once."

My, she's a cold one, Hop thought. Tells me this like she's telling me what she had for lunch. "For their private delectation?"

he said. She stared at him blankly. He tried again. "For kicks?"

"I guess. But Iolene's no fool."

"What do you mean?"

"What, you think she's the heroine of this little story? Those fellas can't even control themselves enough to know that whatever jollies they get from the snapshots aren't worth having those pictures fall into someone else's hands."

"Iolene peddled these pictures?"

"Sure, kid, sure. She wasn't about to let the game end with Jean's disappearing act."

Hop looked at her, trying to see if, or how much, she was lying. "Sutton and Merrel paid?" he asked.

"I don't know how it played out, Mr. Hopkins. Iolene played it long, far as I could tell. She's a confident one," Peggy said.

"Did you see the pictures?"

"No. No, I never did. But . . . but from what Iolene said, those pictures . . ." Her eyes unfocused. For the first time, Hop thought he saw something happening. Something Peggy hadn't copied from the Saturday matinee. She paused for a moment. "They tied a leather strap around her mouth," she said, voice trembling. "The pictures, they must be awful. Iolene, she said she couldn't get them out of her head. She wanted to get rid of them. They were starting to get to her. She said she kept seeing them in her sleep. She said they were in all her dreams."

Her eyes turned red. Neither of them said anything for a minute. Then she looked up at him and there was a fierceness in her eyes. Fleetingly, he thought of Midge.

"You still working for the movie magazines?" she asked.

"Sure," Hop lied.

"Then you must be looking to make some sugar yourself." There was something unloosed in her face. It was unspooling and unspooling.

"Who isn't?"

"I know where the golden egg is. A stash even hotter than this, big names in what they call compromising positions. You and me," she said, setting her hand over the top of her coffee cup, the steam turning her fingers pink. "We could go partners."

"Oh yeah? If it's so hot, what do you need me for?"

"Connections. Muscle—"

"How much muscle you see on me, Ace?"

"Enough," she said, releasing her hand and pressing it on the counter. "I figure you can peddle 'em. To the studios. The chancier gossip rags. Split the take. Get me the hell out of this four-square for good. I've served my fifty-two months. Life's rough all over. Why should Iolene get all the honey?"

"That's your angle, huh?"

"Could be."

"I'll bite. Where's the stash?"

Satin Doll

He told the studio he needed a day—two days max—off. Barbara Payton needed nursing. He was flying out to Chicago and then hopping a train up to Minnesota to babysit the newlyweds. It'd be worth it, honest. Of course he was more than pushing his luck. He really wasn't in that kind of league. And the chances of getting caught showed this was a sucker's bet.

The sound of his own voice on the phone with the studio made him sick.

How could he turn it on so fast, that hot, easy pit-a-pat?

What was wrong with him? He touched his face and it was shiny-smooth, cool, like molded plastic, and if you tapped it, there was the soft sound of a perfectly hollow center.

· · ·

On his way to what he hoped would be Iolene's hideaway, Hop stopped at a dismal-looking diner on Fountain Avenue. He realized he couldn't remember the last time he'd eaten a meal. Was it with Bix Noonan the previous afternoon? Or had he just had coffee? All he could remember for sure was the stale pretzel grounds and stray peanuts he'd scooped up at the Eight Ball.

He sat at a corner table swabbed with coffee stains and made his way through a plate of runny eggs and crushed potatoes, scraping up the last slick yolk with a brittle slice of bacon.

The waiter, a hatchet-faced old fellow with arms like a scarecrow, picked up his dishes with surprising care.

"I could tell you was hungry," he said. "Coming from a funeral?"

"No," Hop said. "Why?"

"You got that look."

Hop tried to summon a friendly rejoinder, even a wisecrack, but nothing came, other than the sour taste of the coffee clinging to his teeth. And the rind of grease coating his mouth.

He paid in a hurry and walked to the five-and-dime next door. He bought a toothbrush and a packet of tooth powder. Without bothering to ask, he pushed into the employee restroom and washed his teeth briskly, messily. Then he ran water over his stubbled face.

He looked into the mirror, and as he did . . .

As he did, he felt something was slowly slipping off him, some silky veneer, a loosening and dropping to the floor of a something—a something he had worn so well.

The waiter was right. There was something in his face. And something missing from it, too.

Oh, fuck, Hop, you just need a good eight hours of sack time, a shower, and a shave.

Maybe a nice alcohol rubdown at the fancy place in Beverly Hills.

Fuck, Hop, you're taking it all too hard.

Now he was snaking his way through random side streets in Hollywood, trying to find Perdida Court. He imagined seeing Iolene again, if she was still there, and how he would handle it. He also wondered how to dance with Peggy Spangler just close enough to avoid making her mad—mad enough to call Frannie Adair, for instance. Or the police.

Poor Jean. Life isn't tough enough for you, you gotta have a green-eyed cuz who stomps over your—dare he think it aloud—your *grave* to try to make a buck off you.

But then the thoughts of what Iolene and Jean may have been up to started to irk him. Less than ten hours ago, he'd been staring at that stained blanket and thinking of Jean Spangler as the wretched victim of a studio-protected sex maniac who, at some point, had veered into bloodlust. Now . . . What could those girls expect, playing this kind of game? They must have had big-league backers. If so, maybe they were strong-armed into it, walking the plank for Mickey Cohen's crew, who were known for running operations like this all over town. And always with starlets on their way up and down and out. But Iolene, really? And if they were so hooked in, how come Cohen couldn't protect them from the likes of Gene Merrel? Maybe they weren't worth the trouble.

He thought about all the things Peggy had said. And the last thing: "Iolene's been sitting on this golden egg for long enough.

Too scared to do anything about it after Jean . . . Somebody might as well skim off that cream."

"How do you know she's not perched on it when I get there?"

"Don't you reporters do stakeouts?"

"Do I look like that kind of reporter?"

"Today? A little bit." She'd smirked, eyeing his crumpled suit and stubble.

She'd handed him a piece of paper with a Hollywood address. Hop had stopped himself from saying that he thought Iolene lived in Lincoln Heights. Why let her know? Clearly, Iolene was not sticking to one place but was darting around, circling and tiptoeing, jumping and running all over town.

"So you'll bring the photos back here? Or should I come to you?" Peggy had said, moving so close to Hop he could smell her coffeed breath, sweet with milk.

"I'll call you," he'd said. "Let me get the lowdown and call you."

"Guess I better give you my number," she'd said, writing it down on the same paper as the address. "You wouldn't double-shuffle me, would you?"

"Me?" He'd tried to put his winning face back on. It wasn't easy.

"You came here looking to outscoop your fellow reporter and look what you get," she'd said, smiling. Hop smiled back so hard his face hurt.

Perdida Court was a series of small, tidy bungalows. The house in question was batter-white with a green roof jutting out over a modest front porch. There was no driveway and the street was dotted with cars, so Hop couldn't be sure if anyone was at home.

Faded green curtains were pulled shut across the front window.

He stepped out of his car and walked up the front path, ignoring a slight wobbly feeling in his legs. Before he could think about what it would mean to see Iolene, or not to, he rang the bell.

No answer.

His collar itched, His hair felt oily, like the pelt of an otter. His feet were swelling in his crocodile shoes. And damn if he didn't want to toss Peggy Spangler out the nearest window for making him lose his temper back there, so rare an act it surprised him.

So, he decided, I go in like the sneak thief I am. How low can you sink, Hop? But then he remembered back in his newspaper days he'd once looked through a councilman's trash cans, the heel of his hand sinking uncomfortably into old spaghetti and coffee grounds.

Broad daylight on a Sunday. Better not try the front windows. He walked toward the back of the house, keeping an eye out for random neighbors watering lawns or hanging laundry. Luckily, a tall fence blocked the view between this lot and the one next door.

As he turned the corner, his leg hit a trash can and the clatter nearly made him jump out of his skin. Christ, Hop, pull it together.

Every window was shut and a quick scan of the latches showed them to be locked tight, despite the warm weather. Come back at night when you might have a shot at breaking one? Could he really wait? Frustrated, he walked up two steps to a back entrance. The screen door squeaked open on its hinge and Hop, for the hell of it, tried the knob on the inner, wooden door. He felt a lock engage but barely. Turning to his side, he began leaning and turning the knob, jiggling it and pressing the door with his shoulder as hard as he could.

He could feel the lock nearly spinning around, just about to give way. He turned with his back to it and gave a quick kick to the spot directly to the left of it. The door flew open.

He felt a gust of something blast in his face, up his nostrils. Walking into a bright white kitchen, he immediately spotted a trash can sitting by the window. The top was slightly tilted and Hop guessed it must've been filled to the brim to give off that smell. Left town in a hurry, Hop figured. Sure looked like it.

Deciding he better not open the windows, he placed a handkerchief over his face. He walked through the kitchen and into a small dining room, which led to a living room straight ahead. The furnishings were simple. A round table and chairs, muslin curtains, a gold-green damask sofa with two matching chairs. Dust motes in the air. A highball glass sat in an evaporated ring on the dining-room table as if someone had set it there for a moment to get a coaster.

He saw a small stack of mail fanned across the sofa cushion. Utility bills. A grocery-store circular. An advertisement for a modeling agency. Hop peered more closely at the address labels. Not Iolene Harper. Not Jean Spangler. The name was Merry Lake. Previous tenant or nom de hideout, Hop wondered.

Then, it hit him. The smell—it was familiar. It was a smell he knew. From back hospital corridors. From a long-ago hunting trip with his father by Lake Ontario. The stench from the center of the enormous devil's tongue flower he stood over at the traveling sideshow his pop took him to when he was five years old. An organic smell, sweeter and heavier and . . . he walked quickly toward the only room left: the bedroom.

The first thing he saw was a neat curl of tan patent leather, the tip of a shoe, jutting out on the floor from behind the ajar bedroom door. As he moved closer, he could see a full-wedge sandal and the bronze stocking foot, graceful, elegant. Lovely Iolene.

At first the stocking looked patterned, but as he squinted and stepped closer to the door, it was as though her leg itself were marbled, green and black wisps winding around her limbs, which looked puffy, straining the seams. Hop felt his body rise out of his skin, hover there a second, and then thud back down to earth.

He pressed his fingers on the door and the smell lunged into his mouth and nose so strongly he saw stars, felt his tongue swell, dry and sludgy at the same time.

As he entered the room, the room seemed to enter him, swallowing him up with the stench, the balm, the sound of the flies buzzing, the sight of Iolene, her graceful, lissome body in a rust-colored dress with black trim, her copper-tinted hair piled high on her head, her wrists and arms patterned with tortoiseshell bracelets, and her face . . . her face he couldn't see. It was turned away, nearly covered by the edge of the bedspread, cheek facing the wooly, worn carpet.

He crouched down, hands covering his face and mouth, still a good six feet from her. No more coffee-with-cream skin. He tilted his head to one side and took a deep breath before peering at her head. That was when he saw the piece of plaster on the floor.

That was the moment before he realized it wasn't plaster but bone, skull.

He didn't want to touch. Didn't dare touch. So he began crawling around.

A circle of soot surrounded the hole neatly, like a tattoo. The hole at her temple, nestled in the delicate whorls of dark hair so artfully arranged there.

He couldn't stop himself from looking more closely. A few green bottle flies stuck in clumps to the hole.

Her eyelids were swollen, and her berry-stained lips.

Her eyelids were swollen but her eyes still looked open.

He could see the glistening between her lashes, or thought he could.

He thought maybe the buzzing sound would never leave his head. He thought maybe the smell would be with him forever.

For a moment, he thought he might never leave this moment.

The shine of the eye, the glitter of the silver bobby pin in her hair. The feeling of something undulating in his stomach, burning in him, making his face hot and sending a strange pulsing rhythm through his own temples. He could feel his collar hanging forward as he kneeled over her and a wetness on his neck as the heat clawed at him. The smell coming harder.

He stood up, startled by the snap of his own knees as he rose from his crouch. He took several long breaths. He walked slowly to the bathroom and turned the water on. Holding on to the sink's edge, he tried to forget about the grinding sensation of his breakfast moving around in his gut. But it was too late. Falling to his knees, he leaned over the toilet and—quickly and efficiently—threw up everything. He flushed the toilet and rinsed out his mouth with water.

He walked out of the bathroom. Then he walked through the dining room and into the kitchen. He almost walked out the back door, but the sound of a neighbor's dog barking stopped him.

Then he got smart.

He walked back into the bathroom and, with his handkerchief, picked up a washcloth and began wiping the sink handles, the toilet seat he'd clutched. The doorknob. He didn't think he'd touched anything else.

Then, he walked back into the bedroom, keeping his eyes straight ahead and holding the washcloth over his nose and mouth.

He looked around. Using the handkerchief, he began opening drawers. They were all empty. Iolene wasn't living here.

It wasn't until this second turn around that he saw the suitcase on the floor on the other side of the bed. It was open, with a few plain dresses streaming out. He looked more closely. A spare pair of shoes. A cosmetics bag. All packed so neatly it made Hop wince. She was on her way out of town. Stopped here to do something, get something, and skip.

The photos.

Where had the photos been, anyway? Had Iolene been killed for the photos? For what she knew about Jean? Both?

He looked under the bed and saw nothing but a thin carpet of dust. He walked to the long sliding closet doors on the adjacent wall. The closet was nearly empty, too, but for a small metal file cabinet with two drawers.

Not the subtlest of hiding places, Hop thought.

He opened a drawer. Empty. He opened the other. Except for a stray paper clip, a few bent staples, empty again. Whoever followed her here found what they were looking for.

Wait. Strike that.

As he began to shut the drawer, something caught his eye, something white wedged in the far corner, just barely peeking through. He tugged it and pulled up an old file tab, along with its paper label still tucked in its sleeve.

The label read:

RX copies 1945

He slid the tab out from the sleeve. Typed on the back were the following words:

Dr. Stillman–1455 S. Hill Street, Los Angeles

This was something. He knew this was something. He remembered:

Kirk, can't wait any longer, going to see Doctor Scott. It will work best this way while mother is away,

Okay. Scott wasn't Stillman, but it was something. Something was there. He could feel it. Why would Iolene have a doctor's file folder in her apartment?

If Jean Spangler was the victim of a botched abortion, the timing of which just coincidentally followed the night at the Red Lily, maybe Iolene was hiding the evidence. Protecting somebody. Or maybe Iolene had done some sleuthing of her own. For which she'd been given this hasty farewell.

At last, in spite of his best efforts, Hop let himself really think about the fact that it was Iolene, sweet Iolene, on the floor. Slowly, he turned his head and looked back at the body.

At her.

They didn't even bother to make it look like suicide, he thought.

He shoved the tab in his pocket. He wiped the drawer handles with his handkerchief once more for good measure. The smell was beginning to rock his stomach again.

He knew he should leave, but he was looking at her. He was thinking about her dancing. He was remembering that once, before everything, when he was still shilling for *Cinestar*, he'd run into her at Fox, where she was shooting a Betty Grable picture. She was a chorus girl in an ole plantation number, wearing a topknot and, inexplicably, a sequined merry widow with fishnet tights. She was tapping her feet and looking bored, waiting for the crew to relight the set. The musicians, also bored, began improvising a ragtime number. Hop, who'd just interviewed Grable about her new baby girl, had spotted Iolene from fifty feet away, and as he got closer, he kept saying things like, "When I get there, Iolene, you're going to dance with me. This is it, you've got to give me a tumble. You know it's time. You're going to dance with me." And finally she laughed and she let him twirl her around for a few minutes, his face pressed against the white netting on her headpiece, the crunch of the sequin and taffeta against his chest, her voice curling warmly in his ear. The smell of . . . of . . . he thought it must have been gardenia, radiating from her body. She always smelled like flowers. And his hand on her back actually met some of her skin and it was like stretched satin, it was like . . . the music was . . . she was . . .

And now this.

He took one last look around. That was when he noticed the front door had been unlocked all along. Must have been how they left, Hop thought. They . . . they . . . What did this have to do with Jean Spangler or Sutton and Merrel? Someone knew about the pictures and wanted them or wanted them to disappear. He remembered what Jimmy Love, Iolene's pal, had told him at the King Cole:

Those boys have been closing in. Boys you don't want to make unfriendly with, Hoppity.

Connected?

Hell, ain't we all? You can't live in this town without it sticking to you like tar paper. But no, these fellas were up some notches.

Sutton and Merrel, back against the wall, could make something happen. It would be no surprise if they had old mob connections from their nightclub days. Could be any number of thugs. Somehow, it no longer seemed to matter. The story of the savaged girl and her frightened friend was turning now, bit by bit, into just another girls-on-the-make-pay-the-price yarn.

Couldn't anyone give him a new scenario? He'd seen this one more times than he could count.

Without even thinking, he found himself outside the house and walking to his car. Without even thinking, he started it and began driving away from the house, lurching along with any number of sick tastes in his mouth.

As he got back on Sunset, his head played nasty games.

How did I get here? Six years ago, working at the *Examiner*, caught by the assignment editor sleeping off a drunk in the display-ad office, he expected the usual punishment, obit duty, and the thought of it made him want to write his own. But the Hollywood-beat reporter picked that night to elope with a San Francisco tie salesman and Hop ended up at Grauman's Chinese covering the premiere of some swooning bedroom melodrama with Joan Crawford and a cast of also-rans. It was afterward, at the premiere party, that he met the gray-haired, tired-eyed senior editor from the East Coast office of *Cinestar*. Nice fella, liked his jokes, ended up buying three rounds of sidecars, told Hop that he reminded him of himself a quarter century ago.

During their second round at Mocambo, the editor had asked him, "If you were covering this party for *Cinestar*, what would be your lead?" Hop had placed his fingertips on his chin in thoughtful repose and said, "Mocambo, where the stars mingle and make hay, was aglow last night. Revelers swarmed there following the thrilling premiere of *Lover for a Day*. Star for a century Joan Crawford drew all eyes as she entered the exotic nightclub on the arm of a dashing young man. Ms. Crawford demurred when asked the name of her mustachioed date, but she did offer the sweetest of smiles when queried about her recent divorce from actor Phil Terry. 'He was a wonderful man, but we'd grown apart. I wish him well.' And we wish you well,

Joan, our forever-bright star, our flapper of yore, now Holly-wood's grandest of grand dames."

"Not bad," the editor said thoughtfully. "Toss the reference to how long Crawford's been in the biz, but other than that, honey, you've got more sweet corn in you than between my uncle Joe's teeth back in Iowa."

Hop had grinned. He had a knack. What could he say? He was going places.

And now, after the nightclubs, round tables at Romanoff's, dog races with movie stars, fluffy beds at the Beverly Hills Hotel, fast rides on pretty costume girls and hairstylists, hat models and manicurists—now this. A separate track he'd careered onto and now there seemed no crossing back over. The other track was gone, its simplicity, the pinwheels and soft lights and perfumed whispers and we two against the world—all gone. No chance of return.

He was driving for a long time, trying to shake the smell from his throat, clothes. A few miles away, he threw his handkerchief out the window.

Iolene, Iolene. Playing far too close to the line and now look. He knew he should be thinking about how he might have helped her. He wanted to be that kind of guy. But how could you stop something like this? These fellows know what they're doing. They'd have found her anywhere.

So that's it, right? I'm done, Hop thought. The last possible squeaking wheel got greased. No one else had any incentive to talk about that night. No one else was talking at all. It was done, deader than Tin Pan Alley.

Who was he kidding? He was going to Dr. Stillman's. After all, the squeaking wheel may be gone, but why not set your foot in that last visible footprint and run your foot over it and be done?

He tried again to think about Iolene and what might have happened to her. But instead, all he could think about was the way these women concealed themselves. Some kind of fan dance. Victim, wave of fan, perpetrator. Angel, whore. They all played it so straight, as if they were just girls, girls with gentle smiles and simple needs. But the truth was they all lived in a gasp of tension. You could feel it like a physical thing around them.

When he met Midge he thought, Here she is. Finally, one of those women like Jerry always has half off his arm. The ones with their own jobs and nice apartments with soft lighting and softer sheets. Women with other boyfriends he never saw but who still liked him best and would break a date if he called but without ever raising a voice, smooth as the martinis they'd pour, as their taut silk dresses and shiny stockings. Women who were ageless, young without a scary eagerness in their eyes, mature without a hint of lines in the face or desperation in the voice. It had been a terrible trick, hadn't it? How she'd made him think it would be so easy.

Driving to the Hill Street address brought him directly past the *Examiner* building on South Broadway and Hop couldn't help but look for Frannie's car, which wasn't there. Jerry's gray sedan was there, though, and before he could stop himself, he'd pulled over. Seeing his friend now, the one solid, fixed thing in his life—that might help him pull it together, get him through the last stretch. But he didn't want to go upstairs, didn't want to risk Frannie showing up, didn't want to do another dance with her. He walked to the fraying coffee shop across the street and found the phone booth. When Jerry got on the line, Hop was embarrassed to hear his own voice shaking.

"Christ, Gil, you sound as lousy as I ever heard you. Stay there and I'll come by and slap some sense into you."

Sitting at the empty counter, Hop ordered a coffee while he waited, his hand wobbly as he lifted the cup. The counterman kept a close eye on him, wiping glasses with a rag, one after the other, like a barkeep in an old Western.

Ten minutes later, Jerry arrived and took a seat beside him.

"You never looked this bad when we were in North Africa," Jerry said, lighting a cigarette and snapping his Zippo shut.

"The salad days."

"You usually play hard to get. Now I see you, what, three times in two days? People'll start to talk," he teased, but there was concern in his eyes and it made Hop worry about himself. Christ, how bad did he look?

"And Midge was up all night," Jerry said, nodding to the counterman as he set down a cup of coffee for him. "Gil, you've got to . . . Gil, she's a wreck."

Hop looked at him, remembering Midge's visit the night before. Frannie's fishing around, trying to get something from Midge. Had that just been the night before? "Because of the call?"

"What call?"

"Frannie—Miss Adair."

"Frannie Adair called Midge?"

Hop tried to conceal his surprise. Midge hadn't told him? Her knight in shining gabardine? He decided he'd better follow suit. "No, no. Frannie was trying to find me and got Midge instead."

"How—"

"Never mind. Never mind. And, listen, about all this . . . I'm sorry I keep flying off. I'm sorry. I don't know why." His head pounded.

"Frannie's got something on you?"

"Maybe. Turns out I've left a lot of fingerprints, footprints, all kinds of prints in my day."

"What's it all about, Gil? The Spangler thing? Is someone shaking you down?"

"Jerry, I've half lost track. Frannie Adair's poking around. She thinks there's something there. It's my own fault for getting her hot on it. And, Jerry, that girl I told you about, the one who came to see me? She's dead."

"Jean Spangler's friend? How?"

"I'm guessing the pistol blast to the head did it."

"Well I'll be. How'd you find out?"

"Up close and personal-like," he said, wanting to tell Jerry all of it. But he couldn't do it. "I was worried about her. I went to her place. The door was open. And she was lying there."

"Did you call the cops?"

"No."

"Did you leave any prints?"

"I don't know. No. Maybe. I tried to be careful."

"Better get yourself a story, boy. You were with me whenever it was."

"I'm not worried about that. I've got too much else to worry about. Believe me." Hop finished his coffee and grabbed his hat. He knew Jerry wanted to talk, but he had to go. He had to go before Jerry saw something. Saw something Hop didn't want him to see. Saw Hop fall to pieces right there.

"Why'd you do it, Hop," Jerry said suddenly, as Hop was almost to the front door.

"Do what?"

Jerry walked toward Hop. "To Midge."

"You're going to have to be more specific," Hop said wearily.

"You know what I mean," he said in a tone too grave for Hop to brush off.

There were a lot of things Hop wanted to say, things that were gathering in him, knocking around, tangling his nerves, rising up under his skin, beneath his eyes. But he couldn't do anything with them. He wasn't sure why. Instead, he just shook his head.

Jerry looked at him for a moment. Then, with a sigh, he said, "She tells me she was never mad a minute in her life until she met you."

"I'm just lucky, I guess." Hop managed a grin and wondered if he'd be able to keep upright long enough to make it to Dr. Stillman's. "See you later, sweetheart."

"Gil . . ." Jerry's eyes were heavy. His mouth was slightly open as if he were going to say more. This was a classic Jerry gesture. Hop knew it meant Jerry was saying everything all at once. Then, finally: "Gil, a thing about Frannie Adair. She got a reputation early on for being willing to roll with some hard boys for a story. Hasn't been able to shake it since. Maybe you can use that. If you need to."

"Thanks, pal," Hop said, head swirling. "I just might."

Dr. Stillman—1455 South Hill Street, Los Angeles.

The address was on a slightly shabby block of cavernous office buildings with worn facades, a small hotel with a barbershop in the lobby, a high-ceilinged Irish bar with wide-open doors spilling mournful tenor lyrics and the smell of balmy beer onto the sidewalk out front.

Hop walked the half block from his car to 1455, a smaller building with a shuttered dental clinic on the ground floor. Opening the heavy, soot-rimmed front door, he entered a dark lobby inhabited only by a newspaper stand. A lone man in suspenders stood behind its counter, dining noisily on a strong-smelling container of what looked like pickled beets and cabbage.

Hop eyed a building directory in a musty glass case.

STILLMAN, DR. MITCHEL........443.

"Pack of Pall Malls," Hop said.

The man reluctantly set down the container and reached under the counter for a pack, which he laid down with a matchbook.

"Quiet today, huh?"

The man shrugged. "Only a few offices open on Sunday," he said. "Hardly worth my time. You here for the locksmith? The dentist closed at two."

"I'm actually looking for Dr. Stillman."

"You're a little late, pal." The man sloshed his container around and the briny smell kicked Hop in the face.

"Gone for the day?"

"Gone for the year. Or close to it. Ain't seen him in a blue moon. He must be paid through the year because the management ain't cleaned out his office or rented it to someone else."

"Where'd he go?" Hop said, trying to sound casual, despite his mounting frustration. To come this far and not know, what could be worse? That file tab, a last faraway whisper.

He raised a bristly eyebrow. "Just a guess but probably someplace cooler, buddy. Get it?"

"Not really."

"You don't know too much, do you, buddy?"

"Less than that."

"He was a lady doctor—you know, a doc for ladies. Things can get hot."

Hop nodded. "You mind if I go up and check it out?"

He shrugged. "I sell newspapers. What's it to me, bud?"

Hop paid for his cigarettes with a five-dollar bill.

The elevator creaked up four floors. He had to use both arms to drag the grated door open, rust pinching into his fingers.

The corridor walls were daubed with smoky amber sconces. The only sound as he walked was his own shoes skating over cigarette stubs, a candy wrapper. He heard a throaty whistle that startled him until he recognized it as his own—a nervous habit left over from childhood, from visiting his uncle in the TB sanatorium in Onondaga, or his grandmother in a charity ward back in '34.

The beveled glass at the end of the hall had M. STILLMAN, MD stamped on it in fading black letters. He took a breath and placed his hand on the knob, which felt cold and greasy and made Hop think of salve on burn wounds.

He wondered what he expected to find. The end of an endless tunnel. The wormy ground at the bottom of a hole. Blood and horror and a churning, red-ringed breach into the void.

Or an empty office as stripped of meaning as anything else?

He turned the knob, but the door was locked. Fuck if this was going to stop him now. Fuck if he couldn't stare down that gaping breach. Spotting an old brass standing ashtray nearby, he lifted it and plunged it against the beveled glass once, twice, three times and the plate knocked out whole, thudding to the floor, and—a ghost of his old luck remaining—cracked into a spiderweb without shattering. He reached through the window frame and unlocked the door, which wobbled open, revealing a dark outer office with one marbled window bringing in faint, diffuse light from the street. Not much to see: a desk and a row of waiting chairs covered with dust. Walking through, he opened the door to the inner office and saw a glass-front cabinet with scalpels, clamps, foamy rolls of gauze. Beside it stood a rolling table with still-full jars of ammoniated mercury, Vaseline, and

Unguentine, glowing red bottles of Mercurochrome. And in the middle of it all sat the metal examination table, with detachable stirrups. A reel of prone women went through Hop's head. Of Jean Spangler torn and desperate. *Kirk, can't wait any longer, going to see Doctor Scott. It will work best this way while mother is away . . .*

But this wasn't Dr. Scott. It was Dr. Stillman. And why Iolene would have his files was far from clear.

He looked around cursorily in the examining room before returning to the outer office and the file cabinets. He pulled open the drawers one by one and, as with Iolene's, each one was empty. He opened the desk drawers and they carried only office supplies, a few open boxes of pens, pads of paper. As he searched, he found himself repeatedly turning his head to look back at the open door to the inner office and the white-papered examination table, which, with its swivel trays and attenuated stirrups, looked disturbingly like a large mechanical spider. Each time he looked he could almost see Jean Spangler's long legs rising from its center.

Hop, you are losing your mind.

Giving up on the outer office, he knew he'd have to return to the interior examining room, but as he did, he tried not to look too closely at the equipment or to smell the uncomfortable mix of heavy dust, mold, and alcohol.

Scanning the other side of the small room, body radiating with prickly heat, he noticed a closet he'd missed before. He opened the heavy wooden door and saw a few old lab coats and, behind them, several large boxes stacked high.

He slid the boxes out of the closet, took a seat on the wheeled chair, and lifted the lid off the top box. Inside were mostly old receipts, utility bills, carbon paper. The second box, however, was filled with brittle brown file folders.

Heart battering around in his chest, he began pulling out file after file, eyes scanning the folder tabs far too fast to take them in. One overstuffed folder he grabbed so hard and so fast that the box fell to the floor with a grunt. The manila folders inside spilled out into a fluttering windmill and at the top was one labeled, in strangely familiar hand, "Employee Records." He fell to his knees, one sweaty hand smearing across the folder. Tax forms, ID forms, JEANNE HORELLY, RECEPT. (1944), CARL HAUS, LAB ASST. (1945–48), LAURA SEIDL, NURSE (1946), and so on. Individual photos of stern-faced employees all posed against the same white backdrop that still hung on the wall next to the reception desk. His damp fingers stuck to one and he shook it loose.

Here was finer metal. Long blonde hair gathered high atop her head, heart-shaped face with a round petal of a mouth. Slanty, sexy-as-hell eyes. All sizzling beneath his fingers. She always had 'em. Looks to make you swoon, looks like murder.

Oh, Midge.

Reno, 1946

Three weeks to the day they met, Hop was driving Midge Maberley to Reno, head pounding already with the hangover that was still six hours away. Driving through the desert relentlessly to get there before he could come to his senses.

They couldn't get married until the last twenty-seven days of her residency were complete. She had to wait out her divorce, a seven-month marriage to a touring bandleader who hadn't made it back to the West Coast since the honeymoon.

In Reno, Hop filed phantom stories at the local UPI office and drank and played cards all night, every night. He kept playing until he lost everything, lost the thousand dollars he came with, and then lost it again. That thousand had been all he had in the world, most of it from a big win at Santa Rosa, the win that started the binge during which he met Midge to begin with. When there was nothing left, Hop, alone and running out of distractions, had the sudden realization that he'd played so that he would lose everything, had dedicated himself to losing. He didn't want to marry this girl, Midge, with one slim dime in his pocket, nor one faint thread of decency or expectation. Each night he clamped his hand on one of her white dimpled knees and pushed it down flat on the rough hotel sheets and tried to fuck all their shared ugliness away. And all her beauty, too. By the time the divorce came through and he propped himself up at city hall, there was nothing left of either of them. Not one bright shock of sentiment or hard-won illusion.

Sitting in his car, Hop stared at the photo of his wife and tried to think, tried to focus. When he'd met Midge she was working at Earl Carroll's. She'd talked about having half a dozen jobs since she'd moved to Los Angeles, from shampoo girl to cigarette girl to third-row-back chorus girl and back again. But she'd never said anything about having worked in a place like this. Maybe it just never came up. Maybe.

He looked at the dates of employment: MAY 1944–FEBRUARY 1945. Not such a short employment that it wouldn't merit mention. And he'd met her in late fall 1945.

Was it all happenstance that Iolene had files from a place his wife once worked? Hell, maybe this doctor was the one to go to for all the girls who ran through the nightclubs. He knew a few doctors frequented by all the actresses at the studio, like their favorite hairdresser or tailor.

Try to talk yourself out of it, Hop, but . . .

Midge at the Earl Carroll Theatre on Sunset. The famous sign out front read, THROUGH THESE PORTALS PASS THE MOST BEAUTIFUL GIRLS IN THE WORLD. He remembered it well. Sitting there, he found himself even saying it aloud:

"Through these portals pass the most beautiful girls in the world."

A chill raced up his back.

Iolene. The last time he saw her, at the bar.

I've known that girl forever, she'd said about Jean. *One of the most beautiful girls in the world. They should have written that for her.*

What? he'd asked.

She'd shaken her head. *Never mind. You never got it.*

Had Jean Spangler worked at Earl Carroll's? Vaguely, he remembered something from the papers. How had he forgotten? Both Jean and Midge. Did Midge know Jean?

Of course.

Before he knew it, he was back in his car, folders strewn across the backseat.

Midge. Fucking Midge. Is there any corner of my life you've left untouched, uninfected?

What could you possibly . . .

At first, his head was too flooded with facts and revelations to form an idea, a theory. Then, as he began driving, scenarios thrummed to life. Almost no food for two days, a few hours' sleep, sure, but he could still put two and two together. The coincidence was too great: she worked at Dr. Stillman's office and files from his office show up at Iolene's. Jean worked at Earl Carroll's and Midge worked at Earl Carroll's. Midge playing so dumb, coming to his apartment, pretending she didn't know what Frannie Adair was digging for ("She asked if I remembered about a girl who disappeared . . . I told her I didn't remember anything like that . . ."). Stringing him along, watching him twist, when all along she *knew* Jean Spangler. God, did Midge work with them? It was a stretch, but not impossible. Why else would she never mention working for a doctor before? He imagined, veins throbbing in his temple, a setup: Jean, Iolene, and Midge all doing the same dance for that hood Davy Ogul back in '44, '45. Jean meets Midge at the doc's office, or Midge takes the job there just to have access to the files. Or Davy Ogul puts her in that job to get access to the files. Had Midge still been in touch with Iolene? Was that why Iolene came to him? Had the two been pulling something on him *now*, ready to blackmail him as Midge's last revenge? He knew he was reaching, but the way his head was jammed, the ugly possibilities seemed infinite. Jean, Iolene, Midge—he wondered, crazily, if they were somehow the same woman with three slippery tentacles reaching out to grab him by the neck.

Well, he was no fucking patsy.

He suddenly realized that he was driving to Jerry's, and he hoped Midge was there alone. He didn't want any interruptions. To stop him. She was going to explain herself. They all were.

Blood pulsing in his head, he was at the front door of Jerry's apartment without any memory of parking his car or entering the building or walking up the four flights. And now there was a man in his shirtsleeves and bedroom slippers standing in the hallway, pointing his finger at him.

"What? What?" Hop said.

"You hammer that goddamned door any longer, I'm calling the cops," the man shouted.

Hop looked down at his fist on the door, at his own red knuckles. For the first time, he heard the sound he was making. Dropping his hand to his side, he turned back to face the man.

"Who the hell do you think you are, buddy?" the man continued. "People are trying to eat their Sunday dinner and they gotta hear you yelling and pounding."

"Take it easy, pal," Hop said. "This isn't the public library." He rubbed his reddened fist with his other hand.

The man, a good six inches shorter and twenty years older than Hop, wouldn't relent. Folding his arms across his chest, he groused, "I should call the cops on you."

Hop felt something rising within him, something popping in his head. Something that made him start walking toward the man, still rubbing his fist in his hand. Walking purposefully.

The man saw something in Hop's eyes and backed up in a dart.

"Where you going, pal?" Hop said, finding himself wanting the man to take him up on his threat. Wanting anyone to.

The man, eyes like saucers, tripped back into his apartment and shut the door.

Hop, two feet away, stopped.

He wanted the popping feeling, that strange flitting in his brain, pressing down and up at the same time in hard bursts—he wanted it to stop.

So, he said to himself, letting his arms fall to his sides, she's not here. No one's home. That's okay. That's okay.

He walked slowly down the stairs, out the front door, and to his car.

You should go home, Hop.

Go home. Clean your head out. You can telephone later. Your head's not right now. Everything's at funny angles. You need to rest.

But instead he ended up driving to yet another drugstore and calling Jerry's apartment. No answer. Of course. Sweet Mary, Hop. Then he called Frannie Adair at the newspaper.

She's out on assignment.

Where?

The Little New Yorker.

Hop called the Little New Yorker.

He could hear the bartender calling out Frannie's name. A few minutes later, he heard her voice on the phone. Direct and lively, like always, but a little breathier. A shade more drawn out.

"You keep close tabs. I'm beginning to feel like my old man's in town," she said, then paused, as if waiting for Hop's rejoinder. He knew he couldn't possibly offer one, and she went on without him. "Well, my boy, as it happens, I've been trying to reach you. This fella I talked to at the studio, turns out he remembered something. Remembered hearing Jean Spangler had gotten lured into some mob-run, picture-peddling racket. And that she had a girlfriend working with her, a colored girl, a torcher."

"Hmm. How Christian of Jean." He cursed himself for letting this Alan Winsted thing get away from him. It was his own fault. Who knew that little studio runt would know so much or be so hungry? I should have, of all people, Hop thought.

"This colored girl, she's the one who came to see you, isn't she? Came for help because she was getting pressure? Someone—maybe some heavies, maybe studio people, maybe both—thought she had something, something she could use to blackmail them or Sutton and Merrel, or both. Maybe she did and maybe she didn't, but they weren't taking any chances."

She paused. He didn't bite. He felt the space between his temple and the earpiece get damper and damper.

"Listen, Hop, Iolene might be as gone as Jean Spangler by now. That's what I'm getting at."

"My, my," Hop said. He was surprised at the sudden coolness in his own voice. To him, it sounded as forced as B-movie tough, but maybe not to Frannie. "You've made a lot of progress, gumshoe. So the cops weren't so far off. Just another girl for hire hustling for Cohen's boys and then trying to work it solo for more dough, right?"

"How do you figure?" she said, her voice bristling.

"Hey, I believed the damsel story as long as I could—the wrong-place, wrong-time girl. Savaged and abandoned for the bad luck of having long legs. But let's face it. She was just another badger girl making bucks on her back. She got greedy and paid the price," Hop said, fast and cold.

Frannie didn't say anything. The phone booth felt 120 degrees. He could almost hear the wood planks spreading.

"Jesus, Frannie, I can practically see your Little Orphan Annie eyes now," he said. "Come on. You've been around long enough to write the end to this sob story."

She sighed. "Just because they may have gotten recruited into some blackmail scheme doesn't mean Sutton and Merrel didn't hurt her, or worse. The one doesn't cancel out the other."

"Well, there's evidence for one and not the other, so you run the odds." Even as he said it, he pictured the stained blanket, its heavy rings of rusted blood, its meaty odor. Had he really seen it? Or was it one of his frenzied dreams, nights shot through with booze, sleeping sitting up in his car, Iolene becoming Jean becoming, somehow, Midge again. The Red Lily itself seemed more and more a fever dream with blurred edges, fun-house grit and pop-up horrors.

"There's evidence for everything," Frannie sighed. "Too much evidence and not enough proof. My editor won't let me run anything until I can get a PD go-ahead. And I could show Jean Spangler and Judge Crater are living in tract housing in Mountain View and the boys in blue would still not raise a paunchy finger. They're bored with my face."

With that face, impossible, he almost said, would surely have said forty-eight hours ago or less. Now he couldn't say a word.

But her face could never be boring. It had too many bright things in it, too many promises of warm hands, knowing smiles, morning coffees on kitchen tables with red-checkered cloths, long car rides in sunny glades, Saturday-night shows with hands touching light and eyes flickering at the screen. Real things with heft behind them, brimming with their own dark wonder. A relentless wonder that stirred him whenever he looked at her.

But something suddenly hit Hop. "Wait a minute. You said Iolene."

"What?" she said quizzically.

"A few minutes ago, you said Iolene might be as gone as Jean Spangler by now. Where'd you get that name?"

She paused. A split second—maybe less—but it was there. Then she said, "I told you. The fellow at the studio. He gave me her name."

"Bless you, Frannie Adair, you're a horrible liar."

"I'm not bad on occasion. But listen, you don't tell me every-thing. Why should I tell you?"

"You shouldn't," Hop said. "You shouldn't." His head throbbed at the thought of how much else she might know by now. The memory of Midge's employee photograph flitted through his brain and suddenly his blood was beating against his skin again. He had no choice. He had to find out. "Listen," he continued, trying to keep his voice from trembling, "can I see you?"

"Okay," she agreed, voice slipping back into a breathier tone. "Meet me at Don's Bar and Grill in a half hour. Hey, Peggy Spangler called. She wanted your phone number. Wouldn't tell me why."

"Did you give it to her?"

"No. She said she called every sheet in town and you didn't

work for any of them," Frannie said, and Hop could almost see her grin. "I told her you were freelance, which is true, after a fashion."

"I'll be there in thirty," Hop said, hanging up. He wasn't worried about Peggy Spangler. She was a detour. Another girl with something hard and metal knocking around in her chest, a can of thumbtacks, a rusty alarm clock. Another blank face with dollar signs for eyes.

Fuck, Hop, can the purple prose. And don't worry about Frannie Adair. Never waste your time worrying about someone who can't even lie over the phone.

He tried Jerry's apartment again. No answer.

He grabbed the phone book and tore out the back page. Grabbing a pen from his pocket, he wrote:

> Midge— Meet me at Don's Bar and Grill,
> Pico and Main, tonight. I have important
> news and things I want to say. —Gil

What if Jerry got the note and read it first? Hop couldn't stop his thoughts from racing long enough to care. Instead, he folded the paper, wrote Midge's name on it, and drove back to Jerry's.

He tried knocking one more time on the door, loudly, half hoping the blowhard down the hall would come out again. He didn't.

When no one answered, he slid the note under the door.

It wasn't until he was nearly downtown that he began thinking about what Frannie might have been doing at the Little New Yorker. The place was a watering hole for mob crews.

When was the last time he'd seen her? A day? An hour? Five minutes? A week ago, he'd never met her, and now she had slipped through the center of every knot, that russet strand curling around every corner, braided in tight.

"Frannie. Frannie." Was all he said. The only woman in his life not out to ensnare him, he thought, before remembering she'd dedicated the last few days to trying to dig his grave.

She was alone at a large table filled with wet rings from glasses recently removed. Her cheeks very pink, like a doll's. Nearly finished with the highball glass in her hand, she was smiling and frowning at the same time. The shiny blue comb in her hair was just a quarter inch askew.

"What's it been? Hours?" she said, gesturing toward the seat beside her.

"Dear heart," Hop said, draping his arm across his chest. Who'd've thought he could still put on a show? Not him. Inside, he felt charmless and mercenary. A sharpshooter with a target in his sights.

He slid down next to her in the booth. Smelling her light perfume, he moved closer without even thinking. And then he was surprised how near she allowed him to come. One whisper of breath from her, heavy with juniper, gave him his final confirmation.

"Frannie Adair's been hitting the nozzle hard."

"I'm okay. Don't you worry," she said, shaking her head. "I've just been working."

"Sounds a lot like my work."

"Hopefully not *that* much."

"So you get your headline yet?"

She shook her head. "But an endless number of unprintable yet completely believable rumors. That tip about Iolene Harper—I've been working that angle with some fellas at the Little New Yorker. That's how I found out her name."

"The New Yorker would be the place for it. Not too many square joes and upright citizens there."

"So," she said, ignoring him. "I guess I don't get a word from you about what this Iolene might have said to you. Now that I know who she is."

"Iolene who?" Hop said, hoisting a smile. He waved the waitress over and ordered a double scotch. If he was going to keep going, he was going to have to forget about everything else, especially the fear he was fighting. The fear was this: nothing, really, matters. These girls, they bloom into these pillowy flowers, inviting him in, then they turn into tinsel, all glittery and rough edges, and then, still later, they turn into something else . . . what was it . . . what was it?

"—Hop? Your drink." Frannie thanked the waitress and slid the glass toward him.

Hop remembered what Jerry said—was it just a few hours ago?—about Frannie Adair: *She got a reputation early on for being willing to roll with some hard boys for a story. Hasn't been able to shake it since. Maybe you can use that. If you need to.*

"Let's get back to the Little New Yorker for a minute. You've been talking to Cohen's crew," he said, letting her have it. "Drinking with them. Consorting just a touch?"

Frannie's eyes widened slightly and crimson fluttered across her face.

"It's okay," Hop said. "Christ. What I do in one day—"

"I know it's okay," she said briskly. "It's my job. I couldn't do my job without it. To get them talking you have to be willing to do one of two things. And this one's easier for me than the other. I spent twelve years at St. Cecilia's with starched shirts and thick stockings and a healthy dose of 'Oh no you don't.'"

"That's charming," Hop said coolly, "and a little worn. I guess that's what you tell those boys as you order up the rye."

She winced slightly. He hadn't meant to sound so hard. Or had he? He took a fast nip of his drink.

"Well, it's true I no longer qualify for St. Cecilia's Purest Flowers Prize," Frannie said, sloshing the stirrer in her drink tiredly. "But girls who jump in with those fellas have too bumpy a road ahead of them for the likes of a slim-hipped gal like me. I stay off the road and watch from the shoulder."

"Okay by me," Hop said, backing off. Who was he to doubt her, the straightest stocking seam he'd come upon in five years? "And what is the word on the shoulder?"

Frannie sighed and took a long sip of her drink, bringing water faintly to her eyes. "I hate it when the whole picture turns out simpler and uglier than the parts. You can forget Sutton and Merrel. They're just cads—maybe very bad cads but not murderers. Forget your big studio draw-up. They're not so interested."

"No?"

"You were right. Word is that Jean and Iolene were working the old badger game for Davy Ogul. Looks like they got greedy. I don't know the details, but one of Cohen's apaches had been casing Jean for two days. Word is they buried her in Griffith Park. Must have missed the handbag."

It was so simple. Was it so simple?

"And Iolene?" Hop asked throatily.

"The pictures they thought Jean had, well, they were suddenly recirculating. Or they thought they were. They could only guess Iolene had taken custody. The call went out on her last week. And these things don't usually take much time. Some goon with a half a C-note in his pocket tailed her and, from what I heard, she got it in the head."

Hop could picture the glitter of the silver bobby pin in Iolene's hair, her heel turned on the floor. The smell, of bruised things, soft things turned steel or plastic or chrome and then soft again, a rotting flower, left to rot.

"I'm sorry," Frannie said, seeing something in his eyes. "I guess you liked her."

Hop looked at her. "I didn't really know her," he said, his voice jagged. He finished off his drink. "Let's get the whole goddamned bottle."

Frannie took a deep breath and twisted a little under her dress. "What the hell."

They talked haphazardly for a while. Once, Hop excused himself and telephoned Jerry's apartment again. Still no answer. As he walked back to the table, he watched Frannie, watched her with those big eyes, her ankles crossed neatly beneath the table, tucking a wisp of ginger hair back into her upsweep. Was she doing it for him? He was pretty sure she was.

He sat down.

"So why did you marry her?" she asked him abruptly.

"Pardon?" He slid closer. He wanted to smell that smell of, somehow, fresh ironed pillowcases, cut flowers, wind through hanging laundry. Something. But it was hard to reach behind the smell of gin and smoke and sawdust and smashed cherries and orange rinds ground under feet.

"I've been thinking about how careful you are. How cautious. And then I think you must have been really unhinged to tell me what you told me that night—when this all started," she said, resting her face on her upturned palm, looking up at him. "Your wife. She must be some number. Why'd you marry her?"

He thought for a second. And at the same time, he considered why Frannie might be asking him. Something told him it was purely personal.

"I don't know," he said at last. "Someone's always trying to get something from you and every so often you just give it to them."

"So it could have been any girl. Wrong place, wrong time."

"For both of us." Hop smirked. "But sure, there were other things, too." He was trying to answer without thinking about what he had just found at Dr. Stillman's office. That was still too much to pull together. Instead, he went with the alcohol, followed it. Made it his own. "I had something for her when we started. It made me a little crazy. But it went away."

Frannie looked at him and in her eyes was the thing, the thing he always tried to conjure in women. A kind of suffuse sympathy and warmth that flooded them but checked itself before extending outward and demanding something, or overwhelming everything. It just seemed to spread throughout her body, behind her face, and slip down her throat, along her arms, tingling at her fingertips—almost visibly—but asking for nothing in return.

But was he so broken? Was he so broken as to deserve this from a girl like Frannie Adair? A girl who'd never worn sparkling netted stockings or held a round card or shaken her ass for coins? A girl who'd not once painted her nails hot magenta and danced them along a sugar daddy's knee for a job or a mink? A girl who'd never stood in a line of other girls and turned her bare leg from side to side for a leering casting director, promising with a wink that she could turn her legs all night?

Those were the girls you could get that look from. Because they were so glad for you. So glad for something fun and carefree and no rough stuff and no grim surprises. But not girls like Frannie Adair.

She said, as if reading his mind, "Maybe it's the hooch, Gil Hopkins. But if I didn't know any better, I'd think I'd gone soft on you."

"Well, I have been turning on the charm pretty strong these last few days," he said.

"Actually I like you better like this. All ragged and desperate."

"Like a cowboy. Or a hobo."

She grinned in spite of herself. "Or a used-car salesman."

"I'd sell a lot of cars."

"The farther you fall, the more I like it. You've lost the . . . the metallic sheen that made you rat-a-tat-tat when you walked in a room. Now you're . . ." She reached out with a slightly quavery hand and poked his wrist with one dainty finger.

"Dented," he suggested. "Broken."

"No," she said. And she smiled and he smiled in that strange sharing of smiles that happens when there is a heavy alcoholic musk in the air and the lights are low and glowing and the chairs are close together and the music is trembling beneath each table in smooth, artful throbs.

That was when he began to think about bringing Frannie Adair home to bed.

She could heal all this, couldn't she? If she, who knew at least half of the sordidness he'd rutted through in recent days and felt only more seduced . . .

And she, with all her slippery Catholicism, was as unsullied a woman as he had known in close to a decade, with a Midwestern sense of right and wrong and crime and punishment and bringing darknesses to light and . . .

Could she fuck him out of his own self-disgust?

Why not try? Why not let her try?

That is, if he didn't mind the risk of infecting her, infecting her maybe in a way even uglier than Merrel's scourge spreading, real or imagined, or both . . .

Before he let himself tunnel into that thought, he took another long drink and then placed his hand, under the table, lightly on Frannie Adair's leg, which was covered loosely in nubby shantung.

"You're so beautiful, Frannie Adair, you make me want to never see you again."

"Now," she said, calm and controlled, but there was no hiding the pinkness spreading at her temples. "Now, I'm just a shade into pretty, far from beautiful. So you can see me all you want."

"I couldn't bear it, Frannie Adair," he said, fingers of one hand on her leg, the other inches from her face. "All I'd think about was putting that sheet crease back on your cheek."

"Is that supposed to be nice?" She tsk-tsked.

"That's what I'm warning you off of," he said, fingers spread, touching, just barely, her jaw, her cheekbone. "That's why I can't possibly see you anymore. And you're stripping all the get-up-and-go out of me. The jackrabbit energy that gets me up the ladder. With you, Frannie Adair, I'd never want to leave you, your twin bed and your bottle of mid-shelf bourbon."

"Quite a picture you paint," she said, trying for sarcasm, but her knees, they were throbbing. He could feel it.

"Frannie," he said. "Couldn't I just lock myself up in there with you for forty-eight hours and then light a match to it so I couldn't ever go back? Your house on fire, I'd have to go back to work."

"You have an awfully funny way of flirting."

"Flirting's for chumps, Frannie Adair. I'm deadly serious. When are you going to slap my hand away?"

"Hand? What hand?"

He smiled at her lightly, resting his chin on the heel of his hand, while the other hand skated along her skirt, dotting the edge with his fingertips, feeling an unbearably tempting warmth. A promise of forgiveness, absolution.

"I get everything I want," he said. "I can't help it."

It was at that moment, out of the corner of his eye, that he saw it. The streak of silvery white.

Midge, head to toe in lamé, her pearly-white skin sweeping
out the top, long tinselly earrings swinging, the head of the white
fox fur around her neck seeming to be on the hunt, teeth bared.

"I got your note, Gil. What the hell do you want now?" she
was saying as she approached their table, her own teeth bared.

In his head, the white turned to its negative and he saw the
dark-eyed, dark-haired, dark-lipped Jean flicker before him for a
split second, then back again. The image, too, of Midge's
employee photograph, as glamorous as the most glamorous of
mug shots, in Dr. Stillman's files.

She'd played him. She'd played him. He just knew it. She'd
held her cards so close, feigning the innocent victim. Somewhere inside him, he'd been hating himself for what he'd done
to her, while all along she'd been playing him. He just wasn't
sure why.

He was on his feet, his heart galloping ahead of himself, his
blood surging hot and frantic through every vessel in his head.

"And that fucking cunt finally shows her face," he said, without even knowing he was saying it, the words singeing his
tongue, and suddenly his hand was around her powder-white
neck and he'd pushed her against a wall post, her head snapping
with a sickly sound. He couldn't stop himself.

There was a lot of noise behind him, chairs sliding away from
tables, voices calling out, Frannie. But his focus was on Midge's
eyes as his hand clenched tighter on her throat, his arm outstretched—he wouldn't get too close. Her eyes were only
vaguely alarmed. Mostly they were flat, glassy, unblinking. It
seemed he really had long ago lost the ability to shock her, even
if he was always shocking himself.

He thought, even as he felt his arms being pulled, his body
being pulled, that he could hold on to her neck forever and he
still couldn't stop her. Her ability to twist his life into knots was

boundless. She had seeped into every corner, every tiny space.

"You're killing me," he was saying, his voice broken, lost. "How did you do it? How long did you know? Did you know all along?"

He felt his body finally wrested so far from her that his hand popped off her neck like a bottle top. Thrown back onto his chair by two fellow patrons, he caught his breath as a manager and two women surrounded Midge, shielding that blinding whiteness from Hop's eyes.

"What's wrong with you, pal?"

"Did you see that guy? I thought he was going to kill the broad dead."

He'd lost Frannie in the melee. Or maybe she'd left. Either way, he allowed himself to be roughly escorted out of the bar and down the street by a bartender and one of the ham-fisted patrons, who socked him once in the jaw, then a blistering crack in the ear to show him "what happens to fellas who roughhouse ladies."

When they felt confident he wasn't going to come charging back, they left and Hop slumped against a shop window, touching his throbbing jaw gently with his fingertips. He was half drunk and all worn out. Had he really grabbed her by the neck? What was wrong with him? That wasn't the kind of guy he was. *The kind of guy he was.* He was the guy who held men back, talked them down, soothed them back to humanity while slipping crisp bills to all the glaring witnesses who saw the Big Star throw a punch at his worn-out wife.

He looked down the street for Frannie, thinking she might try to find him, but instead it was Midge who was walking, in trifling little steps, down the sidewalk toward him. Lit under each streetlight in that dress, she was Lana Turner on her best day.

"Why the hell does she have to be so damn beautiful?" he murmured to himself.

"Come on. Come on, you son of a bitch," she said as she approached him. "Let's go."

They sat in the coffee shop around the corner. She with ice on her neck, smeared with blooming bruises, he with ice on his jaw, swelling by the minute.

"Thanks again for the signature Gil Hopkins necklace," she said.

"Hey, who deserves it more?" Hop said, then felt queasy at having said it. His shame alternated, second by second, with rage at the memory of her photo in Dr. Stillman's office, like catching her in bed with another man. He couldn't seem to stop himself. "Decked out like that"—he gestured to her lamé, hanging from her like Christmas ornaments—"you must be costing Jerry more than his dignity."

"Awfully snide for someone who was seconds away from a night in L.A. County."

"But for the grace of you, right?" he said, then shook his head, telling himself to pull it together, hold on until he could get to the bottom of it. But what could be more bottom than this?

"Listen," she said, fur stole ruffling up like an animal about to charge. "What's the new sin you'd like to hang me for? I'm no angel, but, far as I see it, everywhere I turn these days, you're coming at me like a battering ram. When are you going to find a new girl to batter around? Or have you?"

Hop looked at her, his eyes sore, heavy. He could feel their redness, feel the blood shooting through them.

He let her have it. "When did you work for Dr. Stillman?"

"Oh," she said, twitching visibly. "How did you find out?" She shook a packet of sugar into her coffee, then a second one.

"I better get a drink," Hop decided.

"They only serve beer."

"I'll order a baker's dozen," he said, gesturing to the waitress.

"How'd you find out about Dr. Stillman?" Midge said after the waitress left.

"Maybe you better start talking first."

"I worked there. Before I met you. Before I got the job at Earl Carroll's. I had a lot of jobs back then. What's the big idea?"

"Yeah, but he wasn't just any doctor, was he?"

"You know even better than I do, Gil, that those kinds of doctors keep this town going."

"Why didn't you ever tell me?"

"I probably did. When we started up, if you remember, you weren't paying much attention to my sparkling conversational talents."

"If I'd paid more attention to what you were saying, we'd probably never've gotten married in the first place," he said, then added, without thinking, "But there was the way you walked into a room . . ." He could see her eyes lift in surprise. He'd surprised himself.

The waitress set his beer down. Half of it lapped over the rim and onto his folded hands.

"Gil," she said, "what does Dr. Stillman have to do with anything? Does this have something to do with the reporter? With all that?"

Hop nodded.

"I see. So did you take her to bed, too?" she asked, but her heart wasn't in it. She was thinking hard, staring at her coffee like a fortune-teller.

He didn't respond. He knew something was happening. She was just barely holding on to the coldness, the hardness.

"Look, Midge," he finally said, "maybe I don't deserve the straight story. Maybe I've told too many tall tales myself to earn it. But I'm at the end of something here. Can't you see? I've got one inch of rope left to hang myself with."

"Yes, I can see that," she said. "Oh hell, you're such an awful SOB, but I'm a sucker and always was. A sucker for that ugly face of yours. And no, you don't deserve it, but God, I can't bear it all. I can't bear it."

Hop didn't say a word, didn't dare risk saying something to change her mind.

Squaring her shoulders, she began. "Listen, when that reporter called the other night, I didn't know what to think. It wasn't until Jerry told me that a girl came to see you about . . . about Jean Spangler that I started piecing things together. I started thinking. Maybe you had a hand in keeping things quiet—that's what you do, after all—and now you had to watch your back. The other night, when I came to see you, I realized you were circling awfully close. I was trying to see if I could get up the nerve to tell you."

"Tell me what?" Hop slumped in his chair, put one hot hand under his chin. "That you were kissing cousins to Jean Spangler? How well exactly did you know her, Midge, to give her access to a pirate's cache of blackmail goodies?"

"You're such a fool, Gil," she said, shaking her head. "To you, it's always simple. People want, they take, they make themselves sick about it. Then they do it all over again."

"You talking about me or yourself?"

"Yeah, well I don't do that anymore," she said. "The point is, things are messier. Do you want to know how messy or do you just want to cut me up?"

Hop looked at her, exhausted. "I don't know," he said honestly.

Midge met his eyes, then sat back in her chair, gazing off into some dark space in the corner of the room.

"She was so lovely," her voice tugged out plaintively. "And when she first came to Dr. Stillman's office, she was so calm, so cool. I was more nervous than she was. I'd only been working there a week or two. She'd had a miscarriage and my, was she relieved."

Hop avoided Midge's eyes, even though he could feel her still.

"She told me how she lost it before she even knew it was there — inside her. It happened in the powder room of the Florentine Gardens. She slid on the blood on the floor and cracked her head on the stall door. She had a little white bandage by the corner of her eye. Those dark, sparkly movie-star eyes."

Midge paused a second. "She came again a month later and we talked for a long time and she ended up asking me to lunch. We were just casual friends for a short while a long time ago. She was just another girl on the make. I knew hundreds of them. Yeah, I was one of them, in my own way."

She reached across the table and took Hop's beer in her hands, leaning over it like a cup of steaming hot chocolate.

"When I read in the papers that she was missing, I figured she'd finally gotten too smart for her own good. And I felt sorry for her. And her family, her child." Abruptly, Midge showed a whisper of a smile. "When I read about the note, though, I had to laugh. How they were trying to find a Kirk and a Dr. Scott."

"Why?"

"That wasn't Jean's note," she said, then took a quick sip of Hop's beer and licked the foam off her lips. "I mean it wasn't something she wrote."

"Is this some kind of riddle?"

"One of the times Jean was there, a young girl was waiting. This girl was there for a . . . you know, a termination. She was so nervous and she had this little notebook in her hand and she kept starting to write on it and stopping. Finally, Jean put her hand on the girl's arm and said, 'Honey, unless that's a Latin test, nothing should be so hard to write.' The girl smiled, couldn't have been a day over nineteen, with freckles and a shiny forehead and knobby knees. She said she'd been trying all day to write her beau—she called him her beau—and I remember she said, 'His name is Aloysius Kirkland, but I call him Kirk, like the movie star.' Anyway, she said she couldn't get through with the letter. She rolled back the pages on the pad and showed us all these false starts. 'Dear Kirk: I'm doing what's best for us both. This cannot be.' 'My darling: I'm sorry for the burden I've placed on you . . .' 'Kirk: It is not in the stars, not for us.' All straight out of a Saturday-matinee sudster. Then, the last one—what was it?"

"Kirk, can't wait any longer, going to see Doctor Scott. It will work best this way while mother is away. Ending with a comma," Hop recited. He knew it better than the Lord's Prayer—much better—by now.

"My, my. That's right. Anyway, the girl stopped at that point and laughed. Said she just realized she'd written the wrong doc name. Scott instead of Stillman. Scott was the name of her family doctor she saw back in Louisville or wherever."

"Fuck me," Hop said. Those are the kinds of things you can never think your way into or guess. The puzzle piece you'd never find on your own.

"Anyway, Jean and I tried to calm her down. She never did get the note finished before they took her in. I didn't even realize Jean had taken the note until I read the newspapers."

"But why . . ." But he'd figured it out, too, if slowly. The note reminded Jean of something. Reminded her of the Jean Spangler who stepped off the bus at the Greyhound City station downtown with all the other Jeans, Iolenes, Midges. Hell, he'd gotten off that bus, tipped his hat at the station agent, and dragged his hide-bound suitcase up Sixth Street. He knew what the note reminded her of. He knew those kinds of notes. *Dear Gil, I look forward to the day you can wire me a ticket West. I miss you terribly. Love, Bernice.*

Midge looked at Hop and her eyes seemed a thousand years old. She opened her mouth as if to speak, but nothing came out. Unsnapping her purse, she pulled out a silvery tube of lipstick. After running magenta across her mouth, she said, "That young girl—she got through the operation. But she was back six months later. This time, no note. The shine on her forehead gone, matted to perfection. No knocking knees. And no mention of a beau, Kirk or any other. I saw later that on the place on the intake form where they ask for an emergency contact, she'd written, 'Sodom.'" Midge smiled faintly. "I wasn't worried about her anymore. She'd figured it all out."

"You know, Midge," Hop said wearily. "Contrary to what you might read in *True Confessions*, this town isn't just some platinum-studded meat grinder with fresh-faced virgins going in one end and coming out hard-bitten whores."

She raised one perfect eyebrow. "It's not?"

"Hey, honey, just because it happened that way to me."

And she laughed and it was the first time he'd heard her laugh in a century or more and it was so fizzy and delicious, a hot toddy. It was hard to conceal his pleasure. And hard to feel anything in that moment but the memory of her small bewitching body under his hand, under warm sheets, her laugh in his ear, her mouth tickling his ear and laughing.

"The things you don't know, Gil," Midge said, leaning forward and curling her chin in her hand. "You think Jean was just another starlet grifting her way down. But she had whole other stories to tell. They all do."

"Even you."

"You know my stories."

"I thought I did. Sugar daddies slipping you occasional twists of cash for a slap and tickle. A night on the town. Was there more?"

"Only what you taught me," she said with a blast of coldness. Then: "I wasn't hungry enough to slide into what Jean slid into. But I also wasn't that . . . glorious."

"Glorious?"

"You missed everything," Midge sighed. "She may have been a tramp when she needed to be. Who isn't? But she had something bright and shiny about her. You wanted to rub against it. Feel the shock."

"So did you? Rub up against her?" Hop said, trying, unsuccessfully, to keep the nasty edge from his voice.

Midge shook her head. "I wish everything was as easy as you make it."

"Me too. Why don't you tell me just how hard it was? For Jean. For both of you," Hop said, almost meaning it, although he wasn't sure why. "She got you the job at Earl Carroll's, huh?"

"Yes," Midge said. "She did."

And then she told Hop. She reminded him that she herself had come a long way from the apple-cheeked, starry-eyed girl who traveled from Ada, Ohio, to Los Angeles, California, as Miss Jiffy Muffin 1942. There was a way that she wanted to live. She saw it in the movies, in the movie magazines. No more Saturday nights at the soda shop, killing time—months, years even— sipping on lime rickeys, reading *Look* magazine, rolling her eyes at the local boys with the slack jaws and bumpy skin. Myrna Loy, Claudette Colbert, Hedy Lamarr—they didn't have to live this way. Their evenings were spent shimmering through nightclubs with Cary Grant on their arm, corks popping, band swaying— this is the way one lives.

Just shy of eighteen, she'd packed her bags with the same steely determination with which she'd spent the previous three years shaping her plain face and unremarkable body into a sweet-smelling package of dimples and flutters and perky curves. The stick-straight dishwater-brown hair became long honey locks that, after a few months in Hollywood, became a brilliant blonde to go with her puffy rosebud of a mouth. She knew when she left, even if her warm-faced, openhearted mother didn't, that she wouldn't be returning after the publicity events, the print and radio ads, and the three-week tour of the West Coast (*Once here, I dug my heels in,* Hop remembered her once saying to him, years before, centuries before).

Not that Midge wanted to be an actress. She'd always been much too much of a realist for that. She knew the odds and she also knew the limits of her own talents. Nah, she just wanted to live the good life out here, use her pretty face to get some things, enjoy herself, forever wash the dust of Ada off her.

She knocked around from job to job, and a girlfriend in a rooming house told her about Dr. Stillman. He needed a girl, a nice, smiling Midwesterny girl, to answer phones with kindness and keep the nervous patients in his waiting room calm and comfortable. And Midge thought okay. Shoveling popcorn at the West Hollywood Bijou wasn't paying enough to keep her in stockings. And the other girls she knew, things sometimes got bad for them. One girl sold her hair. Another used candle wax to fill in the cavities in her mouth. Others, you know. That's what they did.

And Dr. Stillman was nice and Midge had never been squeamish, nor had she carried with her from Ohio any judgments.

But one day the doc asked her into his office and his face was sterner than she'd ever seen it. He'd noticed files missing from his cabinet on two occasions, both times after her shift had ended. Was there something she wanted to tell him? She said no, and that she'd never taken any files ever. Why would she? He looked at her for a long minute and said okay. He believed her. But he would be watching.

It made Midge feel lousy. What did he think she would want with a bunch of medical files? Sure, some of the patients were actresses and a few were pretty big. Many more, however, were girls sent by actors, directors, producers, studio honchos, politicians—the list went on and on. Sure, there were secrets. But where would that get Midge Maberley from Ada, Ohio? And yet she felt the doctor's eyes on her all the time now, determined to catch her. Who wanted to spend each day like that, amid that dreadful, awful smell of Mercurochrome?

So when her new pal Jean Spangler said, *Honey, your figure is too fetching for these corridors. Come meet the manager at Earl Carroll's, he owes me more favors than I can count,* she gave her notice.

A week before her last day, Jean took her to meet a photographer she knew who could help Midge learn to use a camera. Then she took Midge shopping. As a shutter girl, she'd wear a uniform of emerald satin with gold flocking and shiny gold stockings. Jean helped her pick out flashing necklaces, earrings, evening gloves, even garter belts to catch the eye.

Then they went to the Roosevelt Hotel for drinks. And Midge was so grateful to Jean and asked if there was anything she could do for her. And Jean dismissed her with a wave of the hand.

Three Gibsons later, however, Jean whispered, "Midgie, you have to take your shot while you still can."

"What shot is that?"

"The doc's office is a treasure trove, honey."

"He doesn't keep any money—"

"You know what I mean."

And then Midge remembered Jean sitting in the waiting room one day, a week or two before, chattering away. Watching as Midge pulled patient folders and refiled them in quick order. "What secrets they could tell," she'd said with a wink.

"That's not for me, Jean," she said now, with an Ohioan's firmness still girded to her somewhere deep inside. And she knew then that it was Jean who had taken those files. She knew it, but hell, why should she care? She had a new job at Earl Carroll's. She was going to take pictures of Errol Flynn and Gary Cooper. And she did. And Jean began getting more movie jobs, was around less and less. They rarely saw each other. And then Midge met a handsome young reporter without two nickels but with a head full of gleaming hair and eyes full of trouble.

"But Hop," she said to him now, her voice turning low, forlorn. "They killed her, didn't they? They killed Jean."

"They?"

"I don't know. The big 'they.'"

"Yeah, I know about the big 'they,'" Hop said, thinking of Iolene. Of Iolene hiding. Knowing her time was marked.

"Funny. Jean was always superstitious about all that," Midge said, stirring her still-untouched coffee. "She said she'd never make old bones."

Hop looked at Midge's eyes and found something in there. Something he remembered, or thought he did. Something old and pure.

"That's why she kept that doctor's note. I'm sure. Some kind of lucky piece, reminding her of things she'd gotten through. She never stepped on sidewalk cracks or opened fortune cookies," she went on. "She had a four-leaf clover she kept in her purse. She'd sent away for it, mail-order, from the back of a magazine. She showed it to me a couple times. She kept it taped to the back of a postcard. I remember it was a picture postcard of a lake she'd visited once as a girl. It was way up in the San Bernardino Mountains. Fresh air, pine needles under her feet, the whole bit. What did the postcard say? Something like 'Come back to Merry Lake' or 'Memories from Merry Lake.' That lake, she said it was her idea of heaven."

Merry Lake, Hop thought to himself. Something was shuttling around in his head. Merry Lake. "So she ever go back?" he finally said.

Midge shrugged. "It was just one of those plans you mean with all your heart when you're on your third sidecar."

"I might know about those plans."

"Me too. Isn't that how we . . ."

"Yeah."

"Gil, one last thing," she said, sensing he was about to go, which he was. Which he knew he had to.

"Yeah?"

"As bad as we were together," she said, her voice delicate. "Why . . ." Her eyelashes lifted and she let those eyes quake through him. She was brutal.

"Because I knew he'd take care of you," he said quickly, glad to have the chance to say it. He'd never said it before, even to himself. "I guess I knew that somehow. And I knew it would be right for both of you. It would be something for both of you."

"How gracious," she said tonelessly.

"I didn't say it was gracious. I just wanted to make things better for all of us."

"The fixer. Always the fixer."

"But I did, didn't I, Midge? Didn't I fix things?" he said, and, mortified that his voice was almost turning into a sob, rose to his feet.

"I missed you my whole life," she said, looking up at him helplessly.

"That doesn't make any sense," he said, because he knew it did.

Merry Lake

He could see the words before him, typewritten on an envelope: MISS MERRY LAKE.

Yes, the abandoned mail at Iolene's hideout on Perdida Court. The old utility bills, the Shopping Bag circular.

So what was the connection? Because there had to be a connection. Every time he thought there were no strands left to tug . . .

He had twelve hours max before he had to show in the office or risk losing his job. He didn't know if he could sell. He even had to think for a long minute to remember what his last lie had been. Ah yes, a trip to Minnesota to work Barbara Payton back into the pretzel he'd sold her as.

"Lil?"

"I've got cold cream on my face, Hop."

"I'm sorry. I'm sorry."

"Are you still in Missouri?"

"Out here, they pronounce it Minnesota."

"You know, we thought you'd be doing better with La Payton."

"What do you mean?"

"Was that quote for real? It was good enough for you to have cooked up, but only if you had a plan we didn't know about."

"Slow down, Lil. Pretend I'm your ole ma calling from Parsippany."

"The quote in the *Duluth . . . Mule Feed Picayune,* whatever it's called. They phoned La Payton at her hotel and asked her how the honeymoon was going."

"What'd she say?" Hop felt the receiver sliding along his jaw, damp with sweat.

"Let me see if I can remember it right: 'I thought it would be forever. But forever is just a weekend, more or less.'"

"Fuck me. Someone muzzle that whore, for fuck's sake."

"Ouch," Lil said. "Sure don't sound like the sweet syrup that usually slides from your lips. Besides, isn't that your job? The muzzling?"

"I've been a little waylaid. I'll take care of it."

"Well, you better. Mr. Solomon saw that quote get picked up by the wires and he wanted to take back his call of praise. Also, he said he'd been hearing some other things he wanted to talk with you about. You best tie her mouth up tight and get back to civilization."

Hop hung up and tried to summon up the snake oil to make a call to Barbara.

"Operator, Duluth, Minnesota. Cloquet Carriage House Inn."

"I'll connect you."

After five minutes of trying to find Merry Lake on the map in his glove compartment, Hop started out, turning the radio as high as the knob would go. Three-hour drive and he didn't want to be able to hear his own thoughts. He didn't want to think anymore. The inside of his mouth felt like soggy burlap, he was still riddled with scotch and beer, he'd long ago forgotten his last honest shave.

He didn't want to think at all. Not about Frannie Adair and her tentative wholesomeness, her awful dance on the edge of doom, of the bad places always just waiting. She was on pins and needles for the slick, sugar-tongued fellow who would yank her over on the pretense of a jitterbug, and he wasn't about to be that fancy man.

And he didn't want to think about Midge and how she could just do it to him, make him crazy, the feel of his hand tight on her neck, fingers splayed on her jaw, he was not that kind of man . . . and which was worse, that rage she inspired or the twitch in his chest as their heads had leaned closer and she showed him that flicker of loveliness that he'd been so sure he'd long ago snuffed out?

He didn't even want to think about Jerry. Jerry who could still somehow rise above it, earnest and melancholy and utterly stead-fast, above the rank turmoil of everyone surrounding him. After all the women Jerry had been with, all the things he'd seen on the job, how did he get off so noble, so uncontaminated and upright? Hop knew damn well why. It was the difference between them, the thing Jerry had that he himself didn't have, never knew to want. He couldn't name it, but it lay there between them like an old promise.

And not about Iolene, not that lost girl . . . and Jean.

And Jean.

The face in the background.

The far-off voice shivering in his head. A voice he'd probably invented. Could he really remember her voice at all? He just remembered it wasn't that taffy pull of Iolene's. No, it was the voice of someone long tired of talking.

He had no idea what he expected to find at Merry Lake. He wasn't sure which Merry Lake—the person or the place—was the original sound and which the echo. But he had this funny feeling that he would know when he got there.

At midnight, he was rounding the mountain roads, rolling down his window to look for any sign of life. It was barely a town, although the sign said, in faux Indian type, POP. 242.

The poplar trees stretched so high that Hop could barely make out the sky. Mailboxes studded the roadway, but the names on them—Gilroy, Canning, Randolph—were meaningless.

As he drove even higher, he passed a scenic overlook and could see the shimmering lake. He stopped his car and got out.

Pine needles crackled under his feet like cut glass and he was suddenly aware of a fresh, rough smell he hadn't experienced since a summer logging job in the Adirondacks when he was fifteen. Was this a place Jean Spangler would dream of? How could he know, anyway? In his head, she was a heady, jagged mix of B girl, good girl, girl next door, victim, blackmailer, damsel in distress, dead girl, girl of broken dreams . . . Christ, she was one of thousands he'd met, no different. But in his head she'd become all those girls all at once—and a succubus no less, holding on tight, refusing release long after he had any reason to be in her thrall.

As he gazed across the open space, the expanse of the lake bleeding invisibly into ring after ring of wooden frame houses, seasonal tourist cabins, logger huts, he realized this was his first moment of real peace, solitude, clearheadedness in days . . . years? He wasn't sure he liked it.

Maybe if Jerry were here, he thought. We could go fishing down there, rent one of those creaky rowboats, lean back and let it bobble. Then he could straighten out his thoughts. Remind himself of what's what. Stop letting these women . . .

Oh, fuck it all, fuck it all.

He lit a cigarette.

As he smoked, he found himself rocking on his heels lightly. Where was that sound coming from? The water? No, Hop, no surf on a lake. No. No. There was music coming from somewhere. Car radio? Open window?

He peered to his left. Walking forward, pushing his way through a few yards of mulchy overgrowth, he saw a cabin with a porch, windows blazing, about sixty yards down a knotty footpath. A bar, God help me. Sweet Mary, if it's a bar, I'll never skip Mass again, he thought. He started walking.

As he got closer, the music took on a familiar feel. Hoagy Carmichael, wasn't it? One of those old songs that Hop remembered dancing to with dozens of women right after the war. A slow song that bands liked to whip into something hot, hectic. He remembered one brassy blonde with a voice low and throaty like Tallulah Bankhead, blowing vibrato into his ear as they pitched around the dance floor in that frenzied VJ Day style, her breasts shuddering against his chest with each twirl. "Love comes along, casting a spell," she sang. "Will it sing you a song? Will it say a farewell?"

That's the one he should have married.

THE HOT SPOT was painted in red letters on a small sign hanging from a nail on the front-porch rail. Hop pushed open the Wild West doors and absorbed a cloud of smoke, old beer, and something that smelled like moonshine. The place couldn't have held more than twenty-five people, but at least forty were crushed in, sitting at the long tables, playing cards, and drinking out of glass jars, perched along the small bar on stools that looked carved out of tree trunks. The jukebox shook mercilessly in one corner. Apparently, the Hot Spot was the only spot in town.

He pressed himself up to the bar, holding on for dear life as patrons wedged in and out of every corner. After waiting two or three minutes for the sweaty, harried bartender, Hop finally reached over the bar and grabbed his own jar. He was seconds away from reaching around to the tap when the bartender finally saw him.

"Sorry, buddy, but it ain't self-serve."

"You sure?" Hop said, watching carefully as the fellow drew his beer, making sure he didn't spit in it.

It tasted awfully nice, but not as nice as a tumbler of bourbon.

A seat opened up at one of a handful of single tables fashioned out of barrels. Hop took it.

Watching the throng, he wondered if there was anything he could do.

Watching the throng, he wondered how he'd lost the big picture. When he'd phoned Barbara Payton before he left, he'd done some very fancy dancing. The kind of thing that can easily backfire. She'd fessed up to talking to a reporter about her wedded woe.

"Maybe if you'd been around, Hop, I wouldn't have felt so lonely and turned to that beetle-browed reporter for a little friendly conversation."

"But B.P., my darling, I thought you wanted this."

"I picked the wrong joe. I miss Tom. I liked lying in bed with him and counting his muscles."

"Then Tom it is."

"For real? The big D for me and Franchot?"

"We can sell it, B.P. The rash actions of a young girl trying to be practical. She meant it when she said those vows, but now she realizes she can't fight her own heart."

"My heart has a lot of opinions, Hop."

"That it does, B.P. Give me a day and I'll make things move like Gypsy Rose Lee."

• • •

Recalling this conversation just a few hours later, he was very unsure how he was going to pull it off. And instead of working the Payton story on Eastern Standard Time, making the calls, cleaning things up, he was in Hicksville Central, having beer spilled on him by men in plaid shirts and suspenders.

His own mason jar long empty, he wondered if there was any chance for table service. He rose and peered above the horde. As he did, he caught a glimpse of himself in a mirror above the nearby hat stand. What was his old man's face doing staring back at him instead of his own pretty mug, he wondered. Fuck me, not even the nice suit helps. His face looked ten years older than a week ago. He hoped he'd be able to wash and shave it off. But what could he do to fix that strange look in his eyes? That empty-eyed look that says, *Whatever you got, I'm ready. No surprises left.*

He sat down, feeling his legs creak.

From a few tables away, he heard a slurred voice shout out.

"Iolene? Iolene? How 'bout one more round?"

Hop turned, a hard, hot tremor dragging from his feet straight up to his chest. All evidence to the contrary, he fully expected to see the lively, lovely Iolene Harper come strolling across the crowded floor, skin glowing toffee, high, tight breasts wrapped in green satin, hips turned toward him, one long arm at her side, hand angled out to him, beckoning.

But instead . . . instead.

A girl appeared, white shirt tucked into a full skirt, hair pulled back in a long ponytail, a long gold scarf tied around her neck, two large jars of foamy beer sloshing over her hands. A white girl, a tall girl, a very, very pretty girl with a walk like a showgirl. *Boom-chica-boom.* A girl waiting tables in a place like this shouldn't have that walk.

As she moved closer . . . as she moved closer . . .

Like the glossy photograph in his jacket pocket come to life.
Come to life.

Jean Spangler back from the dead.

He was suddenly sure he'd lost his mind.

His hand on his mason jar jerked off the edge of the table and
the jar hit the floor, rolling without breaking.

He felt like the whole joint could hear his thudding heart.

He tried to speak, but nothing came out.

She placed the beers on the nearby table with a whisper of a
smile.

This dead girl did.

And then, as if sensing his attention, her eyes lifted and she
looked over at Hop. Walking toward him, a voice spilled forward
from her and slithered straight into Hop's ear, drowning out
everything else.

"You want some more, fella?"

He tried to speak again, but nothing came out.

Jean Spangler. Without all the spangles.

That pearly skin a little less pearly. The posture a little less
bright, less on, less ready to skate around and see what she could
start up. But still without question Jean Spangler. Creamy face.
Fringed, flashing eyes and pouty lip. That thick tangle of chestnut hair. The legs began where they should and ended in forever.

His whole world collapsing from within and she's handing
out drinks, Lazarus-like, in a bar seventy miles away.

Yes, I want some more. A lot more. Goddammit. Goddammit.

"You," Hop snarled, rising to meet her at eye level. "What the
fuck are you doing here? What are you doing aboveground?"

He had lost his mind. He knew it. His mind, it was gone.

He saw her hands grip her tray tightly. He saw her face go
white.

"Who sent you?" she uttered, so low he could barely hear her above the din.

"No one sent me," he said, aware that this all felt more and more like a dream. He was talking to Jean Spangler. In the flesh. He half expected snakes to burst from her head.

She leaned close to him so she could whisper. "Please leave me. I don't have *anything*." She, only a few inches shy of his height, forced them both into the corner, only the tray jammed between them. "I don't have anything to give you."

"You don't understand," he said, placing his hands on her forearms, which rigidly grasped the tray. With one sharp gesture, he knocked the tray out of her grip and it clattered to the floor. He looked down at it and wondered what he thought he was doing. Fuck, Hop. Fuck.

"You're here to finish things, then," she said, her voice shaking. "To finish everything." Her face was so close to his now he felt like he was looking straight inside her, inside those dark, depthless eyes wide with fright. And he could smell bergamot on her skin, almost taste it.

"No, no. Don't you . . . don't you remember me?" He found himself whispering. Against all reason, he felt the anger and aggression slip from him. Maybe it was the perfume. The gleamy skin. The way he could feel her body trembling against him.

He felt suddenly desperate and eerily aroused. He felt he had only seconds to make everything fall together right. How could he possibly make her understand what had happened to him and how close they were now? How intimate. And how Iolene . . . and everything.

"I don't . . . I don't want to remember anything." She shook her head. "I'm done with that."

Hop felt his temper rise again. "Maybe you're done with it, but it's not done with you. It's not done with the rest of us."

She didn't say anything. She just looked at him. Her eyes were pleading.

"Look, we have to go somewhere. We have to talk," Hop said, pulling her closer, pulling her right up against him, his mouth on her ear. Digging his fingers deep into her arms, he could tell he was hurting her and he couldn't stop and didn't want to stop.

"Not now," she pleaded, eyes darting from side to side. "Later."

"So you can take it on the heel and toe again?" His fingers tightened on her arms, pressing her into him.

"No, no. You can wait here. I'll finish the shift. An hour. Just an hour."

"No hour. Now." He didn't want to tell her that he couldn't last an hour sitting there, watching, not knowing. He had no hours left.

She saw something in his face. And she said, "Let me talk to the other girl."

She brought him to an apartment on the second floor of a timber frame house. The stairs ran along the outside of the building, which smelled like tar and mildew.

When they entered, she turned, shook off her coat, and walked across the room to turn on a small floor lamp. The space was furnished sparely with a rattan frame settee, a card table with a fringed tablecloth. A dying jade plant.

"Come here," she said, beckoning him from across the room.

"Why . . ." He trailed off, walking toward her.

As he reached where she stood, leaning over the lamp, he realized she was trying to get a better look, to place him. He moved very close, directly above the lamp with its blonde glow. She looked at him closely and then, suddenly, grinned, the teasing dimples emerging.

"The reporter. The reporter. You're still good-looking but not as pretty."

Hop relaxed a little. "You got me on a bad day."

She smiled again, but then it flitted away. She was remembering things. All kinds of things. He wouldn't want to be in her head. Or maybe he already was. Had been for days.

"Sit down," she said. "You want something to drink?"

"No. No." He sat in a straight-backed chair facing her.

She struck a match on the rattan armrest and lit a cigarette, swatting the edge of her scarf from the red ember. Her hands were shaking. But then again so were his.

"I don't have any money. You can see I don't," she said.

"I don't care about that."

"So what's the game, newsboy?"

The abrupt, hard tone, its similarity to Peggy Spangler's, bristled against Hop. Her face under the light looked beautiful, yes, but like wax. He found his anger rising again.

"How does it feel to leave your family behind?" he said. "They all think you're dead or worse."

She didn't flinch. She was ready for this. "They're so much better off. They're safe. I was nothing but a jinx."

"What kind of mother abandons her daughter?" he said, as if he knew anything about mothers. As if he'd even given one stray, flickering thought to . . . to . . . was her name Christina?

"The kind of mother who knows she's nothing but bad news for her little girl. And I don't mean because I was a lousy mother." She straightened her back, wrapping the edge of her long gold scarf around her fingers. But her voice remained flat. Plain. Toneless. "I was a fine mother, Mr. Hopkins—sure, I remember your name. I was a fine mother who got pulled into something rotten and didn't want to put my little girl in danger for it."

"Pulled in, eh? Is that how you frame it? You know, when you fall into the blackmail racket, you're not falling. You're jumping. Those were some rough boys you were mixed up with. But I didn't see you kicking and screaming."

"What are you talking about?"

"You knew what you were doing, didn't you, doll?" Since when did he call women "doll"? He didn't like the sound of his voice, wasn't even sure what it was, but he couldn't stop. It flew out at sharp angles, shards whizzing through the air. "The biggest stars in town. And ready for a dance with you. You were seeing dollar signs all the way to the back room of the Red Lily."

"That's what you think," she said, with nary a flinch.

"Yes," he replied, watching her, looking.

"You know all about it, huh?"

"I know enough."

"You don't know anything," she said quietly. Then she paused a long ten seconds, face frozen, before raising a hand to her neck and placing it around the scarf tied around it. It loosened; then she gave a hard tug and it slid down quickly to her lap.

Across her neck was a dashed line, pale pink, almost like serration marks, like a girl's paper doll with different heads you could affix, the mark showing where to cut to replace the golden blonde head with the deep brunette one.

As she pushed her hair back, he could see the line ran from behind one earlobe all the way across her delicate neck to the other ear. For a second, he was frightened that her head would simply fall forward, leaving a red-tipped stump.

"There's more, Mr. Hopkins," she said, almost smiling. She turned away from him and placed her fingers on the edge of her skirt, which she began slowly peeling upward. Then she turned back toward him slowly, like some kind of unnatural striptease.

Her full skirt was now gathered at her hips and there were

those long, fulsome legs, which Hop took in, from the straps on her sandals and up, up as she turned to face him. She was pulling the skirt all the way to her waist, and Hop found his eyes lifting slowly from her ankles to her knees to the tops of her stockings, to the tight garters clutching her slender thighs.

She looked at him. "Come closer," she said in that drowsy voice, lulling and hypnotic.

Disturbed and excited and ashamed of his excitement, he leaned forward. What was she going to show him? Did he want to see? How horrible could it be, or was this a come-on? Or both?

His chair skidded loudly as he moved closer. The folds of her skirt grazed his arms as he placed them, tentatively, on either side of her, resting on the seat.

The lighting was low and it was hard to see. There was something pink, folded, tender through the netting of the skirt, above the garters. Something on her skin. At first he thought it was a caesarean scar, but it was too low, too disperse. Then he thought it looked like burns—even branded skin, like a steer's. Soon he was so close that his face was brushing against her skirts, so close he could smell her: not bergamot, no . . . honeysuckle. *You're so much sweeter, goodness knows. Honeysuckle rose . . .*

He heard a scrape and realized he had dragged the whole settee on which she sat closer toward him. He still couldn't quite see and she wasn't going to lift her skirts any higher, wasn't going to stand up to give him a better view. She was only going to let him see this way, her way.

Inches from her torso, he realized what he was looking at. A series of rippling scars abraded on the tops of her thighs, across her hip bones, disappearing behind her cream-colored panties, which she had folded down slightly so he could see.

Letters. Words.

They'd been carved into her and remained in raised scars, pink as rose petals, across her hips.

What did they . . .

What else could they say?

D-E-A-D-W-H-O-R-E.

He kept looking. He was afraid to sit back and meet her eyes. His breath ran hard against her skin. He looked at the words and remembered the blanket at the Red Lily and yes, it was all true. Or true enough. Somehow it was much simpler and much, much more complicated than he'd ever guessed.

His fingers, as if moving of their own accord, were touching the letters gently. He felt her shift ever so slightly, but nary a quiver.

Then, his fingers lightly pressed against her, he heard her voice, slow and strangely sexy.

"He got it half wrong at least. After, I heard both of them tell some fellas who worked there to get rid of my body and they'd get a quick five hundred dollars. This young girl came in while they were deal making. She saw my eyes. She knew. She helped me out the back way. She gave me an old raincoat to cover everything and a few bucks. She said she'd fix it. Later, I figured the men took the five hundred and pretended they'd dumped me in Griffith Park. All they dumped was my purse."

Hop slowly sat up, his fingers burning, tingling.

"Why not go to the cops?"

She looked at him, not even bothering to pull her dress down. The look said everything. But she told him her story nonetheless. She'd never had a chance to tell anyone before. She was dying to tell.

• • •

Marv Sutton, double-breasted and pomaded, all a girl on the hunt could want. He met Jean at the studio commissary, took her to dinner at Chasen's, for a few long ocean drives to far-flung hotels where he'd thrown her down on the softest sheets she'd ever been thrown down on before. He'd whispered the usual promises, and in spite of herself, she'd almost started to believe him. She let him do things to her, things she didn't normally do, not even when she was married. He gave her a three-ounce bottle of Chanel No. 5 and lace-topped stockings from Paris. He bought her pearl-drop earrings that hung so heavy on her earlobes she could barely lift her head. And, not three weeks after the affair began, she felt it starting to turn. She saw a script girl, flush-faced, come out of his dressing room, adjusting the back seam on her skirt. A girlfriend told her she'd seen him taking a tumble with a Tropics showgirl in the club's back parking lot. So when she saw him at the Eight Ball, she wasn't sure how she felt about him anymore. She wasn't sure if she wanted to bother anymore. But maybe she did. He looked handsome and he was with his partner, Gene Merrel, whom she'd never met. The fact that the pair was there together lent a lot of excitement to the place, and everyone seemed to be talking about their table. Her sadsack cousin, what a drag that she'd shown up uninvited. She'd had to do some pretty fast talking to get Peggy to play along. But luckily the fast-talking reporter with the pretty face looked ready for anything and ol' Peg sure was game. Marv paid her a lot of attention and didn't even blink at the luscious Iolene, so things were looking up.

Wouldn't Davy Ogul love me to get some shots of this, she thought. He'd been a lousy boyfriend—dim, short-tempered, and perennially unfaithful. But she liked the sheaves of long-stemmed roses, the bunny rabbit he brought her daughter on

Easter, the emerald tennis bracelet he gave her (and then took back to pay off his gambling vig). When she was dating him, he'd sweet-talked her and Iolene into doing a few jobs. The usual thing: They went to parties where certain men would be and all they had to do, really, was get those men to go into the bedroom or to another hotel room or even, once, to the balcony of a Hollywood apartment, and get things just wild enough to make the photo pay off. If Jean was the one wriggling against the studio exec or the nightclub owner or the big-shot producer, Iolene was the shutterbug, and vice versa. She'd never had to follow through. She'd never done that, not even when it would have rung up gold. When, if it came to that, she'd cut.

Neither she nor Iolene liked the badger stuff, either, truth told. Even if it paid a few bills and once even got her an audition. Davy really brought them in the deal as a love-ya-kid just for her. So when the romance with Davy ended, so did those jobs. And she for one was glad. Not that she and Iolene were stupid. They made copies of every photo they took before passing over the negatives to Davy. They kept them at Iolene's and had no reason to believe Davy would ever know. They called it their insurance files. Insurance in case. Once Jean even jacked up the stash by taking some files from her doctor's office. She was friends with a girl who worked there and once, when the girl left her in the office alone, she'd taken a few fat handfuls and added those to her cache.

But that was all over. Things were easier now, anyway. The child support came more regular. Jobs came. She let it go. Until now, until this opportunity presented itself.

So, when the boys asked her, she said yes to the Red Lily. Why not? She'd heard about it. Who hadn't? She would have been wary, maybe, but Iolene was coming. Still, she knew she didn't want Peggy tagging along, ready to use whatever she saw against her, or, worse still, trying to cut in on the action. So she told her cousin that the reporter was worth her time, knew all the players, and besides, wasn't he darling? Didn't he look like a movie star? Didn't she deserve some hay?

At the Red Lily, Marv and Gene had a favorite room. Marv, he said the junk would really get things crazy. It would be great. She wasn't for junk, but there didn't seem to be a way to decline and keep the game going.

Iolene brought out her camera and said, "Come on, boys. Let's get some shots." And the studio guy, Bix, kept saying, "No pictures. No pictures." But Marv and Gene were so loaded and they didn't care and they started posing. Kid stuff. Marv grabbed her and threw her over his knees and pretended to spank her. He lifted her skirt up. But Gene, he got agitated by the bulb. He kept jumping around and pretending to chew and tear at her clothes like some wild animal. It was strange and she didn't know if it was a joke, but she tried to laugh. Finally, he tore the arm off her dress, trying to pull her toward him on the couch. The more she wriggled, uncomfortable, the more agitated he became. But everyone was laughing and they continued to laugh and that really got him going. In a sweeping motion, he took off his belt and grabbed her and wrapped it tight around her face, her head, wedged it in her mouth. Marv made jokes about steers and cattle. They were laughing and Iolene was not. And Iolene's camera took one last shot before she stopped. And Jean saw that she was frightened. And Jean thought, *I know I should be frightened, too, but I feel nothing.*

Jean no longer knew what her plan was. But she found herself telling Iolene that it was okay for her to leave. She told Iolene that she had to do it, had to keep going. She held Iolene's wrist so tight, like it would break, and told Iolene that she had to do it. It was the only way to end it all. To finally end it.

And then things got kind of hazy, colors swelling, her body stretching like warm taffy, and Iolene was no longer there, and the studio guy wasn't in the room anymore, either.

Marv said, You don't mind if Gene stays. He's just going to sit over there. He won't bother us. Come on, baby, do it like I like it.

She didn't really want to. She didn't much like this Gene, who, so amiable in the movies, so boyish and cheery, the Technicolor Troubadour with the baby face, now seemed . . . off. A funny, far-off look in his eyes. She wondered what he was seeing. And then . . . and then he started singing. Softlike. "Annie Laurie," *I'd lay me doon and dee,* the rolling lilt. Like in the movies but not. Broken or something. Something had turned. The voice, his voice, it echoed, fell in with the creaking sound of water pressing on old wood, lapping on rusty hulls. An old mattress with no spring left, hard thrusts straight through to gasping floors. And that voice, his voice, distorted, as if from an old phonograph, cracked, shuddering, still warbling ancient sea shanties. A siren song. The lost boys.

Marv was whispering, "He takes the pipe because he thinks he's going to die. Thinks he's got the syph, but no doc has agreed with him yet. It's in his head. His head's not right."

She wasn't sure how long it had been—not long—when she looked over, woozily, shakily, barely aware of what Marv was doing, which was as rough and unfriendly as ever, and saw that Gene was crying. Weeping with a strange moaning, wringing his hands. He's not right, she remembered thinking through the haze. Something's not right in his head. Then she remembered thinking, What's right with mine?

And next thing, he was there, with his hands on her neck. Marv made a halfhearted attempt to shove him aside ("Gene, Gene, why you gotta do that stuff?") but was so loaded himself that he couldn't seem to make it stop. Gene's hands were so tight and the smell of burning leaves was everywhere and her own head so swollen with the junk they'd given her.

He was whispering in her ear and there was no other sound, no other feeling, and his breath like something dying inside him, and there he was whispering and saying over and over, "I'm saving you, Jane. I'm saving you. You'll thank me when it's over."

She was thinking, I'm going to die and it's all over. I'm going to die and he doesn't even know my name.

Then she saw the knife drop out of his pocket and onto the floor. And he turned, like a dog with his ears pricked up, and he saw his knife and she knew what he was thinking. And he took one hand off her throat to pick up the knife and she drew a quick breath before he could put it back.

And she could feel it dragging. Oh God, she could feel it.

The last thing she remembered saying was, in that breath, *"Stop, stop, I'm already dead."*

And she was out. Thankfully, mercifully out.

She didn't think she was unconscious for long. When she drifted back, her whole body felt disconnected from her, like a terrible weight from which she could now rise, still tingling from the junk. That was when she heard the voices in the hallway talking about dumping her body. Just outside the door, Marv was frantically pleading ("I'm friends with your boss, the big boss you send the money bags to—they know me and they would want you to help me"), and his words and his promise of money seemed to be enough. And she knew she had no time. And the little girl appeared and she took her chance. The girl found her a raincoat and took her out the back way. Hid her in the cellar until it was safe. Gave her bus fare because she couldn't find her purse.

On the bus, she opened the coat and looked at herself for the first time. That was when she saw the blood, only blood. It was running along her body. It was forming dark spiderwebs on her legs. It was warm and it wasn't until then she knew she was alive.

She took the bus to Iolene's, but Iolene wasn't there, had been staying with her new boyfriend, Jimmy. Iolene's place was where she'd stashed their pictures, the files she'd cadged from the doctor's office. All their sins wedged into a file cabinet. The thought of it now made her sick. She opened a drawer and took out half the files. Pulling a suitcase out from underneath the bed, she dumped them in. After an aching, burning shower, she began changing into one of Iolene's dresses and that was when she looked at the words across her belly. She raised her hand above them, almost as if to touch them. She thought she would faint or become sick. She willed herself to do neither. She wondered now how she did it. But she knew in a flash where she was going. She took five dollars from Iolene's cookie jar and left.

"So I went to see Davy Ogul. He got one of their doctors to come over and clean me up, sew me back together," Jean said, as Hop listened, rapt. "Then I showed Davy a few files I thought might be worth something. I said for a hundred dollars, he could have them."

"And he gave it to you?" Hop managed to ask, his head jammed to numbness with the horrors, with this awful monster movie unfurling before his eyes.

"Sure he gave it to me. He's no fool."

Hop almost corrected her ("He *was* no fool") but then realized she might not know Ogul vanished soon after she did. Then he realized there was a lot Jean might not know.

"Did you . . . did you maybe tell him there were more files?"

"He asked. I said I was leaving town for good, but if he was in the market, he should go to Iolene. I knew he'd do right by her."

Hop felt something drop in his chest. He did the math in his head. Davy Ogul tries to parlay the files to the wrong guy, or his boss Mickey Cohen finds out about Ogul's extracurricular blackmailing. Next thing, Ogul goes poof. The hard boys eventually connect the dots and Iolene has a big bull's-eye on her forehead. Or maybe Iolene, frantic, tries to hustle a little on her own—maybe even hustle those pictures of Jean. Or, most likely of all, Iolene talks up the pictures in a panic, like she did to Peggy Spangler. *Iolene, she said she couldn't get them out of her head. She wanted to get rid of them. They were starting to get to her. She said she kept seeing them in her sleep. She said they were in all her dreams.* If she told Peggy Spangler about them, who else might she have told? For that matter, who else might Peggy Spangler have told? How long does it take for something that hot to get back to the wrong people? And God knows there were plenty of eyes and ears at the Red Lily to set things in motion. Fuck, Jean, you triggered a hundred ways for Iolene to die. And it only took one. Like Frannie Adair said, *Some goon with a half a C-note in his pocket tailed her and got her in the head.*

"But Jean . . . ," he began, but so many questions swarmed his head, he couldn't pick one. Finally, he blurted, "The note. To Kirk." He wanted to be sure Midge had been right.

She looked at him vacantly for a moment, then a flash of recognition drifted across her face. "I forgot that was in my purse. I didn't write that. It's a souvenir."

Hop scrambled for another question. "Your cousin said you were pregnant."

Jean allowed herself a whisper of a smile. "Poor Peg. Did she get her picture in the paper?"

"No. Just you."

She shook her head, still faintly smiling. "I found that note—

just some girl's note, tossed in the trash. I kept it. It made me think of things I might have forgotten."

"The girl coming off the Greyhound bus," Hop murmured. *Hell, he'd gotten off that bus.*

"What?"

"Skip it," Hop said. A hundred more questions danced around in his head, but one didn't come fast enough and he feared she was about to take his pause as her chance to end things.

As if one cue, she smoothed her skirt and adjusted her scarf, and it was like a curtain closing. He could feel his dismissal in the air. He knew he had to hurry.

"So, you can see I've left all that behind," she said.

"Have you?" Hop murmured, distracted by the thoughts racing through his head.

"Listen," she said, leaning forward, winding that scarf back around her pearly skin. "I want you to understand."

"I understand."

"No, you don't. You're one of those who like to stay in the muck," she said, shaking her head. He wondered how she might know that. And then he realized anyone would.

She went on. "What I figured out, from all that, it's . . . it's like this: Sometimes you have to do bad things to get pure again," she said. "Like burning something to make it clean."

He paused, thinking. The moment suddenly seemed heavy with meaning, but he wasn't sure what the meaning was. Then he looked at her and said, "Do you really think you can do that? Make yourself over new? Don't you carry it with you? Doesn't it stick with you, like a scar?"

She looked at him, her eyes hooded.

"I didn't mean—"

She shook her head. "Don't worry about it," she said, her voice turning cool, distant. "Wait here a minute," she said, rising to her feet. She walked into the adjoining bedroom. When she reemerged, moments later, she was carrying a brown, creased accordion file. "I wonder if you can do me a favor," she said, holding the file to her chest.

"What's that?"

"My family, they're better off, you know. Christine is, that's for sure. But Iolene . . . I want Iolene to know I'm okay." As she spoke, her voice changed again. From remote to nearly broken. Her eyes, for the first time, filled with tears. "If you can tell her that I'm sorry for skipping on her and that . . . I wish only the best for her."

Hop looked at her and said nothing. He knew at that moment that he wouldn't tell her what had happened to Iolene. And, looking in her face, he hoped she'd never know.

"And there's something I want you to give her for me," she went on, composing herself. "The files I took from the house— I didn't sell all the ones I took to Davy. I kept a few. The most valuable ones." She shifted the file forward onto her knees. "I wanted them in case I was in a real bind. I didn't know if anyone was going to be coming after me. I didn't know if I could make a clean break. I needed something to bargain with. Anyway, it's been a while now and I'm moving again. Farther this time. And I don't think I need them. Not as much as Iolene might." She looked off to some invisible space over Hop's shoulder. "You see, I left her holding the bag and she . . . she was as close to me as anyone ever was. Closer."

So close you took her name, Hop thought. Before he could stop himself, he said, "You love her." He didn't know where it came from or what he meant by it.

She shook her head vaguely and didn't say anything and it was all right there in front of him. As many questions as he had left, he knew enough to stop asking.

"I'll give them to her," he said, rising. She didn't move. He began walking toward the door. His hand on the knob, he looked back at her sitting there, her forearms posed tensely on either arm of the chair, her fingers wrapped hard around the wood. Her head tilted down, dark hair lit through by the lamp, as if on fire, brilliantly.

He wanted suddenly to give her something, but he couldn't think of what.

"Midge—you know my wife, Midge? She said you were so lovely, that you had something bright and shiny about you. Something special, she meant."

Her head lifting slowly, she looked over at him. Abruptly, he had the feeling you get the split second before the blow comes. Midge taught him that feeling.

"Why'd you do it?" she said, eyes suddenly narrow, like slits.

"Do what?" he asked.

"To Midge."

"You're going to have to be more specific," Hop said, hands turning around the knob damply.

"I ran into her at Good Samaritan back in, oh, '48. Before all this. I was in the emergency room—a boyfriend broke my arm—and I saw her for the first time in two years. She spotted me right off."

He remembered as if it were happening again right before his eyes: Jean and Iolene in his living room that night, October '49. Jean looking over at a set of framed photos. "This is your wife?"

"You saw Midge?" he said.

Jean nodded. "So why'd you do it?"

"Do what?" he repeated.

"She was glad to see me, to see someone," she said coolly. "She looked like she'd been crying for days. Her face was raw. And then she told me how she'd gotten married. To a reporter.

And then she told me how he'd pushed her over a chair and she fell and lost the baby."

"She fell," Hop said mechanically, turning the doorknob right and then left. "That much is true."

"Are you saying you didn't push her or she didn't lose the baby?"

"I'm saying she was never pregnant," he replied, shaking his head. "She just hoped she was. And she fell because she was trying to throw a marble ashtray at me."

She nodded. "That's a big difference. Between your stories."

"Isn't there always?"

On the long drive back, he thought about a lot of things. About Iolene and her last desperate hours. Her unblurred beauty and her tenderness. Her only mistake was judgment. In coming to him, she picked the wrong guy to step up for rescue. For anything. And he thought about fresh-faced, clear-voiced Frannie Adair, so majestic, cool, striding above it all like some goddess, soles of her feet just grazing the ugliness the rest of her kind had sunk into up to the chin or more. And there was Midge. Midge and the half-truth that always lingered, twisting and turning in the hollow between them. And Midge and her stubborn, battered heart because she might love Jerry forever, but she'd never let him touch her where Gil Hopkins had. It was a horrible lesson to learn. He taught it to her a thousand times.

These were the most sentimental thoughts Hop had allowed himself in years and they felt awkward and ill-fitting and he fumbled with them and then let them go. Poof.

He was halfway home when he looked over at the accordion file on the seat next to him. The string had snapped and on his last sharp turn, something had slid out from one of the folders.

He reached over and saw it was a piece of paper. He placed it in front of him and pressed it against the steering wheel so he could get a look.

It was a postcard. A lake lined with fir trees and a fawn at the shore, just about to set a hoof in. In script at the top were the words "Merry Lake Is Waiting for You."

He turned it over and sure enough, behind yellowing tape, was a four-leaf clover.

She must have thought Iolene needed it. She was right. Late, but right.

Hop pulled the car over to the side of the road. He held the postcard in his hand. He could hear his breath, jagged and harsh. He rolled down the window and listened to the wind blowing through the trees, the thudding sound of cars passing, the stillness in between. He looked at his eyes in the rearview mirror for a long minute. Then he dug for a cigarette and match-box in his glove compartment. He shook out a cigarette and tore a match free.

At last, he caught his breath, caught himself. He lit the ciga-rette and inhaled until his chest hurt. Then he blew the smoke out and laughed. A funny kind of laugh he'd never heard from himself before. He started the car, still laughing.

Who was Jean Spangler to think her luck was worth giving?

Four Years Later

"You're going places, kid." The burnished cliché Hop never tired of hearing, held close to his chest at night, keeping him warm. There was a high-breasted, swivel-hipped secretary outside the door. His secretary and his alone, from her fine-turned ankles and buttery locks, to the delicious way she purred "Mr. Hopkins's office. How may I help you today?" in her honeyed Carolinian voice.

The phone, it rang all day, and he spoke, gazing out his large window at the lot—the lot like a circus filled with the most beautiful and fragile people in the world, all dancing, high kicking, somersaulting, tightrope walking just for him.

He spoke to the contract stars and the beauties who floated over from the other studios for a picture or two. They all came to him. Burt Lancaster, Kirk Douglas, too, even Humphrey Bogart. And the women, Jeanne Crain, Doris Day, Jennifer Jones, Jane Wyman, Anne Baxter. They all came. And finer, less flinty fare in the up-and-comers: Janice Rule, Dorothy Malone, Jan Sterling, Carroll Baker. Every day. And, of course, the columnists— the rumor monkeys he worked like a carnival organ grinder. Walter still kicking around, Hedda, Louella, Sheilah, and all their lesser models—all dancing for him.

And he went to premieres with the glimmering girls of the moment, lunch at the Derby, to the track with John Huston and his rough-living crowd. When someone needed to pick up the big-shot buccaneer at the drunk tank and slip some green to the blue, he sent Mike or Freddy or reliable old Bix, whom he'd hired himself. They kicked needles down sewer grates, slipped suicide notes into pockets, gave screen tests to hustlers quid pro quo. Hop had it taken care of. He had it fixed. Mr. Blue Sky. All from his chrome and mahogany office, cool and magisterial and pumped full of his own surging blood. He fucking loved his life. What did he do to deserve it?

He was surprised, if he let himself think about it, how easy it had been to release the Spangler story into oblivion. He tied up all the loose ends. He tipped Frannie Adair to another, hotter story about SAG president Ronny Reagan and his closed-door deals with MCA. Hell, he'd even gotten Peggy Spangler a good job as a thanks for forgetting a few things. She was a receptionist at a snazzy talent agency and got to meet big stars every day. He was happy to help.

And, when Tony Lamont negotiated a better deal for Sutton and Merrel at Universal, Hop was secretly more than glad he would never again have to work his magic for the likes of those two. He'd never do that. *That* he would not do. Truth was, it was Hop himself who gave Tony the idea, on the sly. Even greased the wheels. Hop also did his best to spread the word, discreetly of course, that those two were bad news, especially for ladies. And he tried not to listen when the rumor mill churned, every six months or so, about their peccadilloes, their deviancies, light and dark. *Privately, on rare occasions, he would let himself wonder how long Gene Merrel could go on, shot through with doom, convincing himself he had nothing left to lose so that he could go down those dark, rutted tunnels time and again.*

There's things I can't fix, he said to himself on those long nights, those long nights when he ended up drinking bourbon at his kitchen table after an attenuated evening of premieres and Slapsy Maxie's and Don the Beachcomber's and the Ambassador Hotel. There's things I can't change. You do what you can. *You do what you want. You do what you do.* How could he really help any of them? They all made their own choices. All the girls coursing through the whole bloody story. How could you stop any of them? All you could do was lock the door, close the box, kick the dirt over the hole. He wished he'd figured this out long ago. Maybe he had.

He also took care of something. There was a headstone of camilia-white granite to replace the simple plot: Iolene Harper, 1922–1951, with a gardenia etched on either side. The grandest headstone in the cemetery, cost more than anything he'd ever bought in his life. There was that. He'd done that. You couldn't forget that.

He'd meant to stop by Jerry's place the day they left town. To say good-bye, even offer to help pack the last few boxes, help load Jerry's long, low sofa, his hundreds of jazz records, including his favorite 1925 recording of Bessie Smith singing "Careless Love Blues." He'd meant to slip his arms around Midge's tiny frame one last time, smell the hyacinth in her hair, feel the slenderest tuck of new flesh around her WASP waist. Meant to shake Jerry's hand, his firm, solid hand that he'd seen holding tight to his ramshackle camera during the war, seen rat-a-tat-tat-ing at typewriters, covered with ink, curled around highball glasses, wherever. Jerry, he was it.

They were long gone now, two years gone, Jerry diving into the foxhole at another Hearst rag, the San Francisco *Examiner*. *Can't leave Old Man Hearst without a conscience,* Jerry had said, laughing hollowly. He was ready to get in the trenches again, no more editing from a glass-enclosed office, he'd be covering city hall. First time in the building, though, he'd be saying "I do."

I do I do I do, Midge. Here's to you and to the future showgirl in your belly. You could only give the world beauty queens, showroom models, actresses, jingle singers, round-card girls brokenhearted from too many tries for the brass ring and from disappointments with men. You're one mean son of a bitch, Gil Hopkins. She may give birth to a librarian, a schoolteacher, a social worker in her gut. Even a boy. No, never a boy. Midge . . .

Truth was, he'd been too busy to get over there and say good-bye.

Truth was, he'd rather remember Midge as he last saw her:

I missed you my whole life, she'd said, and that was something else. It was something better than he deserved. That was her gift. The words that came at you so fast, so hard, they almost made you cry before you could stop yourself. Making you weak. Lost. And when he thought of it now, he wanted to laugh. Even she, who knows the worst of me, still can't see what I see just by looking in the mirror.

And Jerry, well, Jerry. He knew he'd see Jerry again. That was in the cards. Jerry knew him. He knew him. There were things Jerry . . . Jerry understood everything. Jerry, he . . .

Sometimes Frannie Adair came over. She'd been engaged to a fellow at the DA's office, but it didn't work out. He was fired for racking up a six-thousand-dollar gambling debt and "compromising the office" when a loan shark showed up at the courthouse to collect his vig. Frannie covered bigger cases now, knocking on doors downtown and bending elbows with the boys who worked for the boys who made things happen, and unhappen.

And she would call and, as long as he was alone, he'd invite her over to his new place in Holmby Hills (sure, he couldn't pay for it yet, but it wouldn't be long). And then he would fix a drink and wait for her, and as he waited he'd always think about the faint line he once saw on her face, the sheet crease as delicate as gold leaf, antique lace. And he would remember it until she got there.

One of the first times, he walked her to the cab stand on the corner. As she slid down in the backseat, patting her mussed hair with trembling hands, she said, "I guess I live here now," and he said, "You've lived here for years," even though he knew what she meant and she was right.

Startled out of his reverie by the buzz of his receptionist, Hop jumped forward in his seat. "Yes?"

"Barbara Payton is here to see you. I told her she needed an appointment. Should I send her away?"

He sat back in his chair. Here was a sad story, a cliché far more timeworn and rubbed to dullness. The girl, she had it all, but her legs went only one way—out. A few more bad headlines—Barbara attracted them like she did bad men—and the parts stopped coming. But the stories never stopped. Divorce from Franchot Tone. Divorce from wife-beating drunk Tom Neal. Paying a two-hundred-dollar bar tab with two fur coats. Rumors of heroin and picking up bellboys at the Garden of Allah on Sunset. A whore who got lucky, someone, not Hop, once called her. Her luck finally ran out.

"You can send her in," Hop said without thinking. She'd caught him in a rare sentimental mood.

"Look at you, as I fucking live and breathe," she announced, walking in, a cloud of teased-out hair, skin mottled, eyes burst through with red.

Oh, Barbara, he thought, all that's left are the tits and your dirty mouth.

"When I met you," she said, sitting down, her blouse pulling tighter across her chest, one button gone, "you were just a fast-talking kid with a slick and tasty way about you. You were good enough to eat, but you only ever looked me in the eye. You never even shot a glance at my rack."

Hop shook his head. "I may have talked fast, but I could look even faster. Besides, your dance card was full at the time."

"Maybe. I would have penciled in an extra line for you. But I was never smart enough about those things," she said, with a half grin. "But look at you now. You're a real world-beater. Maybe if we'd danced back then, you'd be nostalgic now and help a gal."

He knew this was coming. Were there no surprises? "I would do it anyway, Barbara, if I could," he said, with a full grin. "But I've got no pull with casting or production. I'm just publicity."

Raising her eyebrows, she leaned back in her chair. "Yeah," she said, nodding her head and watching him closely. "You know, I didn't just roll in from the pasture. I know what it is you do here. And what you undo. And there's no more precious tackle on the lot. You know where all the bodies are buried," she said, looking him straight in the eye. "You bury them."

Hop smiled vaguely and shrugged. "I wish I had half the muscle you think I have. Haven't you heard? It's all a sinking ship, anyway. The two-eared monster is taking over. Me, I don't own a television set."

She smiled back, but it was a moll's smile, a pay broad's smile. No more shades of cheerleader and homecoming queen. She was all swivel and Hollywood Boulevard now. Where was the soft blonde thing he'd honey-tongued to Minnesota and back?

"You know, I heard things," she said, pointing a torn finger-nail at him. "I heard about the things you knew. The secrets you had on the big guns. They would've promoted you to emperor to keep those secrets kept."

Hop looked at her.

She sighed, rubbing her arm wistfully. "What was I supposed to do? Play the blessed virgin or Betty Crocker? I was having a ball. And I wasn't about to pull the brakes for Louella Parsons or Daryl Zanuck. I know it's hurt me. I've paid. You don't see me on-screen with Gregory Peck or Jimmy Cagney these days. The money ran out. There were some bad men. I hit the sauce. A bottle of Seconal a hotel doctor had to suck back out of me with a tube. Then I took the route, as the junkies say. It started sticking to me. You know the song. You could sing it to me."

Beneath the hard stare, the pancake, the waxy coat of lipstick, beneath that . . . hell, Hop had long ago stopped looking beneath that. Chances were too great that the underneath was worse.

"I can try, Barbara. I can make some calls. I will."

She smiled, sweetly this time. "Thanks, kid. Thanks. I'll say thanks 'cause I need the dough. Truth is, Hoppy boy, I don't know if I want to go back to pictures for the long haul. The shadow life. It never seemed real, you know?"

Hop smiled and looked surreptitiously at his watch.

"Do you ever start to feel like none of it's real, Hop? Like"— she moved forward in her chair, eyes still, behind the skein of red, jewel-blue—"like you're not real. Like I think maybe if I reached across the desk toward you, my hand would go right through you. I know it would. Do you ever feel like that?"

"No," he said, surprised at his own abruptness. Suddenly, he felt like he'd do anything to get her out of his office. What did she mean, her hand would go right through him? What did it have to do with him? "Never. But I know a lot of stars do think about that. About the persona—"

"I'm not talking about that," she said. "I'm talking about the shadow life. The life you're living instead. The life you're living because you can't fight yourself anymore. You're too goddamned tired to fight yourself anymore."

In his head, the familiar volley: What should he have done? A few files that would have come to nothing. No Iolene to give them to. Anyone in his shoes would have done the same. Why not make something from this big, gnawing nothingness? But it wasn't like Barbara was suggesting, a promotion for a clipped lip. He never would have done it that way. He'd delivered those files to the men involved — the studio head's daughter knocked up by a Negro, the thirteen-year-old deaf-and-dumb girl given a dose by one of the studio's biggest stars — so they could dispose of them as they would. It was their overflowing gratitude that gave Hop the big boost from junior publicist to senior publicist to head publicist and a thick and juicy raise. It was a mean, messy thing, sure, but that didn't mean it hadn't all worked out for the best in the end. He was doing a great job; everyone thought so. The on-screen talent enjoyed him, felt comfortable with him, trusted him with their lives. And the brass felt positively serene. Then, through his own grit and guts, from head publicist to, now, this year, nineteen fifty-fucking-five, chief of publicity. He was a climber, yes, but in the best way: the way that meant that what he wanted most of all, all he wanted, really, was to make them happy.

So he said now, pointedly, to Barbara Payton, bleached-brittle hair and toreador pants, smell of bar vibrating off her, "You're the last person, Barbara, that I'd expect to take stock in rumors

"Hey, *I* got nothing to hide," she said, crossing her leg, lipstick-red mule hanging from her twitching foot. "They probably all true, every last one. Did you see the photos N Franchot Tone spread all over town a few years back? Those vate dick shots of me on my knees, all black garters and be before my beloved boxing partner, Tom Neal? How many get out of that?"

Hop nodded his signature knowing, understanding nod

Hop looked at her. He could feel himself bracing. He was ready for it.

"See, me, Hop," she said. "I'm thinking I may go back to fighting."

"Good luck."

That night, Hop returned to his new place, still paint-fresh, at midnight. He'd begged off when—What was her name? Maura? Mona? Mina?—the one with the spangly dress and little-girl lisp offered to fry him up a steak at her little place in West Holly-wood. He was tired. He didn't feel like talking. He was bored.

He poured three fingers of scotch before taking off his dinner coat. Unloosening his tie and collar, he sat in his new Italian leather armchair.

He'd thought he wanted to be alone, but the quiet, the tomb-like quiet of the place made him feel suddenly panicky. Why did he always forget this about himself? When had he ever wanted to be alone?

He thought about calling someone. He could call someone and then she would talk and then she would come over and then there would be no reason to sit in a chair with a drink in the quiet apartment and look out the window and think about things and recall things and recall people and remember stories and faces and feelings and voices that had flitted through him once in a coffee shop, at a bar, in a room smelling sharply of pine.

Iolene, she once said to him, You think you can forget.

And now he couldn't stop remembering. It was the thing he dreaded most. By the time he finished his drink, he was remembering everything.

The pictures, the fast-moving images, the flickering lights like a movie playing in his head. Only by now, it had gotten so mixed up for him, he couldn't separate real memories from things he hadn't even seen, things he'd only been told about. They were all there. A belt across the mouth. A ring of blood. A revolver to the back of a head, pressed against a hair comb glittering. A girl falling over a chair.

There was something lost. There was something lost. He could look in the mirror a thousand times and he would never see it again. He'd snuffed it out. Had he known he'd never get it back . . . Had he known it would be gone forever . . .

He got up and walked into his bedroom. He knew it would be there and he shouldn't do it, but he couldn't stop. He opened the drawer to his bedside table and dug under the handkerchiefs, phone book, cigarettes, matchbooks. There it was.

He pulled it out. It was thin as a cobweb now, this postcard. It had become delicate with time. Postcards, after all, aren't meant to last. They're less than a letter. They're a fleeting thing. A whisper in the ear reminding you, "Merry Lake's Waiting for You."